WORLD IN BETWEEN

WORLD IN BETWEEN

BASED ON A TRUE REFUGEE STORY
by Kenan Trebinčević and Susan Shapiro

CLARION BOOKS
Houghton Mifflin Harcourt
Boston   New York

Clarion Books

3 Park Avenue

New York, New York 10016

Clarion Books is an imprint of Houghton Mifflin Harcourt Publishing Company.

hmhbooks.com

The text was set in Chaparral Pro.

Cover design by Celeste Knudsen

Interior design by Celeste Knudsen

The Library of Congress Cataloging-in-Publication Data is available.

ISBN: 978-0-358-43987-5

Manufactured in the United States of America

1 2021

4500827424

CV 05.03.2021 0445

In memory of
Senahid (Keka) Trebinčević

PART ONE

LOSING HOME

Brčko, Bosnia

ONE

MARCH 1992

I've seen army helicopters before, but only in war movies.

Today is the first time I see one for real.

It happens during recess, when Mr. Miran is lining us up to pick teams for our fudbal game and the copter streaks across the sky above us. I'm excited to be so close—but it's much louder than I thought it would be. The engine sounds like it's inside me, rattling my brain. I put my hands over my ears. It doesn't help. The crazy wind makes my hair stand on end. Even the blades of grass are shaking.

I run down the field with the other kids, my arms stretched out like wings, as if I'm flying.

"Who do you think is in there?" I ask my best friend, Vik.

"Important army generals," he guesses. "I bet they're gonna get all the bad guys."

I wonder who the bad guys are. They must be in big trouble if generals are coming to arrest them from the sky.

"Where are you going?" Mr. Miran yells at us as the chopper flies out of view. "Get back here!"

I'm curious where it's landing, but I don't want to make Mr. Miran mad and lose my chance at a good position on the team. Fudbal is my life. I push to the front of the pack of fifth- and sixth-grade boys and start showing off some of my footwork.

"Choose me!" I wave, trying to get Mr. Miran's attention.

"Kenan, you play right wing today," he decides.

Yes! I squeeze my fists hard, totally pumped. The entire school will be watching our Friday pickup match, I bet — including Lena, the coolest girl in my class. I'll impress her — and Mr. Miran, who never praises anyone. He's reffing our game on the sidelines in his suit and leather loafers, smoking a cigarette as usual. When I've been standing too close to him at school, Mom tells me, "You reek like an ashtray."

"Smoking's bad for you," my dad always says. He's one of the few men I know who doesn't smoke. He's a sports coach, so we're always talking fudbal, which he says people in the U.S. call *soccer*. So weird. On satellite TV, my older brother, Eldin, has shown me what the Americans call *football*: huge guys carrying what looks like a brown dinosaur egg. They run away from even bigger guys to avoid getting squashed. If a giant American player jumped me, I'd break like a toothpick.

I rush to the broken fence to throw my blue sweatshirt on a spike, and I peek over the top, where I can see the military base behind the school grounds. There are soldiers everywhere. Two sit on a bench, taking their guns apart to clean them. The barracks have always been here, but there's more army men than usual. I want to tell Lena about the close helicopter and the troops, but Vik's older brother, Marko, starts shouting, "Come on, Bugs! Chomp, chomp."

Not this again. My stomach sinks as Marko points to my three huge, horrible front teeth. They hang over my bottom lip and make me look like a rabbit. He's been calling me Bugs Bunny, from the American cartoon, because he knows I hate it. Mom makes me wear a retainer so my teeth will move into the right place, but I refuse to wear it at school and only put it on at night. What if it fell out of my mouth when I coughed or Lena saw me drool and the guys teased me even worse? No way. I try not to smile much and put my hand in front of my face so nobody notices.

I'll show Marko. Today I'll prove I'm a great athlete, small but speedy, so he'll shut up about my screwy mouth. But he keeps making that stupid chomping noise, and everyone cracks up. I feel hot all over.

"Just ignore him, Kenan," Vik says, joining me on the field. "I'm in, too."

Of course Mr. Miran wants Vik, the best dribbler.

"Notice more soldiers around today?" I ask as we wait for the whistle.

"Yeah. I saw a sergeant with a stopwatch timing how fast they oiled their rifles," Vik tells me.

Why do they need so many guns ready? I wonder. *How many bad guys are there?*

After kickoff, Vik gets the ball. He keeps it glued to his feet. Like me, he's eleven and small. His two front teeth are twisted, so he has a lisp. If you stand close when he talks, he spits on you. The other kids sometimes make fun of him too, but I don't. I never will. I know how terrible it feels to get picked on. Vik and I have been best buddies since first grade, when nobody would play with me at recess. Then Vik asked me to join his team, saving my whole school career. So I'll always be loyal.

A few days ago, Vik, Marko, and I were at the store to get new numbers stenciled on our T-shirts. Marko snagged 10, the number I wanted — like my favorite players, Pelé and Maradona. Marko's older and taller than me, so I sucked it up and took number 9. Later, I asked my parents for the same red Adidas shorts the other guys had. Dad insisted I stick with blue. When I asked him why, he said, "The Serbian Red Stars wear red. That's Milošević's team. He's a sociopath."

I don't know exactly what a "social path" means, but I can tell it's bad.

We live in Bosnia, and Milošević is the president of Serbia, the republic next door, just an hour and a half away. My family is Muslim, but we don't pray five times a day like my grandmother, Majka Emina. She gets mad when I spend the money she gives me on sports. "Too much fudbal. You should go pray!" she shouts all the time. When I ask my parents why she's been praying so much lately, Mom says, "We all go someplace to feel strong."

I totally get that, 'cause I feel strong here and now all right, rocketing down the field with the ball. I kind of think this is the way I pray, like it's what I'm put on earth to do. I fall, but get up fast, not even winded. I imagine breaking the tie in our game and being the star player. Mr. Miran will tell my father I'm important to the team, and for once, Dad will be prouder of me than Eldin. I'll get tons of fans, and Lena will like me best.

I sprint up and down the rocky ground, focusing on the ball. I can't stop the other team from sinking a goal, but we do get one back, tying the score again. I need to get a shot in.

"Three more minutes," Mr. Miran calls.

Oh no. My time is running out. I'm desperate to show off the new killer kick I've been practicing. Bugs has a few surprises up his sleeve. Luckily, Vik's surrounded, so he passes to me. I hurry up the field. The ball bounces off my shin and hits the huge scab on my knee. I don't even look down, nervous I'll screw up. Everyone crowds around the field, staring at me. The girls quit hopscotching. Even the lunch truck lady leans out of her window to catch the end of the game.

There's Lena! I can see her from the corner of my eye. She's wearing a pink shirt, her shiny brown hair in a ponytail. I dribble the ball down the field fast, knowing she's watching. My teammates chant, "Kenan! Kenan!" The goalie glares, trying to psych me out, but he can't. I wind my leg far back, revving up all the power in my right foot.

Bang. I blast the ball directly at the back corner of the net, so hard the goalie can't block it.

"Goooallll!" I scream, pumping my arms in the air. Vik and my teammates run over, slap my back, and give me high-fives.

"Great work. Keep it up, and you'll play for the national team someday, Kenan," Mr. Miran says.

My heart is pounding against my rib cage. It's the best day ever! As I grab my sweatshirt from the broken fence, my mind flashes to the impressive cleats one of my brother's friends wears to train for his team, the Croatian Outlaws. When I'm older, I'll represent my country wearing official spikes too. I'll be the star player of the Yugoslavia national fudbal team, much more popular and famous than Eldin. I wish my brother and Dad had seen me score. At least Lena did.

As I run off the field with my friends, I see her standing with our classmates on the playground. "Good shot, Kenan," she says.

See, one of the things that makes Lena so awesome is that she isn't shy or stuck-up like some of the other girls in fifth grade. In art class, when I asked her how she made her collage, she moved closer to show me her special glue.

I stop next to the yellow lines she's drawn in chalk on the pavement. She looks right at me. Her brown eyes have long lashes, and when she smiles, all her freckles scrunch up around her nose. She smells like bubblegum.

"Thanks, Lena," I say. I can feel my cheeks turn red.

As I'm rushing back toward school, I hear her tell her friends, "He's good at drawing too."

For years, Vik and I have been trying to get Lena to notice us. We all live about a block away from each other. Last weekend, Vik balanced me on his bike's handlebars and we rode by Lena's house five times. Then we ran over a nail, and his tire blew. I hid in the bushes as she came to her window and peeked out from behind the curtain to see what the noise was. She's the only girl we've ever both liked. We have an oath not to get upset if she chooses one of us. But I hope it's me.

"Did you see Lena watching us?" I ask Vik as the school bell rings.

"She already likes me," he mutters. I hope he's not going to break our Lena pact.

In class, I don't hear the history lesson. I'm too busy reliving the goal, carving Lena's initials into the wooden desk with the needle of my geometry compass. I make sure to hide what I'm doing from Mr. Miran. Goal or no goal, he'll be mad if he catches me.

After school, I bump into my friend Huso at the entrance to our building. He's so strong, he's carrying his new BMX bicycle on his shoulder. Huso's two years older than me and really smart. He's kind of one of my heroes.

"Scored the winning goal in the fudbal game at recess," I tell him.

"Nice." He high-fives me. He has a blond crewcut, and he wears a blue shirt tucked into his jeans and clean white sneakers. Of all the boys in our apartment complex, he's the neatest dresser. His dad is a good friend of my dad's. He's a professor. That's why Huso is the only one of my friends who speaks proper Bosnian and English. His dad is tutoring me once a week so I can learn a little English too, like my father, who says, "You'll be better respected if you know more than one language."

"Let's get a game going later?" I ask Huso. He nods. He goes to a different school, and lately, he's been busy studying. But I always want Huso on my team; he has a kick like a rocket.

When I race up the three flights of stairs and barge into my apartment, I smell peppers roasting. My father and brother are in the living room. "Dad, Dad! I got the winning goal!" I tell him, dribbling an imaginary ball in the air to show him my fast footwork.

"That's super, Kenji." He grabs me close and ruffles my hair.

"It was only a recess game," Eldin says, rolling his eyes. "Calm down."

"Mr. Miran said if I keep at it, I might play for the national team."

My brother snickers. "Yeah, like that will ever happen."

"Take off your shoes and sweaty socks," my mom calls from the dining room. She's ironing shirts, and she has the door open to the balcony, which is filled with her cactus and ferns. She has a green thumb. And she's such a neat freak, it drives us all crazy. The dining room is for eating only. We leave our shoes outside the front door. If my pants get wet from the rain, they have to come off at the door too, so I won't ruin her black and white rug.

"The last thing I want when I get home from work is to spend hours bleaching," she says. Mom's the office manager at Velma Clothing Company. Vik's and Huso's mothers work there too.

As she irons, Mom sings along to Madonna on the radio. "Rescue me ... Baby throw out your rope ..." She claims her plants like the music.

"More crazy girl crooning?" Dad teases her.

"Better than your old-man music," she fires back with a smile.

My dad is sixteen years older than my mom. He listens to worn-out albums from his jazz band days, which he keeps in a wooden case. It's hard for me to imagine Mom meeting him when she was just eighteen. That's the same age Eldin is now. My Uncle Ahmet says Dad "robbed her cradle."

Everyone says she still looks young, even though she's about to be thirty-seven. Maybe it's because she's short. The last time Dad measured me, I was five foot two, as tall as she is.

"Old-man music?" Dad says, raising his eyebrows. "One day when I take you to hear the greats on the other side of the pond, you'll understand."

Now my mother rolls her eyes. "America? Yeah, what a dream." She laughs as she keeps ironing. "When we're rich and connected enough to get visas."

When we were studying geography, Mr. Miran told us that America is 5,500 miles from Brčko and has fifty separate states. It's gigantic compared to Yugoslavia. We only have six republics: Slovenia, Macedonia, Montenegro, Bosnia, Serbia, and Croatia. They add up to the size of a yellow square on the U.S. map called "Oregon." Bosnians are situated right in between Serbia and Croatia. We're smushed in the middle, like the jelly inside a doughnut.

I go to our bedroom, bummed but not surprised that Eldin's still avoiding me. We used to hang out all the time. He was the one who taught me how to play ball. He's six and half years older than me and eight inches taller, but I'm catching up. Eldin can lift way more weights, though I already run faster. But now that he's a senior, he doesn't talk to me. He's always on the phone with his friends. Since he's eighteen and almost done with high school, he's too busy hanging out with kids his age and dating girls.

Last weekend, after he complained, "I'm not missing a party to babysit Chicken Arms," I got really upset. If there's anything that annoys me more than getting teased for my teeth, it's being teased for my skinny arms. I tried to kick his leg but accidentally hit him in the crotch. He fell to his knees, yelling, "I'll kill you!" I ran to our room in a panic, but he caught me and shoved me to the floor and kicked me in the back with his huge foot. Then, when I cried, he called me a baby. He took down our bunk beds and put my frame and mattress on the floor, across the room from his. He shoved my car collections aside and taped a poster of the Croatian Outlaws fudbal team over his bed. Now we barely speak, except when he's insulting me.

"Dinner's ready," Mom calls after a while. "Wash your hands."

We all hurry to the table. I forget to dry my hands and wipe them on the back of my pants, hoping she won't see and make me go back and wash again. Mom serves chicken soup, fried okra, and my favorite, moussaka with beef. After my fudbal triumph, I'm starving.

"Guess what I saw today? A giant helicopter, like the one in *Airwolf*," I say between forkfuls. "It landed at the army base. And Vik saw a sergeant timing the soldiers to clean their guns faster."

Mom flashes my father a worried look, like I've said something wrong.

"Stay away from them," Dad snaps. "They're not good guys."

What does that mean? I'm confused. He always says the army's there to protect us. He spent twelve months in the military when he was eighteen. So did mom's brother, Uncle Ahmet. Now that Eldin's eighteen, he'll be doing it soon too. It's a requirement.

"When do you go back to the reserves?" I ask.

"Never," Dad says.

What changed? I'm about to ask when Eldin interrupts. "Can I take the train to Croatia with Tomo to see the championship game tomorrow?"

"No," Mom answers. "That's seven hours away."

"We can stay overnight with Tomo's cousin," Eldin pushes. "Please? I'll get the early train back Sunday morning."

"He is eighteen now," Dad jumps in, which means *he's going.*

"Can I come?" I beg, though Eldin's still mad at me.

"No extra ticket." He shuts me down.

I know he could sneak me in if he wanted to. He's such a liar.

"Too far," Mom repeats, shaking her head. "It's dangerous."

"Eldin's old enough to take the train to see a game with a friend," counters my father.

"Keka, stop," she says.

That's Dad's nickname. He's the owner of Fitness Keka, the best gym in town. To him, sports are serious business. He's in great shape. Whenever we're out walking around, guys stop to talk to him and ask advice. People call him "the unofficial mayor of Brčko." It makes my chest swell with pride.

Sometimes, during volleyball games at his gym, I help out the players with him, holding the cold spray to numb their pulled muscles and other injuries. After the game, I wait for my dad in the locker room. Once, the guys were goofing around, hoisting me up on their shoulders. My head felt so dizzy I was sure it would fall off, but I didn't want to scream *put me down* 'cause they'd think I was a wimp.

Mom raises her voice. "This is not the time for Eldin to travel so far."

"Your mother's a worrywart," Dad tells us, smiling.

Eldin nods, happy to have Dad on his side, as usual.

"Keka, the climate's changing," she replies. There's a line between her eyebrows, like she's frowning with her whole face.

I look out the window. It's sunny, so I'm not sure what the weather has to do with anything.

"He'll be fine. Stop being a nervous Nellie." Dad has the final word.

"You leave me the phone number of Tomo's parents and his cousin," Mom tells Eldin, looking annoyed.

Eldin grins in victory. My mouth droops. I'm so jealous. He always gets to go everywhere and do everything with his buddies, just 'cause he's older.

After three helpings of rice pudding for dessert, I go to my room to try to forget my brother, the big-shot showoff. I draw a picture of Lena, the sun and birds floating above her long hair. I'll give it to her for her birthday on Monday and ask if I can walk her home from school.

As I'm getting ready for bed, I hear Mom and Dad arguing. My parents hardly ever fight. I put my ear to the door, hoping to figure out what's going on.

"It won't affect us, Adisa. This is our home, everyone here likes us," Dad is saying.

"When trouble is walking by, don't offer it a seat," Mom says loudly. "We have to get out of here fast."

Get out of here? But why? Where would we go? Who would I play with at recess? I wouldn't be any good on another fudbal team without Vik. And what about Lena?

"You're in *denial,*" Mom tells Dad. I'm not sure where Denial is, but it sounds scary. Especially the way she says it, stretching out the last sound so it hums, giving me the shivers.

TWO

The next morning, Eldin writes down some numbers on the pad by the phone as Mom hands him a brown bag with a salami and cheese sandwich inside. "Be careful. Don't drink or mouth off. If anyone bothers you, run the other way," she says, kissing his cheek before he leaves.

That evening when we turn on the TV to catch the game, I look for Eldin in the stands. But it's too crowded. When his team, the Croatian Outlaws, lose to the Serbians, the spectators boo. After a Serbian player pumps his fist in the air, Croatian athletes chase him into the locker room. Fans charge the field. It's a mob scene. Someone burns the Yugoslavian flag as the Serb team waves a red, blue, and white one with a two-headed eagle and cross, the kind they've been waving at political rallies on TV. I've never seen chaos like this at a game. It freaks me out a little, knowing my brother is there. The broadcast ends, and Dad turns off the TV. I can't sit still, and pace around the living room.

Mom's getting scared too. "Why did you let Eldin go?" she keeps asking Dad at dinner. She phones Tomo's house and his cousin's, but nobody picks up. She opens our curtains to look down the street. Dad turns on the TV again to watch the news.

"Don't worry," I tell her, trying to chill her out and stay calm myself. "Fights break out at games between crazy fans all the time." Then the newscaster says the National Army just bombed a train station in Bijeljina, with a hundred casualties and "bodies blown everywhere."

I'm stunned. Bijeljina is only about sixty miles from Brčko. It's where we have our karate practice. The bottom of my feet feel cold. I picture a zombie movie where people are walking around without arms, legs, or heads. But Bijeljina wasn't on Eldin's way. I don't believe that our soldiers would hurt their own people. It must have been a foreign army.

"What if Eldin can't get home now?" Mom screams at Dad. "Or if he got rerouted there? I told you he shouldn't have gone!"

The tips of my fingers are tingling. I chew on my thumbnail. Dad goes outside, and I trail behind him. Our neighbor Hasan comes up to Dad and says "Did you hear? Houses near the train station were set on fire with gasoline. Government tanks are in the streets!"

Eldin can be mean, but he's still my brother. He's the one

who takes me swimming and to karate, who shares his comic books and frightens off kids who threaten me. What if he was at that station? Then who'll protect me?

I usually go to bed by nine, but tonight nobody cares. It's late when I go to sleep.

I wake up the next morning to hear Mom clanging dishes around the kitchen. When I come in, she's making breakfast for Dad, slamming his plate of eggs down on the table. They both look like they haven't slept at all. Dad turns on the TV and radio for more news, but there's nothing new. Mom pours me cereal, but nobody is hungry. We sit on the living room couch all afternoon as Mom keeps calling the numbers Eldin left.

"Why isn't anyone picking up?" she yells. "Are they in a hospital or jail?"

"They're on the train back," Dad says quietly. "I'm sure he'll be home soon."

My knees are bouncing, and I keep checking the door. It isn't until after eight that Eldin finally walks in. His face is dirty, his hair floppy.

"Where have you been?" Mom cries, hugging him tight.

"Yeah, where were you?" I ask, relieved and tired, not telling him I'm glad he's back.

Dad touches Eldin's arm. "What happened?"

"I'm fine," he says, pulling away.

"We were terrified. Why are you so late?" Mom demands.

"There was a freaking riot after the game last night!" Eldin says in an excited voice. "The police broke it up with tear gas. Guys ripped the seats right off the stands and tossed them like Frisbees. I got caught in it 'cause I was wearing an Outlaw scarf. Tomo got hit in the back with a stick, and I almost got smashed in the head. A bunch of people wound up in the hospital with broken bones. You wouldn't believe it—they went nuts! The whole brawl was caught on tape, and now the government's going after only the Croatian fans. It was insane. All the trains and buses were running late today, with cops everywhere."

Man, I wish I could have been there.

"Is Tomo okay?" Dad asks, and Eldin nods.

"You could have gotten hurt. Or arrested!" Mom yells. The vein in her neck is bulging.

I don't understand why, since Eldin's Bosnian, not Croatian, and didn't do anything wrong.

"From today on, you'll watch sports from the couch," Mom decrees.

My shoulders slump. *No fair!* Now I'll never get to see a live match, one of my dreams.

Eldin makes a face. "Don't overreact. You know how crazy the fans get."

"Didn't you hear about the train station?" Dad asks.

"They said the trains were backed up for hours, so I took the bus. It's not a big deal, Dad."

Mom's words come out in a rush. "You didn't hear that there was a bombing — and fires, too?"

"What? Where?"

"Bijeljina," Dad says.

"That's less than an hour from here." Eldin sounds shocked.

I want to hear more about the game and the bomb so I can tell my friends how my brother was really close to all the trouble.

But of course, that's when Mom turns to me and insists, "Go to bed, you have school tomorrow."

The next night before dinner, Eldin returns home from karate practice looking freaked out and breathless.

"What's wrong?" Mom asks.

"I heard that masked men went door to door in Bijeljina, ordering Muslim families out of their homes," Eldin says, his face pale. "Everyone's saying it was paramilitary Serbs."

I pull at his sleeve, a lump in my throat. "What does *paramilitary* mean?"

"Guerrillas," Eldin explains. I think of King Kong banging his chest with his fists.

Mom looks as confused as I am.

"Enemy soldiers, not with the army," Eldin goes on. "They made everyone kneel down; then they fired. Seventy people shot dead."

Mom's mouth opens. She turns to Dad. "We have to get out of here now, Keka."

My throat tightens as I stare up at my father. "Do we?"

"No. They won't hurt us," Dad promises.

"How do you know?" Mom snaps. "It's only one hour away! Those people were shot in cold blood." She puts her arm around me, but it makes me feel worse.

"We're not political. We don't wave our flag," Dad says. "I have lots of friends in this town. Nobody would hurt us. I'll go talk to the police chief."

That night, I can't sleep. I stare at the ceiling fan. "Why did they kill all those people?" I finally ask my brother in the dark.

"The Croatians want independence," Eldin answers. "The Serbs don't want Bosnians to leave either."

He's actually speaking to me without insults. Things must be way worse than I thought. "Why?" I press.

"Everyone's divided politically — the Christian Serbs, Catholic Croats, and Muslims from Bosnia, like us," he reminds me.

"But there's Bosnian Christians too," I say.

"The Christians don't want to be associated with anyone Muslim anymore."

"Dad says the Yugoslavian army's supposed to protect us all."

"Now it's run by the Serbs, and they hate us," Eldin says.

"Vik's a Serb, and he doesn't hate me!"

My brother's quiet for a minute. Then he says, "Don't be so sure."

He's wrong. He doesn't understand that Vik and I are blood brothers forever. So what if Vik paints Easter eggs at an Orthodox church and has a Christmas tree? Eldin's Catholic classmates go to midnight mass and fly a red and white flag. My Muslim relatives cook a feast on Ramadan and wave a green flag. Nobody ever cared what color flag we had before.

"On Republic Day, Mr. Miran had us pledge allegiance to our country that unites all Yugoslavs," I remind Eldin.

"Well, the Serbs who control the army want to rule the whole country, and some Croats and Bosnian Muslims just declared independence from Yugoslavia," my brother explains.

"What are we gonna do?" I ask, my voice getting squeaky at the thought of having to move away.

"Keep our heads down, I guess," Eldin says. "Go to sleep."

I bring Lena's birthday picture to school on Monday, but her seat is empty. I keep turning around to look for her during class. She never shows.

Later my brother tells me that her older sister didn't come

to school either. Some Muslim families are going to stay with relatives in other cities and countries, he adds. But Lena wouldn't leave without telling me. Would she?

The next day, when she's not in class again, I get up the courage to ask Mr. Miran where she is.

"Just do your work," he growls.

That night, when we're choosing teams for a pickup fudbal game outside our building, Marko and Vik put Huso and me with our Croat neighbor, Leon.

"Only Serbs on our side today," Marko announces.

What? I can't believe they don't want me on their team. After I scored the winning goal at recess and won the game? That doesn't make any sense.

At dinner, Mom tells Dad, "I've seen strange men in dark uniforms lurking around. My brother and Maksida are sending their kids to stay with her relatives in Vienna. There's room for us to go too."

"Milošević's a power-hungry psycho. No one takes him seriously," Dad argues.

"You saw his stupid new flag with the eagles?" Eldin asks.

Milošević is Orthodox Christian, like Vik. Suddenly I remember seeing Vik, Marko, and their dad at a Serbian rally in town, waving that same eagle flag. I didn't think anything of it at the time.

The phone rings, and I get to it first. "Hey, Kenan, we got

new slingshots," Vik says, as if nothing happened this afternoon. "Want to go shoot some pigeons with us?"

Usually only Marko and his posse go bird hunting. I hate the thought of hurting any animals. But this has to be a sign that the conflict is blowing over, like Dad says. Hope balloons in my chest. Maybe no one is taking this seriously after all. "Hey, Mom. Can I go play with Viktor and his brother?"

"Stay close by," Dad tells me.

"I'm visiting Majka Emina tonight, to make sure she's okay," Mom adds. "You should come."

"I'll call her instead," I promise.

Mom has a big, close family. We see her mom and her brother and sister, my Uncle Ahmet and Aunt Bisera, every weekend. This is my chance to straighten everything out with the guys.

Mom sighs. "Don't go far," she repeats. "And be careful."

Vik comes by with Marko and Ivan, Marko's best buddy, who asks Eldin to flex his muscles for them. As usual Eldin loves the attention and takes off his shirt to reveal his arm bulges. He works out every day with weights to get those huge, dumb muscles.

"Great biceps, Triangle." Ivan uses the nickname he's given Eldin for his wide shoulders. Then he nods at me. "Let's go."

Ivan's a bossy jerk who gets in everyone's face and likes to bully people. I breathe through my mouth when he's around, because he smells gross. Vik thinks so too, and it's worse for him because Ivan's at their house all the time. Huso told me that Ivan's dad beat him with a belt once, after he got busted for ripping off someone's bike.

Ivan leads us to the dark basement in a nearby building we call the Catacombs. It's where he stashes everything he steals —and he steals a lot: bike parts, marbles, candy, cigarettes. He hands us slingshots he's made from tree branches and strips of old truck tires.

I'm nervous as we walk the two blocks to the railroad tracks near school to collect round rocks for ammo. Pigeons roam the rail yard. Vik, Marko, and Ivan aim their stones at the birds, hitting a few and laughing. I fake giving it a try, missing on purpose. As soon as we get near, the birds fly away. I'm secretly glad.

"Don't be a wuss, Bugs," Ivan says, watching me closely.

"I'm not a wuss." I spot a pigeon who strays from his flock. I stay quiet, creeping closer, and aim at his wing to show Ivan I can do it. I pull back the strip of tire and let the rock fly.

It makes a soft thud when it hits the pigeon, sounding like something broke.

"Good shot! You nailed him," Marko says, punching my shoulder too hard.

The bird stumbles like he's drunk. Then he flies sideways to the top of the building. I might throw up, but I don't want the others to know. I feel dizzy, praying the pigeon is okay. What would Lena think?

I act like it's no big deal as I watch Ivan load up his slingshot and aim at another one. He misses, and he's so annoyed I've outshot him that he throws rocks on the ground. I think of the hurt pigeon swaying on the building's ledge.

I swear I'll never shoot any other living thing again.

When it gets dark, we head back. On the way, we see a mangy dog I'm about to pet when Ivan kicks its face. It whimpers and runs away. "Why did you do that?" I ask. I feel like crying and taking the dog home with me.

"Shut up, Bugs," Ivan snarls.

I put my head down and walk faster to get away from him, so he doesn't kick me too. I've never been so relieved to get home. I walk up the stairs to our apartment and creep toward my room. The slingshot is still in my pocket. Before I can stash it, Dad sees.

"What's that?" He points.

"This? Um, it's Ivan's. We were shooting cans down the street."

"Stay away from that kid," Dad says. "He's bad news. We don't need another problem right now."

I don't get why bad things are happening to us when we haven't done anything wrong.

THREE

"What? That can't be true," Mom says into the phone later that week. Her mouth opens and she's shaking her head as she hangs up. "The army burned down Vukovar," she tells us slowly, as if she doesn't believe it. "Djilla says busloads of survivors escaped, and they're in the park."

Djilla is her coworker. Vukovar is a Croatian city not far from us. I don't understand what they escaped from. Mom rushes to the window, and I follow. We look down to see a crowd gathering in the park right across the street, getting off a bus and sitting together on benches.

"Those poor people. Let's go help," she tells me and Eldin, spinning around our apartment.

My mother likes to do charity; she's always helping whoever she can. For the first time, I want to join her. Maybe I can also make a difference.

Dad's at his gym. I think we should call to ask him too,

but Mom's in a hurry. She and Eldin pull old jackets from the hall closet and take cash from the drawer where we keep extra money. As I put on my coat, I grab my favorite blue sweatshirt with the fudbal logo, thinking someone might need it more than me. On the way out, I fill my canteen at the kitchen faucet in case anyone's thirsty.

Before we head to the park, we go to the grocery, where Mom buys a twenty-four-pack of cold bottled water, loaves of bread, aspirin, and baby supplies. We carry it all to the boulevard, where there's a long row of parked white buses. The wheels are caked with mud, their sides pocked with dents. The windows have been cracked by bullets. Who would shoot at buses filled with passengers?

I expect to see a small group, but there are tons of Croatians here, like a whole city. I guess seven or eight hundred people, all looking battered and dazed, some with bandages. It really is like I'm in the middle of a zombie movie.

One guy takes a whiz against a tree, and I quickly look away. It's weird, but then I realize there's no bathrooms here or on the buses. A lady on a bench cradles a baby. She has red hair like Mom.

"The soldiers took my husband. We don't know where he is," she wails.

"I'm so sorry," Mom says, handing her diapers, baby wipes, formula, and water.

"Thank you for your compassion, ma'am," the lady says between sobs. I'm about to cry myself.

An old man in a felt hat puts a towel against his bleeding forehead. A boy tapes his own broken eyeglasses. Then he wraps gauze around the hand of an older woman. A blond lady who looks my mother's age whispers, "They murdered my son. He's dead!"

I feel a chill growing in my chest. I've never seen anyone this sad before. Their eyes look so frightened, it hurts my heart. I help Mom hand out the money and medicine, wishing we had more clothes and cash to give away.

"Who did this to them?" I ask Eldin. I think of all the bad guys in the World War II movies I watch with Dad. Could it be the Hungarians or Germans?

"The Serbs occupying their town," Eldin says, his jaw clenched.

But my best friend, Vik, and lots of my classmates are Serbian. So is Mr. Miran, my favorite teacher. I'm sure they'll be really mad when they find out all the damage their soldiers have caused. I bet they'll throw the guys who did this in jail.

I feel horrible. Standing in the middle of this swirl of exhausted, sobbing strangers, I try to keep up as Eldin fills me in on what he's heard on the radio: Serb soldiers forced the Croats to leave their own city, Vukovar, two hours north of us. They threw rocks and shot at the buses filled with fleeing refugees. I'm stunned when Eldin tells me it took three days for them to get here because they were forced to drive through Serbia and kept getting stopped. How could a two-hour trip take three days?

I picture the map of Yugoslavia from geography class, with Croatia bordering my home of Bosnia at the top, and Serbia surrounding us at the bottom. To get the Croatian passengers from Vukovar to their capital, Zagreb, Eldin explains, the drivers felt the safest route was through Brčko.

"We're caught between two warring republics, stuck right in the middle," he says.

"What's going to happen to us?" I ask.

He shakes his head. His lower lip is twitching. I've never seen my brother scared. His face lets me know: being the jelly in the doughnut is bad. Really bad.

I turn and notice a girl my age sitting on a bench near the playground. She has a bloody sheet wrapped around her head. I walk over and offer her water and my fudbal shirt. She takes my canteen and sips from it. Her long, dark hair is the same color as Lena's.

"Are you okay?" I ask.

"No," she bawls. "Serb soldiers with machine guns ordered us out of our house. They shot at us in cold blood. I don't know where my mother is — I have to find her!" She glances over at my mother handing out bottles of water and food, then she looks me in the eye. "Be careful, you could be next."

This is flipping me out. I used to be sure my parents wouldn't let anyone hurt us. But what if they can't protect us anymore? I watch a bunch of neighbors from our building bring out jackets, blankets, and food. The survivors keep telling us what they've been through.

"The Yugoslav Army set fire to our homes," a man with a gray beard mumbles. "They burned everything we owned. My dog, Staza, was in the house. They didn't care."

I picture a puppy stuck in a burning room, not able to get out.

"All that remains is ash," he goes on. "My whole life savings, gone, my poor Staza . . ."

It's too hard to hear. I want to put my hands over my ears and make him stop talking.

I find a spot away from the crowds to get my bearings. As I look around the park, I notice something odd. I only see the Muslims and Catholics I know helping out the Croatians. Vik isn't here. Or Marko. Or Ivan. None of my Serb friends or their relatives come.

"What's going to happen to these people?" I ask my brother.

"The buses will take them to a refugee camp near Zagreb, I heard," he tells me. "They'll be safe there."

I want to believe him. At home that night, I sleep with the lights on until Eldin comes in and flips the switch off.

On Monday morning, walking to school with the gang, I plan to ask Vik if he heard what happened to the Croatians over the weekend. But before I can, Marko says, "Did you hear about those filthy Croat traitors? They got what they deserved."

Everyone laughs, including Vik.

I don't. The back of my neck is tingling. "What makes them traitors?" I ask in a calm voice.

"Duh! They're rebels trying to overthrow the government, Bugs," Marko answers.

Vik and Marko don't know what they're talking about. The people at the park were just like us.

"Why did the army shoot at those passengers on the buses?" I ask Dad that night, sitting on the couch after dinner. I want to make sense of it. I'm sure there's something I'm missing.

My father shakes his head and clicks his tongue in disgust. "Remember I told you how our country is made up of families from different backgrounds who don't think the way we do?"

"But you said President Tito taught brotherhood and unity. And we should treat everyone the same," I say quickly. "That's why we gave out food and clothes to those poor people at the park."

"Well, after Tito died, in 1980, leaders from the Serb Republic decided they wanted to control the Croatians and the Bosnian Muslims," he says. "They're causing stupid fights that harm the innocent. It's despicable. This is how history repeats itself."

"But why are they doing it now?"

"They're mad because Croatia and Bosnia want independence," he explained.

"Is that why Vik and Marko were happy those Croats got beaten up?"

"They were?" Dad looks horrified. "They must be listening to their parents."

On the Croatian TV station, it sounds even worse than what we saw. "More than one thousand Croatians were relocated to a makeshift migrant shelter in Zagreb," they report. The conflict is escalating, with Serb soldiers committing atrocities, burning towns and villages, attacking civilians. Murdering entire families. They give a microphone to a young woman, who says, "We'd like to thank the Muslims and Catholics of Brčko who came to our aid, brought us water and blankets, and emptied their store shelves to feed us."

"That's us! We did that!" I tell Dad proudly. I secretly hope our good deed might keep us safe. The reporter and the woman are singling out the Muslims and Catholics as the good guys and Serbs as bad guys on television, in public, for all to hear. But I'm still nervous as I remember the words of the girl with the head bandage: "Be careful, you could be next."

"This fighting won't go on much longer," Dad assures me. But now he looks spooked too.

On Saturday morning I wait for Vik to holler for me to come down so we can play ball, like we do every single weekend. Nobody calls. When I walk outside, I see him and the other guys in the parking lot, already choosing teams. *What's going on?* I rush over.

"Vik, why didn't you call me? Don't you need my ball?" I'm talking too fast, too loud.

"We have our own," Ivan yells back.

"Yeah, we don't need yours anymore, Bosniak!" Vik holds up a ball that's ripped and a little deflated.

Vik has never called me a *Bosniak*. He says it like it's a dirty word. "Come on, I really want to play with you," I beg. I know the political stuff in our country is getting weirder, but I can't believe Vik — of all people — is trashing and benching me.

"Fine. We're on the army's team and you're on the rebels' side," Marko decides.

I don't like being called a rebel, since I'm not. But I jump in anyway, annoyed that Vik chooses Nizar and Ivan over me, even though they're lousy players. Their fathers are in the Serb army, like his.

Vik knows I'm not a traitor. I try to figure out if I've done anything to make him say that. I picture all the times we biked, swam, and played ball and marbles together. It's always been like this, ever since we were little. I know them, and they know me. I don't see Vik and Marko as "Serbian" or think of myself as "Bosniak."

I decide to play my best, show him I'm the same guy I've always been. I hope he'll lose, realize he needs me, and pick me next time. But as I dribble, Vik and Marko pull my shirt and kick at my ankles so I'll fall.

It's no shock Marko's a jerk. He hangs with Ivan, after all.

But — my best friend?

"Vik — why are you —"

"Shut up, Bugs Bunny." He tries to trip me again.

I can't believe this. I won't believe this. I stare at Vik, trying to make my eyes ask him *why?* But he looks away.

Of course, the "army's team" wins. Afterward we stand in the street, watching the real army trucks pass by. They kick up dust as they turn into the base. Vik and Marko wave at the drivers. Black smoke blows from the trucks' tailpipes. The smell of diesel fuel makes me cough.

I don't want to be here, but I can't leave. I keep glancing over at Vik, waiting for him to say he's sorry, nod, or give me a sign that he just can't talk now in front of the others. That he has to act this way in front of his brother and Ivan or they'll beat him up.

Still, he avoids my eyes.

"They'll be coming soon to slit the rebels' throats," Ivan says, sliding his finger across his neck, smiling at me.

A shiver runs through my body as it sinks in: I'm not safe here anymore. I turn and head back into our building, thinking of Lena and her sister, gone. I have a bad feeling and keep remembering the girl with the head bandage. I hope Lena's okay. None of Eldin's friends are calling or coming around. Other Muslim families have been sneaking out of the country too. The problems are not blowing over, like Dad keeps promising. They are blowing up.

Early the next morning, the doorbell rings. I run to answer, hoping Vik has come to say he didn't mean to screw up yesterday's game or call me names.

It is Vik, but he's with Marko.

"Give us our marbles back," Vik says with his chest puffed out.

"What? I've been the marble keeper the whole year," I say. I even spent my allowance on a bunch of sets and won most of the glass and ceramic ones myself.

Marko gets right in my face. "We don't want them at your house anymore."

"Why?" I feel my voice shaking a little. I say it quietly, since I don't want Mom to hear. My eyes prickle. No way am I going to cry. Not in front of them.

"Because you're a traitor," Marko insists. "We're not sharing anything with you."

"I am not! I never did anything bad to you," I tell him, adding, "My dad says the Serb politicians are lying."

Vik is quiet, but Marko sneers, "You Muslims are the liars."

I know we aren't, but can't think of how to prove it.

Vik and Marko follow me to my room. I get the canvas bag from under my bed. They snatch their share of marbles. Marko lifts his shirt, using it as a pouch to carry the loot.

My head pounds. Vik can't really hate me for my religion. That doesn't make sense. He's never even mentioned it before. It has to be something else. Is he jealous that Lena likes me better? Now I worry that he's only been pretending to like me since first grade.

That day I shoot the leftover marbles by myself for hours, feeling homesick in my own room. All week, the guys ignore me. I sit alone at recess, eating beef sausage from the food truck lady, watching everyone play without me. It sucks. I feel like I'm being punished, but I'm not sure for what. I'll have to switch schools to find new friends. Where will I go?

When Ivan comes over to the bench where I'm sitting, I expect him to call me more names or keep threatening me. Instead, he points to the fence. "Hey, come check this out," he says, as if we're still pals.

Surprised, I throw out the sausage wrapping and follow him across the field. On the other side of the fence, soldiers from the base are unpacking new rifles outside the warehouse. Every year a fresh batch of eighteen-year-olds do their mandatory service in the barracks, like Dad and Uncle Ahmet did. All the boys in my neighborhood look forward to turning eighteen so we can do our year of service. Staring at the new weapons being unloaded, so close, I wish I could touch one.

"Last week when I was swiping a bike, they were bringing in more equipment," Ivan tells me. He talks about stealing as if it's an everyday activity, like turning on the TV.

"What else do they keep in there?" I ask.

"Uniforms, gas masks, helmets, and duffle bags," he says, fixing me with his bugged-out blue eyes. "I know a secret entrance. We're sneaking in tonight. Meet me, Vik, and Marko here at nine. I'll bring bags to cart out the stuff." It's creepy how excited he looks.

Still, I'm pleased to be invited. Though I wonder if it's a trap. Or a test, to tell if I'm a traitor? I hope they just forgot they're supposed to be jerks to me.

I don't get why they'd rob from the army they like. Everything's upside down, but I want to prove to Vik that I'm still one of them. If we're caught, my parents will be really upset.

Mr. Miran might make me stand in the corner all day and never choose me for another recess team. I know robbery's a serious crime I could get thrown in jail for. But I really need to win my friends back.

FOUR

It's dark out and raining. Ivan is waiting for me with Viktor and Marko.

"Hey," Vik says, nodding.

"Hey." I'm glad he doesn't seem to hate me anymore. But I'm still not sure if they're messing with me. I hope his brother and Ivan made him call me names when he didn't really want to. I nod, like nothing strange went down, pretending everything's fine.

Vik hands me a plastic shopping bag. Ivan leads the five-minute walk to the edge of the school playground. My stomach is doing jumping jacks as we sneak through the hole in the fence, squeezing in sideways, one at a time. I slip in easily.

Ivan points to the new army recruits in the distance, patrolling the base. I'm nervous as we crouch down and hurry to the dark warehouse, getting wet from the rain. Ivan speed crawls to a window that's open. We follow without a sound. Are the soldiers so confident they're not even guarding their own guns?

It feels like we're on a spy mission. Ivan squeezes through the window. He reaches down for Marko. One by one, we boost each other inside. I'm last. As soon as we're all here, Ivan turns on the lights. I can't believe it. I want to scream, "Stop being stupid! Someone will see us!" But I don't say a word. I'm not gonna challenge the ringleader on my first heist.

The place is packed with shiny, cool military equipment in mounds stacked taller than we are. There's a raw, new smell, like wood. I stare at the fresh uniforms, tools, and gadgets. I wish I were eighteen and could wear a soldier's uniform and fire a rifle and ride in a tank, like Dad and my uncle do in the reserves. I try not to remember I'd be on the opposite side from Vik, Marko, and Ivan. Right now, we're all just plainclothes spies.

"Grab what you can," Ivan orders.

I work fast, putting bandages, a canteen, a green flashlight, and a small shovel that folds in half into the shopping bag. Wow, this stuff could be really useful. The gas masks are black rubber with big goggles to protect your eyes. I take four for me, Dad, Mom, and Eldin, so we'll be prepared in case the war comes. Viktor and Marko take shovels too, along with combat sweaters, socks, and gun holsters. Ivan seizes a helmet, camouflage pants, a gas mask, and some shirts. Nobody spots any guns or ammunition the way we'd hoped. We all find backpacks and stuff more stolen goods inside.

Each of us takes turns as lookout. My throat is dry. It's

nerve-racking but thrilling to be back on the same team where I belong.

"A soldier is coming," Viktor hisses. "Hide!"

We look around frantically, then burrow under a pile of blankets that are thick and scratchy. I almost pee my pants. A soldier who looks Eldin's age stares through the window, but he doesn't see us. He probably thinks another recruit flicked on the lights.

"Let's get out of here," I whisper. What will my mother do if she finds out? I don't know who's more scary—the militia or Mom.

"Let's come back again tomorrow," Ivan says loudly, like we're hanging at home and not about to get arrested. Of course he isn't nervous—he's been ripping off things his whole life.

We hurry toward the window and climb back outside. It's raining harder now. My breath is fast. It's a struggle to move quickly carrying so much stuff. Ivan goes through the hole in the fence first, and we hand him the backpacks and bags, then squeeze through after him.

The rain hammers down on our heads, and there's no one around to see or hear us. I follow their lead, and we dig ditches in the mud with our new shovels, stashing our take along the outside of the fence. I put mine under a bush near a weeping willow tree that I'll use as a marker to find later. Ivan takes a whiz near another bush. I do too. What a relief.

We run back to our apartment complex, and I wave bye to Vik. He nods back! Does he think I did a good job?

At home, I dry off and put my wet clothes in the hamper, acting like I've just been out playing. Mom, Dad, and Eldin barely notice me. I go to bed but can't fall asleep. I stare at the ceiling, watching the shadows move. I've just gone against everything my parents believe. But I'm psyched to get away with it.

The next day during math, the principal, Mr. Nikolić, walks in and says, "Kenan Trebinčević, come with me."

Everybody is watching, even Mr. Miran. I follow the principal with my eyes on the floor as I pass rows of desks and walk out of the classroom and down the hall. My palms are wet. My mind is shouting questions: *Is this about the army stuff? What else could it be? What's gonna happen to me? Will Mom freak? What if Lena finds out?*

Two military policemen stand in the principal's office. Both Serbs, I figure. Ivan's already in a chair across from Principal Nikolić's desk. I swallow hard.

I can't figure out why Marko and Vik aren't in trouble too. Are they taking me to jail? Could this ruin my chance of a fudbal career? Worse, will they beat me up like they did to those poor Croatians in the park?

"Where were you last night, Kenan?" the tall soldier demands. His voice is rough, like sandpaper.

"We were playing hide-and-seek," Ivan jumps in.

If I didn't know better, I'd believe him. I'm awed by how easily he makes up stories. To him, lying comes as naturally as breathing. He slouches in his chair, not looking afraid at all. He's been here before. Or maybe it's because he's a Serb too? I nod in agreement.

The principal leaves, then returns with my classmate Aleks Vojnović. He has food stuck in his braces, as usual. What's he doing here?

"I overheard them talking about breaking into the base last night," Aleks says proudly, like he's some big hero for snitching.

I've never liked him. My dad used to go skiing with his father, but now that Dr. Vojnović is president of our town's Serb party, they aren't friends anymore.

"When this is over, I'll get you," Ivan hisses at Aleks, who looks terrified.

Ivan spits at him, and the principal pulls Ivan out of the chair by his ears and slams his head to the desk. My mouth drops open. This is ugly. I've never been in trouble like this before.

"You boys have ten minutes to bring everything back," the officer says calmly, but his glare could cut through steel.

The back of my neck drips with sweat. I was nine the last time I got scolded by the principal — for kicking a new kid who'd called me Bugs Bunny and making him cry. My parents made me apologize. If they hear about the robbery, they'll ground me forever.

Two more uniformed men appear in the hallway and escort me and Ivan out of the school and into a military jeep. "Where is the contraband?" one asks.

We reveal where the spot along the fence is. They drive us there and wait in the jeep as we walk to the bush and dig up the stuff with our hands.

"I bet they don't know what we stole," Ivan whispers in my ear. "They can't see much from here. Let's just give a few things back."

He has a point. I decide to keep the gas masks my family might need. And if I return everything and Ivan doesn't, they'll suspect something's up.

I don't want to be a wimp. I decide to act chill so I'll be asked to go on more secret missions with Vik.

I lift out the shovel, flashlight, and backpack, but leave the bandages and masks behind, shoveling dirt back over them. Picturing the war movies I've seen with Dad, I worry that if there's black smoke, fires, or fumes from rockets, my family won't be able to breathe. I could save us.

The soldiers take the loot and yell, "Get in the jeep!" We drive back in silence. They stop in the middle of the school's courtyard, and we get out. My classmates are all staring down from the second-story windows. Shaking, I wipe my dirty hands on my jeans. My parents are going to kill me. Mr. Miran will never pick me for any of his teams again.

"We are so screwed," I tell Ivan.

They put us in two separate small classrooms with no windows, like the cops on *Law & Order* do when they're interrogating perps. There's a rectangular table with chairs around it, and Milisav, a Serb friend of Dad's, is standing there. They serve in the army reserves together every year. I'm relieved to see him.

"Oh, it's little Keka," he says, but without his usual smile beneath his goofy mustache that hangs down to his chin. He's not happy to see me. This is not good.

I reach out to give him a handshake as I always do. He keeps his hands to himself.

"I know his father," he tells the two other soldiers who brought me in. "Sit down," he commands.

I obey, sitting on the edge of the leather chair, my feet barely touching the floor. I feel tiny as the tall men hover above me. "Did your dad put you up to this?" Milisav asks.

"N-n-no," I stutter. "We just thought it would be a neat game to see if we could sneak into the base."

Milisav shakes his finger in my face. "Wait until I tell him."

I can't stop tears from pooling in my eyes.

"Do you support the army?" his young comrade barks.

I'm not sure what to say. "I love our country," I tell him.

"Are you a Bosnian, a Yugoslavian, or a Muslim?" Milisav asks.

Is it a trick question? "My country is Yugoslavia. I'm from the Bosnian Republic. My religion is Muslim," I say. I'm being honest. I think it's a good answer that proves I'm not a traitor. But Milisav's sour face tells me it's not the response he wants.

"Take him back to his class," he orders the younger guy.

In the classroom, Ivan isn't there. Vik looks worried that I've been a tattletale. I raise my eyebrow, trying to signal that I didn't give anything away.

"What did you do?" Mr. Miran asks. I can tell he's disappointed in me. He's never scolded me before. I'm usually a good student who tries hard. He once said he expected a lot from me because he respected my dad so much.

"I'm sorry, Teacher," I tell him, embarrassed.

"Now is not the time for apologies." His teeth are clenched tight. At least he isn't screaming like he sometimes does when other students screw up. I hope it's a sign I might be forgiven.

When Ivan comes back to class, he nods at me, then at Vik, making it clear I'm not a rat.

After school, I straggle home, keeping my head to the ground. I'm too ashamed to look up. I don't even want to think about my mother. I pray she doesn't know.

At my building, I lift my eyes to see Mom glaring at me from our balcony. "My hands will be around your throat!" she shouts down at me.

They must have called her from school. I've never seen her this mad. I take a deep breath, then bolt upstairs to get it over with.

Her face is red with rage. "I was at work and heard your name on the radio!" she yells. "They said you stole supplies from the army!"

I was on the radio? For a minute I feel like I'm a famous crazy outlaw, like Billy the Kid in the Val Kilmer movie. It's exciting — until I catch Mom's puffy face and realize I've humiliated her in public. Majka Emina always says the worst thing you can do in our culture is smear your family's good name. My heart drops to the floor.

I imagine that none of Dad's friends will shake my hand anymore. The owners of the candy store won't trust me — they'll watch me like a hawk so I don't steal, like Ivan does. My friends' parents will whisper: *Stay away from Kenan Trebinčević.* No fudbal team will ever scout me as a player. Wherever Lena is, she'll no longer like me.

"I wasn't the leader, Ivan was," I try to explain as I enter our apartment. "I just took bandages and gas masks for us, in case anything happens."

She doesn't hear a word. "Go to your room. You're grounded forever! What are people at work going to think of my son the thief?" she shrieks, swatting at me.

I race to the bedroom. Eldin and Dad aren't home yet. I bet they'll be angry at me and ashamed too. Everyone probably heard that radio broadcast. What will the people at Dad's fitness center say?

The minutes crawl by. I can hear my mother banging pots and pans in the kitchen. No music tonight. Finally I hear my father return from work. He storms into my room without knocking.

I freeze, sitting on the corner of the bed. Neither of my parents have ever hit me, but this time I'm in for it.

"Why did you do this?" he hollers, hands on his hips.

"Everyone says the war's coming. I'm scared. I want us to be ready," I tell him.

"You do this by stealing?" he yells. "What did you take?"

"A canteen, flashlight, bandages, shovel, and four gas masks, one for each of us. To keep us safe." I need to prepare us for the war. My parents aren't doing it. *Somebody has to,* I almost say.

Dad doesn't speak for a minute. Then he looks worried. "Listen, Kenji, that's not your job," he says in a quieter tone. He pats my head. "Don't leave your room or make noise, or your mom will murder you."

I'm relieved he's not that angry, but I'm still nervous about my mom and brother.

Eldin drops his books on his desk when he gets home and stares at me. I'm waiting for him to punch my arm and tell me I'm an embarrassing idiot.

"Hey, that was wild. Your name was really on the radio?" he asks. "How did you sneak in there?"

Turns out I don't need to worry about my brother after all. He's impressed with my new tough guy rep!

"Like Sylvester Stallone in *Rambo III* invading the Russian base in the dark," I say, feeling taller. "But without any German shepherds."

"Get any guns?" he wants to know, like he's sorry he wasn't in on it too.

"I wish," I tell him. "There weren't any. I checked."

Mom hasn't changed her mind, though. For the first time ever, I'm not allowed to eat dinner with my family. I sit on the floor of my room like an outcast, starving. When I hear my uncle's loud voice, I open my door. Mom's bossy older brother Ahmet is my favorite. For my birthday he brings me miniature cars, plastic army men, and milk chocolate.

"Can I please see my uncle?" I call from my room, hoping he'll get her to forgive me.

"No! You stay there, you thief!" Mom yells.

"Get out here, Kenan!" Uncle Ahmet calls. He's strong and always in charge, even at *our* place. Knowing she won't argue with him, I slink to the kitchen, where they're eating without me. I stare at Uncle Ahmet's plate of chicken, okra, and rice, my stomach growling. "What did you do?" he demands.

"I stole from the army," I confess, head down. "Aleks Vojnović told on us."

"You know who Aleks's father is?" Dad asks Uncle Ahmet, his voice filled with disgust. "The doctor who heads the Serb radical party."

"They're the ones with the red flag with the double-headed eagle and cross," I say.

"That's what you're punishing him for? You're not grounded anymore," my uncle declares, magically pardoning me. "Let him steal from those unscrupulous bastards who keep attacking us with our own weapons." He lights a cigarette and tells Mom to bring me food. I look at Dad, who nods his okay.

Mom pushes a plate of okra and rice at me, scowling. "Here, eat, *ti žvotinjo*," she says, rolling her eyes at her brother. She's never called me an animal before. I feel dirty.

"Bosnian workers haven't been paid for months — teachers, lawyers, doctors, municipal employees," Uncle Ahmet explains. "Those corrupt Serb bastards put the money they owe us into guns to kill us."

"Despicable murderers," Dad spits out.

I shovel food in my mouth fast, before Mom can change her mind. When I look up, Uncle Ahmet winks at me. Does that mean stealing back from the "corrupt Serb bastards" is allowed?

As soon as I walk into school the next day, I'm sent to the principal's office a second time. None of the other boys are there. I sit on the bench in the hallway and miss my first class. Then Principal Nikolić opens the door and tells me to come inside. The wooden floor squeaks as I sit in the chair across from him.

He leans forward and asks in a harsh voice, "Did your father get you to do this?"

"No." I shake my head violently. I can't bear to cause problems for Dad. "I was just fooling around with my friends."

He phones my father to come get me. Twenty minutes later, Dad barges into the office. "Why do you keep interrogating my son?" he shouts, looking around. "What about the other boys?"

Principal Nikolić seems embarrassed. "It's standard procedure now."

"He keeps asking if you talked me into it," I tell Dad, more confident now that he's here to protect me. "Yesterday your friend Milisav wanted to know if I was a Yugoslavian, Bosnian, or Muslim."

Dad shakes his head. "What did you tell them?"

"I said I'm all three."

"That's right, you are," Dad says. He turns to the principal. "Is that why he's the only kid here? Because he's Muslim?" I realize that Principal Nikolić is a Serb. "Don't you *dare* call him into your office again!"

Dad slams his fist on the desk, then takes me by the arm, and we march out. I hold my head high.

At home, he grabs his army beret and captain's uniform from the closet.

After his mandatory army service at eighteen, Dad has kept volunteering to stay in the reserves. Every year he puts on the uniform and heads off for a whole month, promising to write. Every year when the month has passed, I wait downstairs for him to return. He looks powerful coming up the street in his green shirt and beret, with his pants tucked neatly into his boots. When I was a little kid, I'd jump into his arms and he'd put his cap on my head before carrying me upstairs.

"You're coming with me to the military base," he tells me now, shoving his uniform into a bag. We walk there in silence. I glance up at him. He's cursing under his breath, still furious.

At the gate he announces, "Tell Milisav that Keka is here."

The guard does as he says, then lets us enter.

In the one-story yellow brick building, Milisav leads Dad into his office and says, "Keka, we need to talk. This is not good for you."

"No, this is not good for *you*." My father points his finger at his face. "You're harassing my son because he's Muslim? How long have we been friends? How long have I volunteered to serve in this army?" My father rips the red star from his beret. He forces it into Milisav's hand. Then he gives him the rest of his army greens. "I don't believe in this nationalistic nonsense. I resign."

This is upsetting. Dad has always told us to respect the military. Each spring my buddies and I wave at the new Yugoslavian recruits marching around the base. We even hand out candy to the young soldiers.

"I thought I could count on you," Milisav says.

"It's not my army anymore," my father tells him, turning to leave.

He doesn't look back over his shoulder as we walk away, but I do. Milisav just stands there, stunned, holding Dad's uniform and shaking his head.

"I bet they didn't ask Ivan what religion he was," I tell Dad on our walk home.

"It wasn't that kid Aleks's idea to snitch on you," he says, like he's thinking out loud. "It was his father's dirty work."

I'm honored that my dad is standing up for me. But I hope this doesn't get him into trouble too.

Ivan and I are famous now. At lunch the next day, people crowd around, firing questions.

"Did you hide any of the guns?" a short kid wants to know.

"How did you manage to sneak by the armed soldiers?" a tall blond girl shouts out.

Even the teachers are curious. "When did you become a thief? Aren't your parents beside themselves?" asks Mrs. Kusturica, the math instructor, clicking her tongue and staring at me, like she's trying to solve the equation of how a good kid could go rotten so quickly. Overnight I've become a dangerous celebrity. Now I *really* wish Lena was still here.

I kind of enjoy my new troublemaker status. But I keep thinking about what Dad and Uncle Ahmet said at dinner. If the army hates Muslims and attacks innocent people, why aren't *they* considered the bad guys? Nothing makes sense anymore.

"You won't need braces. I'll fix your teeth for you," Ivan hisses at Aleks the Rat right before he jumps him on the fudbal field after school. Marko and Ivan punch him. Aleks is a creep who was happy to tell on us, so he deserves it. I add a kick — just a light one on his arm, but still. It's the first time I've ever been a bully.

I get in trouble for that too, but I don't mind, since we all get scolded.

"We beat up Aleks for snitching," I admit to Dad at dinner.

"Good," he says, and I smile, happy to please him.

FIVE

APRIL 1992

On Sunday night, the fathers from our building hold a meeting in the courtyard. I stand on the balcony, where I can hear every word.

"We have to watch out for the Serbs running the army," yells Hasan, my friend Huso's dad.

Our next door neighbor Obren shouts back, "We Serbs are peaceful people. It's the damn Muslims and Catholics we need to protect ourselves from."

Hasan lunges at Obren. I stare, surprised. I've never seen well-dressed Professor Hasan fight with anyone. Dad jumps in between the two and pulls Hasan away, taking him off to a corner to talk him down.

Why is Dad taking Obren's side? Obren's a Serb. He and his redheaded wife, Petra, aren't very nice neighbors, barely speaking to us when we pass in the hall. They bang on the wall when Eldin and I are loud.

"I'm sending Huso out of the country," Hasan tells Dad. "You should send your kids away too."

"Stop overreacting," Dad answers, patting his shoulder. "Showing your temper now can get you killed."

On Monday morning, as we're eating breakfast, the local radio station announces that school's been canceled indefinitely. My parents exchange a look. Dad tells us, "It's for security reasons."

"You boys won't be going back for a while," Mom says, nervously wiping the kitchen counter.

I'm thrilled to not have class or exams. I want to go outside and celebrate with the guys, get a couple of extra games going now that I've passed their test of courage and I'm in again.

But Dad tells me and Eldin, "Listen, something bad might happen. If it does, we'll be okay and it won't last long."

What's he talking about? I think of the Croatians in the park and feel a pang in my gut. Who'll get hurt next?

While Eldin stays to talk to Dad, I run outside. My friends are by the gate, so I go over to say hi to Vik. But Ivan blocks my path. He crosses his arms.

"We don't hang with rebels," Marko says. Then he spits on me.

The warm slobber runs down my cheek. I can't believe it. The four of us survived our army mission and the fallout from the authorities together. I didn't tattle or break under pressure. Some of the stuff we took is still under the weeping willow — and they're back to treating me like the enemy? Oh, come on!

I harden my expression and wipe his slime off my face with my shirtsleeve. I clench my fists.

"Play by yourself, you separatist turncoat," Ivan says.

That must be a new Serb insult for Muslims and Catholics. I stare right at Vik, waiting for him to stick up for me and tell his brother off.

But Vik won't meet my eyes. "Yeah, play your own game," he mumbles.

Then they turn and walk away, laughing at me. My teeth are clenched so hard my jaw hurts.

I broke my parents' rules to do their robbery, got into trouble with the school, and was hauled in front of the army — all for Vik. And this is how he repays me? I did *every single thing* they did, but *I'm* the turncoat? I think of how Vik and I were closer than he was to Marko and Ivan, and how I can't even talk to my best friend now. I'm done being betrayed by him. *I'm* not the traitor, Vik is!

The next day, as I'm walking down my building's stairs, I see Ivan sitting there. I can't avoid him, so I try to go around him. But he trips me, laughing when I fall on the cement.

My palm gets scratched and the scab on my kneecap is bleeding. I look up at my balcony to check if Mom is watching. I don't want her to see me weak. I picture her screaming at my friends, humiliating me more. Luckily, nobody from my family can see how they're treating me.

I go back upstairs to wash the dirt off my hands and put on a bandage. I'm madder than I've ever been, swearing inside my head. I can't figure out if they already hated me during the army theft. Did they set me up, use me to steal stuff and take the fall? I'm sick of how mean they are.

With school closed, there's no homework, no early bedtime, no getting up at six a.m. But when I look out the window, there are no kids out playing—not that my ex-friends would let me play anyway. Only Serb soldiers standing at the end of our block.

In the living room, the TV is on. I used to have to plead to watch more television. Now they never turn it off—but all it shows is the stupid news, over and over.

Mom insists we stay home. "Everyone's keeping their kids inside," she tells Dad. They don't go to work, either. We sit on the sofa, watching the news for hours. I'm bored out of my brains. The next day's the same dull story. So is the day after that.

Later that week, Uncle Ahmet comes by. I'm happy to see him, but he says he can't stay. He's in a hurry to drive my Aunt Maksida and cousins Minka and Almira six hours to the north so they can escape to Vienna. I don't want my uncle, aunt, and cousins to leave.

"The battles are getting worse," he tells Dad. "The army's slaughtering more Muslims each day." He isn't hiding adult things from me anymore.

"Why would our National Army do that?" I ask.

"It's just the Serbs' army now," Uncle Ahmet says. "I can take the boys with me," he adds, gesturing to us.

We both turn to Dad. I want to go with my uncle and cousins. With no school, and friends who aren't my friends anymore, there's nothing to stay here for.

"Keka, maybe it's a good idea," my mother says, her voice tense but pleading.

"No!" Dad shouts. "I will not break up my family. We are all remaining here under one roof. I've lived in peace my whole life. I am not leaving my business — or my home. This will blow over."

"You're being stubborn and pigheaded," Uncle Ahmet argues. "It's too dangerous for the kids to stay here."

For the first time ever, I believe my uncle over my father. My neck gets hot and scratchy. I feel guilty, disloyal.

Dad folds his arms. "Nobody will hurt us."

My mother glares at him. "How do you know that, Keka?"

His face is set and stubborn, like when he orders a player to get back in the game. "Because I did nothing wrong. I didn't join a political party. I didn't even vote!"

Later, when we're lying in our beds not sleeping, Eldin explains the backstory. "The Serbs won't let Bosnia or Croatia get independence from Yugoslavia. That's why they're going to war."

"Against who?" I'm still not understanding how the Serb

army can fight Bosniaks and Croatians when we're all Yugoslavs who live together.

"Against us," he says.

Vik and Marko's and Ivan's fathers now wear a different kind of green military jacket, with Serbian flag patches. Dad says all the Serb men are quitting their jobs at the factories and construction sites. They're being paid by the army to be soldiers. When they leave in the morning in their uniforms, I'm scared they'll do the terrible things to Muslims that Uncle Ahmet and Dad talked about. I hear Vik, down in our courtyard, bragging that his dad's joined up. I notice the only guys out there playing with him now are Serbs.

Alone in my room, I divide my green plastic army men into three teams.

"Boom! *Ksshhhh!*" I drop a marble bomb from my tin airplane onto a fort made of matchboxes.

The news stays on, even through dinner each night, which we now eat while sitting on the couch in front of the TV. Mom gives me and Eldin extra napkins so nothing spills.

Tomo calls to tell Eldin that his family's leaving town. Then we hear all the phones of Muslim families are being tapped, so Eldin stops calling everyone altogether.

We're eating moussaka as a news commentator says, "Separatists who aim to overthrow the government must be stopped.

These traitors are causing civil unrest and trying to destroy the country."

I don't know any "separatists," and I can't figure out how my family has ended up on the wrong side. Except for my one-time robbery with the gang, I follow rules and laws. Dad always makes me and Eldin act like "polite gentlemen." We aren't "overthrowing" anything. None of my relatives have ever hurt anyone.

This is pissing me off.

"Are the TV news reporters lying?" I ask Dad.

He tosses an embroidered pillow at the set. "That station's controlled by Serbs!" he yells. "The politicians are brainwashing everyone with this bullshit propaganda."

It's the first time I've ever heard my father swear. I'm too shocked to ask anything else.

By the last week of April, I can tell that something terrible is about to happen. Eldin says all the Muslim people we grew up with are sneaking themselves and their families out of the country any way they can, by bus, train, plane, or car.

One morning over breakfast, Dad says that Huso and his family have fled in the middle of the night. They've lived in the apartment below ours since I was born. I go out into the hallway and look at the stairwell, not believing they're gone.

"But why didn't Huso say goodbye?" I ask Mom.

"They had to leave fast," she says, throwing an angry glare at Dad.

"And he couldn't even knock on the door or call me?" I say, stung. I'm getting used to being betrayed by my former Serb friends — but not Muslims like us.

Dad takes a deep breath and says softly, "Hasan learned they were on a blacklist to be killed." He looks pale and scared.

What? People are doing that? I picture my friend Huso, his smiling mom and kind dad, Professor Hasan, who teaches me English. His younger sister, Nadina, is in my grade. "Why?"

"Hasan voted in the party elections last February and spoke up for Bosnian independence," my father explains. "But don't worry. I didn't vote, and we're not on the list."

Is that why Dad broke up the fight between Obren and Hasan? To keep Hasan's family safe? I feel like I'm not getting the real story. They're hiding something.

All I know is that Huso and Nadina are gone, just like my cousins Minka and Almira. And Lena and her sister. And all my brother's and parents' friends and their families. Are Eldin and I the only Muslim kids still here?

From the window I see Vik and my old gang hanging out by the stairs. I used to love that this building was our meeting place. Not anymore. Every time they're in the courtyard, my stomach hurts from being reminded they hate me.

I decide to go out anyway. Vik is sitting with his legs stretched across the stairs, and as I pass him, he trips me. Marko spits on me again. Ivan laughs.

I wish I could punch them, but I'm outnumbered. If I get jumped by the gang and defend myself, Mom will yell at me for fighting. If I tell Dad or Eldin, they'll think I'm a loser for not defending myself.

I go back upstairs.

That night my father and I are out on the balcony, watching flames rise in the sky in the distance. The sound of bombing thunders down from the north, and I flinch. I've only seen these kind of explosions in war movies, never in real life before. My heart pounds so fast it's like an explosion in my chest.

"Don't worry. We'll be okay staying here." He pats my arm. "This won't last very long."

I love my Dad so much, but I don't believe him anymore.

I know he's not lying to me on purpose. He thinks everybody is kind and honest, like he is. But those Croatians from the park were good people too. And they still got beaten up, shot at, and driven out of their towns.

We aren't safe here, not even in our home. I know we should have gone with Uncle Ahmet to my aunt's family in Vienna. But my father won't budge, and Mom refuses to leave without him. Nobody asks Eldin's opinion, or mine.

We're the only Muslims left in town. There's nothing I can do but wait until they come for us.

SIX

My father storms into the apartment one afternoon like an angry tornado. "I was just at the bank. You won't believe it! Our account's completely empty," he rages. He's panting, his hands shaking.

My mother rushes to the foyer, Eldin and I following right behind her. "What happened?"

"Thousands of dinars erased. Those greedy Serb bastards. Damn them all to hell!" Dad's voice keeps getting louder. I'm getting used to his cursing.

Mom puts her hands over her heart. "But how could all our money just disappear?"

"It's gone. Our life savings, wiped out." He looks shocked, his eyes bulging. "The Serb government stole it for supplies and weapons. They think they're above the law."

"They *are* the law now," Eldin says.

Mom's face turns the color of ashes. "How . . . How will we survive? What will we do without money?"

The room feels hot and cold and blurry and bright all at once. I want her to stop asking horrible questions, though I'm wondering the same things she is. Who can just steal a family's money like that—from a bank!—and get away with it? Bank robbers in old movies like *Bonnie and Clyde* get chased, put in jail, or shot. But in our case, the police, soldiers, and bankers are the ones doing the stealing.

"All we have is in our wallets," Dad says, opening his. He empties it right there on the dining room table. Then he goes to the liquor cabinet, where he keeps extra cash. He pulls out six bills, dinar notes showing President Tito's picture.

My mother goes to her purse, and then to the drawer where she keeps spare cash, and gathers up what she has. I run to my hiding place in the bedroom closet, my heart pounding, and take out the birthday bills and coins from Majka and Aunt Bisera. I hand it all to my parents. Eldin offers what he's saved from his birthdays and allowance too.

We count out the bills and coins. Seven thousand dinars altogether. It isn't much, about the cost of the BMX bicycle Dad's supposed to get me for my twelfth birthday. I have the awful feeling that's not gonna happen.

"Wait, I have some cash at work!" my father says. There's a cash register for when he sells sports drinks, and he keeps a safe in his office. "I'll be back as soon as I can." He puts on his jacket as he rushes out the door.

Mom tells Eldin to clean up his side of our room and me to do my homework, forgetting there's no school. We're all on edge, waiting for Dad to return.

Then the lights go out. Mom tries to turn the lamps back on, but they won't work. We walk around the apartment, flicking all the switches. Nothing. No TV. No light on in the fridge. We have no power at all.

What's going on? Is this happening to everyone in our complex? Next, the faucets go dry. The toilets stop flushing. How will we live with no water? Where's my dad?

Mom lights a candle in the living room, even though it's not dark out yet. Her face looks pale and trembly. I don't know if it's the candlelight flickering or her fear.

"What if I go get us some water?" I ask, picking up two empty jugs in the kitchen. I'll go to the well we use after playing street fudball games.

"Good thinking," Eldin says. "I'll come too."

"No." Mom stops him. "Obren said men over eighteen are being rounded up. Eldin should stay here."

"I'll go myself." As I walk down the stairs, I feel proud to be useful.

"Be careful, Kenji," Mom calls.

The street's weirdly quiet. It's four p.m. but nobody's outside. Where is everyone? My heart races as I hurry through the deserted streets to the well a few blocks away.

As I'm filling the jugs, I look around at the store windows and telephone poles, plastered with political posters for Croats, Serbs, and Bosnian Muslims, and it hits me: my whole country has divided into three rival teams.

Eldin is standing outside our building when I return. Without a word, he takes one of the heavy jugs to carry upstairs with me. Dad still isn't home.

"Just drink a bit," Mom says, pouring us little cupfuls. "We don't know how long it has to last." Her voice is shaking. She's trying to act as if everything is okay, but we know it's not. I grab her hand and squeeze.

We wait for almost an hour. Finally we hear footsteps in the hall. It's Dad! He's home safe. Mom rushes to the foyer to hug him while I swipe away the tears leaking from my eyes so Eldin doesn't call me a wuss. I'm so relieved we're all here.

"It's bad," my father tells us. His jaw is clenched. His shirt's wet under his arms. He smells sweaty, probably from running. "I heard gunfire and bombs going off on the street next to the gym." He takes out more bills from his pockets and counts all we have. "Not even enough for plane tickets." He shakes his head, looking crushed.

He never imagined getting ripped off by the bank or pushed out of Brčko. He knows he's waited too long to get us out of here. I feel sorry for him. I knew we should have gone weeks ago. Why didn't he?

Eldin takes out his old ham radio. We spend the night listening for the latest news. The ice cream in our freezer melts, so we drink it from the container. Mom and Dad forget to send me to bed. I'm excited to be up so late with Eldin, but hearing what's going on makes my insides jumpy. It's hard to stay calm when everything's getting crazier. The radio announcer says he's "Senad Hadžifejzović, with battle updates from our capital Sarajevo." From his name, I can tell he's Muslim. They're getting bombed too, he reports. All airports are closed. Cabs and trains aren't running either. Brčko is surrounded by Serbian troops.

We can't leave now, even if we try.

The next morning, Dad hears that Uncle Ahmet and other Bosnian Muslim men have formed a resistance army miles away, on the outer edges of Brčko. I'm impressed my uncle got Aunt Maksida and my cousins to Vienna, then came back to fight. What a tough guy he is.

Dad and Eldin want to join up, but Mom warns they'll get killed walking outside or driving now. And even if public transportation were running, the cashiers would ask to see ID before selling tickets. While Serbs, Croats, and Bosniaks like us all look alike, the name Trebinčević might give away our religion.

I wish I were old enough to be a soldier like my brave Uncle Ahmet, my hero.

SEVEN

MAY 1992

On Friday, May 1, I'm eating dry honey flakes cereal for breakfast when I hear a blast so loud, it's like thunder inside my head. Mom, Dad, Eldin, and I hold each other close. The floor rattles beneath us. We wait to see what happens next, but it goes quiet. Mom eventually lets go and opens the door to find out if there's been any damage to our building.

"The war is here," I overhear a Serb neighbor tell her in the hallway. "Don't let your husband go outside. Or Eldin, since he's fighting age. They'll definitely take him." *What about me?*

"It's not safe for any of us to go out anymore," Dad says. He locks the door, shuts the windows tight, and pulls down our shades.

Explosions in our subdivision come at all hours, off and on. You never know when they'll hit. I thought I'd be happy with no school, but now I miss my classmates and Mr. Miran. I hope he's okay. I just want to go back to normal, but we can't. I'm not sure we ever will.

We're the only Muslim family left in the building. I'm afraid they'll shoot us or blast us to smithereens.

"We're actually lucky so many Serb soldiers live here," Eldin says. "They won't blow up their own people."

Living with armed bad guys on all sides of us makes us lucky? At least my family's not sugarcoating everything, treating me like a dumb kid. I feel like I'm an adult now too.

Senad, the radio newscaster, seems like a courageous friend we can trust. He's caught in the crossfire too, he tells us. He announces that our city is officially occupied by the Serb army and we're under curfew.

"What does it mean, they're 'occupying us'?" I ask.

Eldin's face is grim. "It means our enemies are in control of everything and we're being held hostage."

I wish I could be a hero like Uncle Ahmet, or like Bruce Willis in *Die Hard*, flipping cars over and charging through the fire. But even Bruce couldn't save all those poor hostages.

We wake up to gunfire at four in the morning, our apartment rumbling from bombs. It gives me a headache. I peek through the blinds to see masked men with assault rifles driving up and down our street in jeeps.

"What do they want?" I ask my brother.

"Us," Eldin answers.

But we're all Yugoslavians, I think. How could our own people be hunting us down like animals?

Mom moves us into the living room so we can all sleep on the floor together. In my nightmare, I'm in a truck that turns over, and I wake up with my ears throbbing.

I try to act as calm as Dad and Eldin, but I'm twisting into knots.

The sanitation department has stopped coming to take away the trash. It piles up outside our building. Soon the air smells like rotting garbage, even through the windows. With the shades drawn and no sunlight, Mom's plants are wilting. We're all wilting.

My mother portions out the well water carefully. We're each allowed to drink half a cup a day. After we wash our hands, we use that water to flush the toilet.

We're lucky she went food shopping last week, when we had money. She makes us salami sandwiches and gives Eldin and me three gingersnaps each for dessert.

By the end of the first week, we've eaten everything left in the warm fridge: the chicken, turkey, salad, vegetables, and fruit. Next we eat the canned fish, tuna, soup, dried fruit, and baked goods from the pantry. Some of the meat in our freezer goes rotten and we have to throw it out. The days and nights crash into each other as we all sit on the couch, hearing our city getting destroyed.

Keeping all the windows closed makes it muggy inside, too.

I'm antsy and sweating. I hum "I believe in the power of love," from the Madonna song Mom likes, swaying and spinning around. Mom ignores me. Then I sit on the rug, playing cops and robbers with my toy tank, army truck, and police van.

"Crash! Bang!" I smash my miniature cars into each other.

"Don't act like a baby. Keep quiet, somebody will hear you," Mom scolds in a wobbly voice.

At least I got her attention for a minute. "Who?" I ask, putting the toys away and taking out my playing cards. "The building's half empty."

I shuffle my deck and beg Eldin to play poker. He's the one who taught me five-card draw. But he says no, so I switch to solitaire. Then I get out my notebook and colored markers and draw pictures of Lena in the pink shirt she was wearing the day I scored the winning goal at school.

When nobody's watching, I peek outside through the slits in the blinds. I hear footsteps outside and sneak to the front door to figure out who's walking in the hallway. My brother keeps trying to find the latest news on the radio. Luckily we have extra batteries. We ration the box of beige candles. We ration everything. I'm thirsty. My feet are fidgety. I miss the sun, running on the field, stretching my legs outside.

"Get away from the windows in case of stray bullets," Mom warns. "Keep the radio low. Be still."

I go to my rocking chair in the bedroom and rock back and

forth as fast as I can until I get really sweaty. The chair is on a thick rug, so it doesn't make the floor squeak. I don't know what else to do.

I crave Majka's lemon cake, a juice box, warm toast, eggs, and jam. But I get used to having cereal without milk. Mom and Dad are hardly eating. I don't know if they've lost their appetites or if they're saving everything for my brother and me. I feel guilty with each bite and make Mom eat a spoonful of my cereal, though she pretends she's not hungry. What will we do when all our food runs out?

Eldin spends hours listening to his radio for news from Senad. I know my brother can tell how caged up I feel when he asks, "Game of marbles?" I can't believe it. We haven't played since our big fight when I kicked him in the crotch.

He's my only friend now, though I'm pretty sure he doesn't even like me. We're just stuck with each other.

Sitting on the floor in our room, I fire my blue marble into the hole, a circle on the carpet.

"Good shot!" Eldin says. If he's being *this* nice to me, I know: he thinks we're goners.

"What's gonna happen to us?" I ask.

"Some people are predicting the war will end in a few more weeks," he tells me.

"What do you think?"

"I dunno," he says. "Senad's saying the fighting is spreading all over the country."

"I heard Obren say the covered trucks driving around our neighborhood are packed with dead Muslims," I tell him in a hushed tone. "Think it's true?"

My brother shrugs, returning to his radio like a robot who only has one trick, trying to get a signal. I feel like I'm going to puke.

We eat smaller meals, with more hours in between. I'm more thirsty than I am hungry, so I sip my water slowly and swallow my spit. The water in the jug is getting lower.

By day six, all we have left are some stale crackers and canned sardines. But worse than my hollow stomach is living every moment in fear that my father and brother will get taken away.

We're surprised when there's a knock on the door the next morning. It's Obren. Is he turning us in? But he just slips us butter cookies, jam, and coffee grounds.

"That's so kind of you," Mom whispers. She hands the food to Eldin and me.

I put jam on a cookie and eat it quickly. Obren's a Serb. I bet he's helping us because Dad stood up for him at that meeting.

Mom asks if he's heard what's going on in my Aunt Bisera's village a half hour away, or in Majka Emina's town ten minutes in the other direction. All the phone lines are down, and it's been weeks since we've talked to them. Obren shakes his head and sneaks back down the hall before anyone sees he's helping Muslims.

Eldin and I tear through the cookies and jam in one day.

"We're almost out of everything," Mom tells Dad.

"I'll go to the grocery to get some bread," Eldin offers. "I think it's still open."

"No," snaps Mom. "If you or Dad go outside, they'll throw you into the army or a camp. Or just kill you like a dog." Her lips are quivering. "I'll do it," she says, going for her purse.

Dad stops her. "I won't let you. A woman can't be alone on the street with all the enemy soldiers."

"Let me," I break in, acting braver than I feel. "I used to get snacks and juice there on my way home from school."

"No," my father says.

"Please," I beg.

"It's too dangerous," Mom tells me. She bites her nail and looks to Dad for help.

It's been a week since I've been outside, smelled fresh air, or felt the sun on my face. "It's just two blocks. I've done it a hundred times."

"I'm not sure," Dad tells Mom. "I mean, he's small and looks young. Maybe he'll be the safest. Who would hurt a little boy?"

"I don't want to find out!" Mom says.

"Come on. I'm fast. I'll be fine," I promise, trying to convince her and myself. "I want to go."

I don't know what it's like on the street, but this is my chance to see what's going on. And to help Mom, Dad, and Eldin. It feels kind of good to be needed.

Mom hands me a few dinars from her pocket. "Do not stop or talk to anyone," she says. I can tell how nervous she is. "Go fast and be careful. And come right home. Quickly."

I lace up my sneakers and dart out the door. I'm on fire with an important mission.

The ground is covered with broken glass and churned-up asphalt from the blasts. Zigzagging around the sharp edges, I hear my heartbeat thumping in my ears. I see a Serb soldier carrying the espresso machine out of the pizza place on the corner. Another guy in uniform is holding bags of blankets and toys looted from the kids' clothing store. Funny how I got into so much trouble for stealing supplies from the army, but weeks later they're all ripping off anything they want. I thought my parents would be angry forever that I stole. Now it's like they don't even remember it.

A couple in normal clothes walk by, not looking scared. They must be Serbs. Then there are loud explosions and smoke up ahead, and they duck inside a building. I crouch behind some overturned trash bins. Green military trucks speed by. Army men on top of turrets hold machine guns in ready positions. I shrink down and hold my breath until they pass.

Finally I make it to the small supermarket. I'm so dizzy from fear and hunger, I forget what I'm supposed to get. I look for cookies or chocolate. The shelves are almost empty. I spot two loaves of bread and remember. I take one to the counter. I know the cashier from stopping in here so often. "Hello," I say, trying to smile at her like it's just another day.

She shakes her head and mutters, "You Turks."

Turks has become another slur for Muslims. *The Turkish people first brought Islam to our country in the fifteenth century,* Eldin, always an ace at history, had explained to me.

Being called mean names doesn't faze me anymore. I'm just relieved she's letting me buy the bread.

I head straight home, as Mom told me to do, clutching the loaf. On the way back, it's quiet. No cars anywhere, only military jeeps. I run across the street beneath broken traffic lights, shards of glass crunching under my sneakers.

I'm halfway home when a swarm of soldiers and men in plainclothes rush around behind me.

Bang! Bang! Bang!

I see two of the plain-clothed guys fall to the ground. Are they Muslims trying to escape? *Keep it together, Trebinčević,* I tell myself. *Keep moving.*

I break into a sprint. Voices call out. More shots fire.

Then a bomb detonates a few yards ahead of me. An angry flash of orange lights up the sky. The street explodes, debris stinging my face. I hurl myself toward the sidewalk and keep running. My armpits are drenched. My throat clogs up with smoke. Mortars are whizzing back and forth in front of me, blasting the pavement when they land. I see someone on top of a building shooting at a soldier on the ground. He fires back. Suddenly my forehead burns. *Oh my god, a bullet has nicked me!*

I press myself against the side of a building and touch the wound just above my left eyebrow, then look at my finger. No blood. Maybe if I stay here, they won't shoot again. I can't think. I can't move.

Until I spot Mr. Miran on the sidewalk. He's walking with another guy. They're both in green uniforms.

"Hey, Teacher!" I yell. I'm so overjoyed to see him, I could cry. I rush over, hoping to hide behind him. He's holding an AK-47 assault rifle, like the one Stallone carried in *Rambo*. It's good he's armed. He can protect me.

"Teacher, Teacher! When I was getting bread, a bullet almost hit me!" I tell him as he turns my way.

"Your kind doesn't need bread," he snorts. His eyes are wild. He swats the bag out of my hand, and it falls to the ground. I freeze, realizing his uniform is the kind the Serb fighters now wear.

Mr. Miran holds his gun to my head. I try to stop my legs

from quaking. My body is drenched in sweat. The metal barrel feels cold against my skin. My teacher is going to shoot me right here, in the street. Nobody will stop him. I thought he liked me, that I was his best student. How could he hurt me?

I watch his finger on the trigger. Everything is spinning upside down. His weapon clicks.

"It's jammed," he mutters to his comrade standing behind him.

I snatch up my bread and race home across the railroad tracks, sprinting faster than I ever have on the recess field. The air is dark and smoky. It's like I'm underwater, trying not to drown, my ears clogged. Everything is vibrating, moving in slow motion around me.

I can't believe my favorite teacher since first grade is my enemy. Nobody can be trusted anymore, only my family. I feel filthy and drained, clutching the bread under my arm. I brush my hair over my brow so my parents won't know the bullet nicked me, a secret I'll have to keep. If they find out, they'll never let me outside again.

Before I turn onto my block, I look back one more time at Mr. Miran. I want to think he faked his gun jam to save face in front of that other soldier, but he catches my eye and holds up three fingers. It's a creepy salute I've never seen before: a peace sign ruined by the added thumb. I don't know what it means, but from his smirk, I know he wants me dead.

—

"You're okay?" Mom stares at me.

"I'm okay." I hand her the loaf, trying not to shake.

I keep questioning what just happened. Has Mr. Miran hated Muslims all along? I'm sure he liked me. He must be getting brainwashed by the politicians my father calls "power-hungry egomaniacs."

I decide never to tell Mom or Dad what happened. If they confront him, he'll probably accuse me of lying and throw me out of school forever. I don't want to get into more trouble. Though we're all in deep trouble now.

A week later, there's banging on the door of our apartment and a voice says, "It's Miran."

Mom, who knows him from parent-teacher conferences, looks at Dad and says, "Stand back. I'll get it."

I can tell she thinks he'll be nicer to her.

"Good day, Mr. Miran," she greets him. I can see from where I'm hiding in the corner of the dining room that he's holding that same AK-47.

"If you don't leave your apartment within twenty-four hours, we'll kill you!" Mr. Miran yells, as if he doesn't even know us.

Mom can't understand why my teacher is armed and threatening our family. I feel bad I never told her he pointed his gun at me, but I'm relieved my parents will now know the truth about him. My mother is so sure it's all a mistake, though, she walks out into the hallway to try to reason with him. When she comes back, her eyes are filled with fear.

"We have to pack—this second," she says, rushing to the hall closet. She takes off the sandals she's wearing so she can move faster, handing me and my brother a striped duffle bag each. She pulls out the heavy valise for Dad. He doesn't say a word, just follows her orders. She's in charge now.

Eldin and I run to our room. He grabs pants and shirts from his drawers. I look at my clothes and toys, trying to decide what I'll need most, but I don't know where we're going or for how long. I go to the chest under my bed, my eighth birthday present that Mom said was "a magical vault that once held valuable loot stolen from pirates." I grab my stack of special fudbal trading cards, marbles, my G.I. Joe, and my favorite miniature cars.

"What are you doing?" Mom asks when she comes in and sees my bag.

"Packing my stuff."

"You can't take all this!" She removes the trading cards and G.I. Joe.

But if I leave my cars and marbles, my old gang could break in and steal everything. With no friends or toys, how will I play? I'm about to argue with Mom when she says, "K-K-Kenan, you won't be needing any tttt-oys."

She never stutters. Her hair is frizzy from sweat. She's more afraid than I am.

I put everything back in my chest and cover it carefully with a blanket, shoving it against the wall beneath the bed so any thieves ravaging through our home will miss my treasures and steal something else.

"Kenan, come on." She opens my drawers and takes out underwear, socks, a sweatshirt, jeans, and sneakers, which I stuff into my bag. "Here, take this too." She hands me a thick red family album. "We can get new toys and clothes, but pictures can't be replaced."

I don't want to leave my marbles and cars. But I do, making room for her dumb album, *her* treasure. It's not fair.

When she leaves, I open the album to the first page, to my baby picture. The last time I saw Majka Emina, she'd pulled it out. "You only weighed four pounds when you were born, much smaller than your brother," she'd said, telling her favorite story of my birth. "The doctor said you were so small, you might not survive. Your mama said, 'You're wrong. I'm taking my boy home to make him fatter. You'll see.' Three months later Kenji was eight pounds with big fat cheeks." Majka had smiled, kissing my forehead as Eldin and my cousins laughed.

Now I feel guilty that I didn't visit her after my fudbal win. I don't even know if she's still alive.

—

Mom wakes us the next morning at six a.m. Our bags are over-stuffed, so she says to dress in layers so we can bring more clothes. I put on a T-shirt, a button-down shirt, a sweater, and a jacket over it, feeling like a marshmallow. When we walk outside, it's really warm. I'm too hot. I'm glad nobody else is around. If my old friends saw me like this, they'd make fun of me.

"I forgot my retainer," I whisper to my mother.

"Your teeth are the least of our problems," she says.

"But my friends call me Bugs Bunny," I admit quietly.

"They're not your friends anymore," Eldin snaps. "You won't be playing with them again."

Who else will I play with?

"We don't even know if the papers we have will work," Mom mumbles.

What papers?

Along with our passports and Mom's and Dad's driver's licenses, Eldin tells me we have a new permission document stating "You are allowed to leave the country in exchange for all your property and belongings and promise never to return," signed by the local Serbian police chief, a man Dad knows. Hopefully it will be enough to get us out of here until everything blows over. After we win the war and come back, it won't matter.

The four of us creep quietly from building to building, away from the main street. It's a mile walk to the bus stop. We cut through an alley, spot two Serb soldiers with the double-headed eagle patch on their shirts, and hide behind a corner until they pass. At the station, we buy four tickets on the first bus going across the border to Austria, a safe country. Nobody stops us or asks questions.

As we board, I count ten other passengers. No families who look nervous, like us. In the middle row we see Ljilja, the wife of Milisav who was also Eldin's art teacher, wearing all black, with a long silver cross around her neck. Eldin waves to her. She looks down, pretending she doesn't know who we are.

The bus pulls out of the station, and we sit silently in our seats for fifteen minutes. Then the driver stops at a checkpoint. I'm sweating so much, my hair is wet.

A tall paramilitary soldier stomps aboard. They're like war gangsters, forming their own special units, Eldin says. Some are criminals just released from jail, more lawless than other Serbian troops.

This one is demanding to see our IDs. Mom shows him the papers, but he is not impressed. "Get the hell off!" he yells. He has a beard down to his chest and dark glasses. Despite the heat, he wears a hat and a black uniform buttoned above his Adam's apple. The bayonet knife in his holster hangs halfway down his thigh. He gives me chills.

We climb off the bus and wait by the side of the road, like he commands.

"Ultranationalist Chetnik," Dad says quietly to Mom. "You can tell from the knife and the crazy hat."

"They were a brigade of Serb psychos from World War II that they're bringing back now," Eldin explains to me.

"Hey, that's my coworker, Slobodan!" Mom says, spotting a man in a car stopped at a nearby intersection. Good timing! I remember him as the nice prankster from her company's fudbal tournament. He called me Little Keka and showed me dribbling tricks.

Mom waves, and Slobodan rolls down his car window.

"We need help," Mom says. "We don't know if this paperwork will get us out of the country. Would you vouch for us?" She's sure that if he says these papers are legit, they'll let us go.

He takes the papers through the window and studies them. "These are no good," he sniffs, throwing them back at my mother and driving off.

She picks up the documents from the ground, her hand shaking. I have to remember that everything is flipped around. Friends are enemies. My parents are powerless. Religion rules. We're nobodies now.

"I can't believe that piece of trash," Dad mutters.

As we stand outside near the bus station, I realize there isn't anyone to help us. The bearded "Chetnik psycho" returns, and he tells Mom, "Hey, lady, you can come and cook us some bean soup." Then he makes a kissing noise and laughs.

I want to punch him. From the looks on their faces, so do Dad and Eldin, but we all know to keep still and quiet. Another soldier nearby says, "Let's just take them to River Sava and shoot. You haven't killed anybody recently."

Mom is tense, breathing heavily, but she doesn't flinch. The psycho raises his rifle and orders us to march forward on the road, in the same direction the bus is going. We line up single file, holding our bags by our sides. As we walk up the one-lane highway, I hear him cock his gun.

"Just keep going. Don't stop," Dad says. "Don't turn around."

Petrified I'll be shot in the back, I'm sweating buckets and my legs are jelly. I smell stale, worse than after playing sports.

We walk for a long, flat block, and then the road climbs. I can't keep up with long-legged Eldin. Mom is crying, exhausted, falling behind. I take hold of one strap of her bag to help. Sweat stings my eyes.

Once we're at the top of the hill, I dare to look back. I can no longer see the psycho. Maybe he was distracted by a car pulling up or another fleeing Muslim family he can terrorize. I put down my bag, try to wipe the wetness off my face with my shirt, and exhale slowly, relaxing my shoulders.

I don't understand why they don't want us here but won't let us leave.

EIGHT

We have no idea what to do. I wish we could go home, but the only way back to Brčko is blocked by the psycho at the checkpoint behind us. "Be careful," Eldin warns. "I heard on the radio there's land mines around here now."

We're afraid we could detonate them if we step off the pavement. Trucks full of soldiers pass, waving. Are they mocking us? One flips us the three-finger salute that Mr. Miran held up.

"What is that?" I ask my brother.

"It used to symbolize the Orthodox Christians' Holy Trinity of father, son, and holy spirit," he says.

"Now it's a sick sign of Serb nationalism," Dad adds.

"Hey, isn't this the road to Aunt Bisera's village?" my brother asks.

"Yes!" Mom exclaims. "Let's go stay with my sister!"

Dad nods. "I hope she's okay."

It's only a half hour car ride from our city apartment to her rural neighborhood, but today it takes hours to walk, carrying our bags in the heat.

When we finally arrive at the entrance to Bisera's subdivision, we find a guardhouse, with a Serb soldier stationed inside. "This whole village is now a detention center," he says. "Once you enter, you can't leave. There's an eight p.m. curfew. All men over eighteen have to sign in every morning at the school and get a number." Eldin and Dad promise. I feel a little left out.

On the twenty-minute trek uphill to Aunt Bisera's, my brother fills me in. "Serbs are occupying the entire village. They're guarding the only two roads out, so none of the remaining Muslim men can escape to fight in the resistance."

I'm exhausted. My arms are weak and shaky from carrying our luggage. My hands are so wet, I'm losing my grip on the duffle bag's handle.

Stray dogs and chickens and cows who've been freed from their pens roam around. They look as lost as we are in this farm country. The redbrick house Aunt Bisera recently moved into is on a main road, overlooking the river. The backyard borders a corn field and is filled with pear, apricot, and apple trees, but the house has an unfinished roof and no garage door. Aunt Bisera lives there with her second husband, Halil. He's a riverboat captain who doesn't make much money. *But he has the sweetest heart*, she always says.

Standing on her doorstep, we're very happy to see Halil now.

He's tall and quiet, with bushy eyebrows. He takes our bags and gives us cold towels to wipe our faces, along with glasses of water from the nearby well. Bisera kisses me and Eldin, hugs Mom and Dad, and tells us that Majka's side of town is destroyed. Thankfully, she says, Majka and my cousins have escaped to a Bosnian safety zone nearby that's protected by the newly formed Bosnian army.

"But the Muslim men who stayed behind were murdered," Bisera cries. "My friend Fadila, she was shot on her own doorstep. Dear God, what did we do to deserve this? Were we throwing rocks at you?" she asks the Lord. Then she turns back to Mom. "We have twelve other Brčko refugees staying with us too."

We go into the living room to find some of Aunt Bisera's friends, people of all ages, sitting on the floor, sobbing. A husband and wife who look younger than my parents take turns holding their toddler. They are all sharing stories of husbands, wives, and teenagers who were herded onto buses, taken to jail, shot, or used for prisoner exchange. Mom hugs Katica, her Croatian coworker's mother, who once baked us Christmas cookies. She's Catholic, on our side. I think the rest of these refugees are all Muslim. I'm now sorting everyone by their religion, to be safer.

In the backyard, two parakeets in cages squawk like maniacs. Aunt Bisera loves animals. I say hi to her birds and turtles, the pretty fish in her aquarium, and her neighbors' roosters and chickens prancing outside. They make me feel better.

"You're all right?" my aunt keeps asking Mom when I go back inside.

"Better with you," Mom says as her sister strokes her hair.

That night we crowd into Aunt Bisera's extra bedroom. Mom and I share the small bed. Eldin and my father take the couch, lying head to toe. Dad snores like a bear. The rest of the refugees sleep on the living room couches and on the hallway carpet between the front door and the main bedroom, couples and families huddling together.

I feel pinched and airless. There's no electricity here either, no phone service. I miss my bed, my room, with my marbles, miniature cars, and fudbal. Nothing here is mine.

But I almost forget the war in the morning, when Aunt Bisera greets us with creamy eggs frying on her wood-burning stove. She serves us warm bread and sweet corn and a juicy salad with tomatoes and crunchy cucumbers from her garden. Aunt Bisera is a wonderful cook. It's been almost a month since I've had a good meal, and I eat too much, too fast.

Halil gathers peaches from their trees for us, milk and cream from the neighbor's cows. We drink sweet rose juice that my aunt has made from flowers. She gives us clean shirts and robes to wear while she washes our clothes with soap and water from the well and hangs everything outside to dry.

"We signed in at the school two hours ago with Halil, while you were still sleeping," Eldin says to me as we eat.

"They called the names of twelve other Muslim men staying here and took them away," Dad adds. "But luckily they let us go."

"Why?" I don't understand.

"It's only a month into the war. They haven't figured out what to do with all of us yet," Halil says.

"What are their choices?" I ask.

"Kill us. Use us for prisoner exchange. Force us to dig trenches." Eldin lists the possibilities. "They want to keep checking that we haven't fled to Muslim-controlled territory, where we can get arms."

I really wish I'd stolen weapons from the army to protect us.

After our feast, I play alone in the backyard, staying out of everyone's way, feeling lonely. A neighborhood kid comes up and says hello. He has a dark crewcut. I'm not sure what this new kid's deal is, and after being betrayed by Vik and the gang, I'm not going to be friendly to somebody I don't know. But his hunting dog sniffs my feet, and I can't help petting him.

The boy smiles at me. "I'm Almir."

It's a Muslim name. He's safe.

"My family's friends with Bisera. We live up the hill. Want to see my cows?"

As we make our way up the road, he introduces me to

another kid, Omar—also one of us. Omar's hair is longer, like mine. They're both eleven, and not much taller than I am, but they look rugged and strong compared to the guys back home.

When we reach the small farm, I'm happy to see a fudbal on the grass. I pick it up and say, "Let's play a game."

Almir shrugs. He doesn't seem that into sports. He leads me to the barn instead. I've never been in one before, and I don't get why he puts on rubber boots before we enter. Then I get a whiff of the horrible smell and realize the mud on the ground is mixed with animal crap. *Yuck!* I zigzag around the hay and debris so the only sneakers I have won't get stinky.

Almir introduces me to his dad, who is peeling the green husks off ears of corn. His mother is milking a huge cow. "Ah, you must be Bisera's nephew," she says, showing me the udders she squeezes to extract milk. How does she know who I am?

"Want to try?" Almir asks.

It grosses me out. I pray he doesn't ask me to touch those bloated-looking balloons. The cow flops her ears, shooing away a fly. She seems mean. I shake my head no, worried if I get any closer, she'll kick me.

"Go get some fruit for Bisera," Almir's mom tells him.

Almir and Omar lead me to a tall pear tree they start climbing. "Come on," Almir prods.

"No way." I'm afraid of heights, and I get queasy just staring up at them. At home, Ivan was the only one I knew who could climb a tree; I never dared.

"Oh, a city boy," Almir says, and I feel wimpy. Omar laughs, but not in a mean way.

"You can see the whole world from the top," Almir says, trying to convince me.

But I won't budge. So he tells me to hold a plastic bag to catch the pears he starts throwing down, one at a time.

After catching a few, I have an idea. I take his fudbal and punt it into the branches with my foot so several pears fall.

"Good job, city boy!!" Omar says. "Do it again."

My foot blasts the ball into the tree again and again, knocking a bunch more pears to the ground. The fudbal kick I worked so hard on is still good for something. We repeat my new trick to get apples and apricots too, gathering our spoils in triumph.

"We'll go fishing tomorrow," Almir says as I wave goodbye to him and Omar and head down the hill toward Aunt Bisera's.

"Where the heck were you?" Mom yells when I get back.

"With the neighborhood boys, getting fruit," I say proudly, handing her the pears and apples I have in my shirt. "They invited me fishing tomorrow. Can I go?" I'm excited to have new friends.

"We'll see," Mom says as we walk into the living room. A group of the old women are sitting at the table, smoking and wailing.

"Dear God, why did you take my son away from me?" one cries.

I immediately feel guilty I've had fun horsing around with my new buddies while the adults are crying. I keep quiet about Almir and his dog and cow, not wanting to be disrespectful. I wish I could cover my ears to stop hearing all their sadness.

"Two Muslim men who signed in at the school today were taken to Luka port," an older man says.

"Why Luka?" I ask, picturing the port, a ten-minute walk from our Brčko apartment. My brother and I used to play there on the docks.

"It's a concentration camp now," the man answers.

I think of the prison camp in the movie *The Great Escape*, wishing I had Steve McQueen's motorcycle.

"They're murdering Muslims and Catholics there," one of the women says.

Nobody watches what they say in front of me anymore. I wish they would. I feel sick.

That week, Almir and Omar show me around the village. We see local Serb soldiers patrolling the streets, but they never stop us or ask questions. On Friday, after it rains, we go fishing. Almir knows which rocks to lift up to find worms. Now's the time, since they come up from the wet ground," he explains.

"You do it," Omar says to me.

I don't want to pick up a worm, let alone kill it. Almir baits my line for me, and I feel bad for the squirmy creature who's getting the hook dug into its brain.

"Scaredy-cat," Almir teases.

"We're so much bigger. They're tiny with no power," I say. "Isn't that torture?"

Omar rolls his eyes. "We need to eat."

"How else are we gonna catch dinner?" Almir asks. "We can't put in an empty line and wait for the fish to hook itself on."

They're right. I'm embarrassed — but not enough to try baiting one. I've already maimed a pigeon. That's enough.

Omar hands me the pole, and I dip it in the water.

The fish start to bite at Almir's and Omar's lines almost immediately, but not mine. After a half hour I finally feel a pull.

"I think I got one!" I yell. "What do I do?"

Almir grabs my hand and helps me reel it in.

"That's a baby trout. Good work," he says, taking it off the hook. The fish wiggles, still alive, as Almir throws it into the bucket of water with the other fish they've caught.

I bring it back to Aunt Bisera's and Halil fillets it and cooks it on their wooden stove. Mom and Dad say they're not hungry, so I share it with Eldin.

"Remember when we went fishing on the boat with Dad?" he asks. It was just last summer, but it seems like a hundred years ago.

Over the next few days Almir and Omar teach me to use a bow and arrow they make from branches, gather eggs from the chickens and hens, and pick cornhusks from the fields to feed the livestock. They give me eggs and a bottle of milk to bring to my aunt.

If I spend the rest of my life here, I could share their farm chores every day. I still miss school, but I could get used to having friends who are nice to me again.

NINE

JUNE 1992

One Monday morning, two weeks after we arrive, Dad and my brother go to town for their daily sign-in at nine o'clock.

"Why aren't they back yet?" Mom asks at nine thirty, staring at her watch. They usually return within ten minutes.

By ten o'clock Mom is pacing. Halil comes back alone, looking sweaty and disheveled.

"After doing chores, I was late for signing in," he says, breathing fast. Bisera gets him water and wipes the sweat from his face with a washcloth. "Something bad was going on, with more cops and soldiers around. It seemed like a trap. So I ran back here on the side road. They didn't see me. I didn't get there in time to warn Keka or Eldin."

"Where are they?" Mom cries.

Halil shrugs.

Mom runs outside to look for my father and brother. I follow her. The streets are deserted, like a ghost town in a Western. All the doors and gates of the houses we pass are open. Aunt

97

Bisera warns us about this new rule imposed by the Serbs so they can get in easily and take anyone or anything they want.

We see a thin blond soldier who looks Eldin's age. The Serb soldiers like him who grew up in the village are much nicer than the ones the army brings in from other towns. Halil told me they're mostly poor farmers being forced to police their neighbors.

But they're all working together, and they seem to know who we are. When we ask the soldier about Dad and my brother, he tells us that all the Muslim men have been taken to the Luka port. My heart stops. Mom's frantic eyes bug out from fear.

"Don't walk any farther or they'll take you too," he warns.

We stumble, crying, back to Aunt Bisera's, where Mom falls into her sister's arms. I rush to the bathroom, my whole body convulsing with the runs. It only stops when Aunt Bisera feeds me leftover grounds from the coffee filter, her home remedy.

By Friday, we've still heard nothing of Dad or Eldin. I'm sick and scared every minute. I continue doing chores with Almir and Omar in the mornings, but we barely speak. Their dads are at Luka too.

At night, it's pitch-dark, ninety degrees, no air conditioning. Mom and I share the twin bed, sleeping feet to head for more room, with nobody on the small couch Dad and Eldin used, like it's waiting for their return.

When we hear gunfire, Mom worries someone will walk past the first-floor window and shoot us, so she stays awake all night being our lookout, taking only a short nap at sunrise. I can't sleep either because of all the sounds — crickets chirping, frogs croaking, ammunition blasting.

"I'm sure they're okay," I lie, trying to comfort Mom, telling myself that since everyone in Brčko knows and loves Dad, nobody will hurt him in Luka, out of respect.

One morning I go to Almir's house to do chores, but no one's there. I search the orchards and the barn, yelling my friends' names as the animals silently watch me. Back at Aunt Bisera's house, Mom tells me that Almir's and Omar's families and the other farmers must have fled in the night.

They didn't even say goodbye to me, just like Huso and Lena.

We hear cow and chicken noises around the clock. With nobody feeding the animals, they're dying. I want to run back to the barn to save the starving livestock, but Mom says it's too dangerous, I can't go that far from the house now.

Soon there's a cow's body rotting in the middle of the road, and three dead chickens. Halil buries the animals in the backyard, while Aunt Bisera weeps.

The grownups don't talk about it, but I know food is running out. My aunt is upset she can't serve us much, just bread, corn, the last ripe apples and apricots Halil picks from their trees, and the trout he catches. We're hungry and tired, petrified that

Dad and Eldin might be dead. Though I haven't known Almir and Omar very long, I miss my new buddies. But I keep quiet, trying to be brave for my freaked-out mom.

One day while I'm playing by the road in front of the house, I see a black Mercedes speed by, driven by a Serb soldier in aviator glasses. When I hear shooting a moment later, I dive down to the ground and watch as the car screeches to a halt and the soldier — wearing dark jeans and a military shirt — steps out to see who shot at him. When he can't spot them, he pulls out a rocket-propelled grenade and launches it across the river, at nothing, just because he's angry. The trees on the opposite shore explode in flames. I run inside to tell Mom.

"You could have died!" she yells, then hugs me close. "From now on, stay behind the house."

The next morning, when I wake up, I forget where I am for a minute, ready to play fudbal for a smiling Mr. Miran at recess, as if the nightmare were over. But it's only been six weeks. Dad said World War II lasted six years.

A friendly visitor stops by Aunt Bisera's with a message of hope: my cousins have made it to non-Serb territory with Majka Emina. I think about whoever shot at that soldier in the Mercedes, and about Uncle Ahmet, fighting to defend Bosnia. I wish I were old enough to join and could find a way to get there. I'd rather be a fighter than helplessly living in fear.

We hear nothing about Eldin and Dad. Aunt Bisera tells me to pray, but I don't really know how. Nobody I know covers their head or follows conservative Islam. I've only gone to the mosque once, with Uncle Ahmet. I don't fast for Ramadan or know the official prayers. Dad studied the Koran in school when he was young, but I never did. Mom's grandpa was a popular imam, but we only celebrate major holidays.

Every night when I get into bed, I shut my eyes and hope someone is taking care of Eldin and Dad. I try not to imagine that they're being tortured or lying in a meat truck, which is where we hear those who die in the camp are stored before getting dumped. I picture my father and brother here when I wake up in the morning, my own kind of prayer.

One night, as explosions echo down the river for miles, Mom is extra antsy, tossing, getting up, and pacing. I follow and find her mopping the kitchen floor. I help move the plants and garbage bin out of her way.

"We should escape on a rainy night by swimming across the river," I tell her.

"You're too young." She bends and wipes the tiles with a napkin, sweat dripping from her forehead.

"I took swimming lessons last summer."

"You never went into the deep end without Dad," she reminds me.

I also wore inflatable water wings, which we had to leave

behind. Mom and I look out the window at the river's currents. Along the banks, armed soldiers hide in the bushes.

"We'll think of something," she says.

One day, two Serb policemen we've never seen show up at the house, one fat and one skinny. Spying from the kitchen, I see the cops looking around, like they want something to steal. I overhear Mom begging for information about my brother and Dad. She assumes all the local Serbs know everything going on around here — and she's right.

"I think they were in the group of men that were released from Luka," the fat cop tells her.

"What? They're alive, then? They're okay? But where would they go?" she asks. "We're from Brčko, not far from the port."

"If you really want, I can get you back to Brčko," the thin cop offers.

"Yes. Please," she begs. "I hardly have any money left, but . . ."

"Jewelry?" asks his partner.

Mom hands him her gold wedding band, and he nods. But what will Dad say? I wonder if she's mad at him for not getting us out of Bosnia in time. Does this mean she doesn't think he'll return?

As she runs to get our belongings, I just stand there, helpless.

"What's happening?" Aunt Bisera asks, stopping her in the hall.

"We're going to look for Keka and Eldin," Mom whispers. "I bribed those pigs with my wedding ring to help us."

I'm relieved she's angry at the cops, not Dad. Now I understand: material things don't mean anything anymore. All she cares about is getting my father and brother back.

Within minutes we're standing at the door, Aunt Bisera hugging us goodbye. The chubby cop winks at my aunt. Then we're climbing into the back of the Serb police car.

This feels insane. But even my mother isn't crazy enough to barge into a concentration camp, so I don't know where she's taking us. She gives the cops our Brčko address. She still has the keys.

We live on the main street in town, so they know it. As they speed there, I relax a little. These cops don't seem dangerous, just happy with their bribe. I'm more afraid we'll run into the nasty soldier who threw us off the bus. But since we're driving in a Serbian police car, we're waved right through the checkpoints.

"Think your pretty sister will go out with me?" asks the fat cop as he drives.

Mom doesn't answer. Yuck. Is that why he's helping us?

He drives so fast, it takes only twenty minutes to get back

to our apartment. When we pull up in front of our building, we get out quickly.

"Thank you," Mom says. I'm relieved when the cops speed off.

Everything looks the same, except for the bags of garbage piling up near the side of the building. It's quieter too, with nobody outside, though it's around noon. I wonder where Vik, Marko, and Ivan are.

We rush to climb the stairs before anyone sees us, and Mom takes out her key—but the door is unlocked. We creep inside slowly, scared soldiers are living here and could shoot us on sight. Silently we inch forward and peek into the living room.

I can't believe what I see—Eldin and Dad! They're sitting on the couch, in shorts and T-shirts.

"Oh my God, you're here. You're safe!" my mother cries. "You're alive!" We all run into each other's arms.

"They let us out of Luka after two weeks, but we didn't know how to get back to you." My father grips Mom tightly, not letting her go. "So we walked back here, since it's so close."

They're both much thinner than they were just three weeks ago. Eldin is wearing his big yellow-framed glasses, and his cheekbones are sticking out. Dad's hair is grayer, his face is pale. I've never seen him look so small and confused. It's like he's lost all his power.

"We heard buses full of women and kids from Bisera's village were blown up. So was the bridge near Majka's," Eldin explains.

"We thought you were dead, or given to the Serbs for prisoner exchange. We wanted to go look for you but couldn't chance any more checkpoints and get sent back to Luka. Or worse." He picks me up high, hugs me, and messes up my hair, all our old fights forgiven.

"Didn't they feed you there?" I ask.

"Bread and water," Dad says. "They murdered so many men . . ."

"It was a miracle we got out," Eldin adds. "They intentionally released some of us, right before the Red Cross came. They didn't want the world to find out what they're doing."

"The Red Cross?" I repeat.

"It's an international charity, trying to help us," he says.

Oh yeah. I remember their TV ads showing workers feeding starving kids in Africa. I'm glad the rest of the world knows what the Serbs are doing. Maybe more good guys will come here to save us soon.

"Why don't you go change your clothes?" Mom tells me.

In my room, I rush to the treasure chest, afraid my old friends might have snuck in to steal my toys. I inspect my trading cards, marbles, action figures, G.I. Joe, miniature car collection, notebook, and colored markers, happy to see they are all there, untouched. My clothes are still in my closet and drawers too, exactly the same as when I left.

It's so weird to think that while I was lying awake at Aunt

Bisera's, scared about my brother and Dad, they were safely sleeping here, in their own beds. I change into clean underwear, shorts, and T-shirt. It feels so nice to be in clothes that aren't stiff from being dried in the sun. But then I go to wash up and remember we have no water. There's no soap or deodorant either.

At least my old retainer is here in its green case. But when I put it in my mouth, it's too tight. I'm supposed to get it refitted every six weeks.

I come down the hall to show Mom. "Feels too small," I tell her.

"That's the least of our problems." She takes it from me and throws it out.

"Here," she says, handing me some baking soda from the kitchen. "Use this for deodorant." I remember the day last year when I came in sweaty from playing fudbal and Mom told me that I was turning into a teenager and had to prevent my armpits from smelling. "We'll use it for toothpaste too."

"We're staying here?" I ask.

"For now," my brother says. "Where else can we go?"

Mom sits on the couch between Dad and Eldin, asking about everything that happened in the weeks we've been apart. I sit on the floor, so glad we're all alive and reunited.

"Anto was in Luka with us," Dad says. "We slept on the same cardboard."

I love Anto, Dad's Catholic buddy who was the best man at my parents' wedding. He's a butcher, and whenever we visited his apartment, he and his wife, Ruža, would serve us steak, salami, beef sausage, and lamb. The thought makes my mouth water.

"So they took Croats to Luka too?" Mom asks. "Even though Anto's married to a Serb?"

"Ruža came to get him out," Dad says. "Rumor was a guard attacked her first."

Mom gasps, then puts her hands over my ears, though I already heard. I know, from some of the movies I've seen, what they're talking about.

"Anto's hiding at home now too. He said if we can get there, they will have food for us."

"I'll go," I offer. Their apartment is only a fifteen-minute walk from our place.

"We'll talk about it later." Mom turns to Eldin. "We had bread at Bisera's this morning. Did you eat today?"

"We stopped at Aunt Fatima's place on the way here. We've been eating the cereal, Spam, sardines, and canned chicken pâté she gave us," Eldin says. "She's okay. So is Majka Emina, but we didn't get to see her."

Aunt Fatima, my Majka Emina's sister, lives a few blocks from us. I'm so happy she's all right and we won't starve. "Mr.

Miran was the one who took us to Luka," Eldin adds. "He walked by and sneered at us every day. Wouldn't help us get out or bring us any food, because we didn't have enough money to pay him off."

This time I'm not surprised.

"I hope he gets killed and his flesh rots in his grave," my father mumbles.

I've never heard my father wish someone a bad death before; in my culture, it's our worst curse.

I know now that Mr. Miran is a bad man, and I'm still hurt by the way Vik, Marko, and Ivan treated me. But I'm not wishing anyone dead.

TEN

JULY 1992

On Monday afternoon, as Mom and I open the door to take trash bags to the dumpster, our next-door neighbor Petra, Obren's wife, slinks out of her apartment like a snake. She's wearing a beige nightgown and has on too much makeup and stinky perfume. She leans against the wall to light a cigarette. When Mom sees her, she shrinks back.

"You have to keep your door unlocked now, otherwise it'll be kicked in by looting soldiers," Petra warns, exhaling smoke. "And it's mandatory to put your last name on the door, in Cyrillic."

Petra hands my mother a piece of paper and watches her scrawl *Trebinčević* in the script the Serbs use. Mom is so nervous she forgets a few letters, which Petra immediately corrects. In school, we learned the Cyrillic alphabet—along with the Bosnian alphabet. They're very similar and share a lot of the same letters. Now the Serbs are even trying to erase the way we write.

Mom tapes the paper to our door.

"A paramilitary commander was living in your place, but he disappeared," Petra adds.

So that explains why Eldin and Dad found everything a mess when they returned home. They said our door was unlocked, and there was a sign on it that read PROPERTY OF THE POLICE. Mom's black and white rug was wrecked by combat boot prints, and a bath towel with caked-on dirt was draped over the couch. The dining room chairs had been dragged into the living room. The toilets were unflushed. In both bedrooms, the beds were unmade. Dad and Eldin had straightened up and taken out some of the garbage the strangers left behind, but our once-spotless house still reeks.

"Petra's wearing the nightgown my sister gave me — that thief," Mom says when we're back in the apartment, her neck turning red. "She snuck in and helped herself to my closet when we were gone."

I hate to see Mom so upset. It's gross to picture Petra in her bedroom. It creeps me out to think that someone could have been under my covers, touching my things. The TV and all of Dad's jazz records are also gone. Is that Petra's handiwork too?

"Wait. So she can just come in without permission, take anything she wants, and not get in trouble?" I ask.

"Her husband's a Serb guard. They control the town," says Eldin.

"Lucky their tiny studio apartment couldn't fit all our furniture." Mom tries to joke.

"Serbs don't have to follow the laws anymore." Eldin sounds resigned. "They won't get arrested for stealing from us. We can't call the police on her or try to do anything about it or she'll call Obren or one of his Serb soldier friends to have us taken away again."

"I wish those evil monsters would drop dead already," says Dad. It's less shocking to hear him say it this time.

But Mom shakes her head. "Stop wishing people dead, Keka."

"So we have to give Petra whatever she wants, whenever she comes over?" I ask.

"For now, but it won't last," Mom says. "God's watching. His hand will take their power away."

I wonder what God's waiting for. I envision him as an invisible man, looking down on the earth, who has to be addressed respectfully. Once, when I was with Majka Emina, I broke a toy and muttered, "Goddamnit," and she yelled, "Don't use God's name in vain. He's always listening and watching you." But if that's true, why is he letting so much bad stuff happen to us?

Mom sinks to her knees and scrubs at the footprints on the floor. I feel like saying, *We could be shot any second and you're worried about your rug?* I'm hungry and angry we're not allowed to leave, forced into hiding in our own apartment, surrounded by enemies. But I keep my mouth shut and stomp into my room instead.

"Walk softly, so the new tenants below don't hear us," Mom orders.

We don't know which of our Muslim neighbors escaped, who is detained or dead. Serb military men and their families are now living in the empty apartments in our building, since it's the newest complex in town. Some have houses in the suburbs, with second homes here. At least the soldiers won't bomb or burn down our building, Eldin figures.

The street fighting has died down, and the canned food from Aunt Fatima won't last much longer. "Want me to check if the store has any food left?" I ask Mom.

She looks at Dad, who nods. She hands me a few dinars from the little cash we have left.

I'm glad I kept the gun incident with Mr. Miran to myself, so they'll let me outside. The grocery is open, and luckily a girl I don't know is working the cash register. There's no candy or cookies, but I find a can of beans, a tin of sardines, and a bag of lentils on the half-empty shelves. Mom's Serbian friend Ankica walks in, and I freeze, afraid she'll be mean. But she puts her arm around me.

"Hi, honey. What are you guys still doing in Brčko?"

"We're trapped," I tell her quietly. "They don't want us here, but they won't let us out."

"I'll come visit," she whispers. "Stay inside. I'll bring you something better to eat. Be careful."

On my way home, I pass apricot and cherry trees I've never paid much attention to. I grab a branch and whack them the way I did in the village, dislodging fruit to carry back for my family.

Mom is pleased with the food and thankful for Ankica's message. She sends me back out to the fountain to refill the empty jugs with water. When I return, she takes out the propane tank and lights the flame under a pot with matches, then makes bean soup, which Eldin and I eat with pieces of bread.

"Why aren't you eating?" I ask Mom and Dad.

"It's for you guys," Dad tells me. "Don't worry about us."

"You have to eat too, or your stomach will growl," I say, pushing my soup toward Dad. He takes a few slurps with the spoon.

"Please," Eldin says, handing Mom a slice of bread, which she finishes slowly. For dessert, we have three cherries each and save the rest.

My brother's transistor radio was still in the drawer under the missing TV. He turns it on low for the latest news: missile barrages fell on a nearby village, forcing hundreds of Muslim refugees to flee. We need to escape soon. But we can't go anywhere now without a Serb escort or the official papers we don't have enough money to buy.

"Even if we had the cash, how the hell would we make it two miles to the police station without getting shot?" Dad asks.

They've stopped saying, *Everything will be fine.* We know it won't.

The authorities have canceled summer camps, outlawed boating, and closed the pools and beaches. Last July, I went fishing with Dad on the river, watched sailboat races, and took swimming lessons in the city pool. Now they're all abandoned battle zones. I sit inside and draw pictures of camouflaged tanks and Bosnian soldiers in the trenches blowing up the Serb attackers with bullets and bombs.

Behind our building, the piles of trash have become mountains. Green flies buzz around, and it smells gross in the hot sun. On my way back from tossing a trash bag onto the pile, I see Vik, Marko, Ivan, and another kid I don't know sitting at the entrance to my stairwell, holding a fudbal. For a second I'm excited, about to rush up and high-five Vik, forgetting how mean he's been. But he won't let me.

"Oh, look who's back," he says in a nasty voice. I'm surprised he even noticed I've been gone.

Three others guys who live nearby walk up. Their fathers are soldiers too.

"Let's get a game going," says Stevo, a fifteen-year-old Serb kid who lives in my building. His dad has a Doberman that scares me.

There are seven kids. They need eight for two equal teams.

"Need another player?" I ask, scared but acting casual, desperately wishing we could forget the war and just kick the ball around.

"I don't want him," Vik yells. "Trebinčević's yours."

It hurts to be rejected by my former friend again, but I'm still glad to get in the game. I miss fudbal. I run upstairs to tell Mom I'll be outside playing for a while, so she won't worry.

"It's not a good idea," she says. She's cleaning the floors with a dry mop.

"Listen, I'll have to keep going out to get us food and water from the well," I bargain. "I might as well try to be friendly so they won't stop me."

She's not convinced. "I don't know." She shakes her head.

"You can watch me from the balcony," I tell her.

She sighs. "Okay. Be careful, Kenji."

For the first ten minutes of the game I take it easy, dribbling but not taking a shot. We use the stairwell as the goalpost, and my team is pretty good. Then, when I get the ball again, Marko stomps on my foot. The next time, Ivan elbow-jabs me in the waist while Vik pulls on my shirt.

"Hey, no fouling," I say, jabbing Ivan back.

"Foul on Kenan," he shouts.

His call they listen to. "How come everyone else can call a foul but me?" I ask.

"Muslim traitors don't call the shots," Vik answers.

Of course, Ivan's team wins. Frustrated, I turn and start up the stairs, and Vik yells, "Hey, where you going, Trebinčević? Get down here."

But I hurry inside, feeling stupid for thinking we could go back to normal.

After sunset, Mom lights candles and I sit in the rocking chair in our living room, bobbing back and forth. A knock on our door makes me jerk to a stop, scared that Mr. Miran has returned to get us. Or that Petra's back to snatch more of our stuff.

"Can I come in?" a lady asks when Mom peeks out into the hallway. "I'm Zorica. I knew your father."

Mom opens the door. Zorica has short, puffy brown hair and wears jeans, a T-shirt, and sandals. No lipstick or makeup. She seems about my mother's age. A shy little boy hides behind her, holding her hand. "This is my son, Dejan. He's six."

Zorica says that she's a Bosnian Serb who had been living in Croatia. But now they've moved in right below us, into my old pal Huso's two-bedroom. My back stiffens. I don't like that Huso had to leave and that she's taken his home, but Mom invites her in.

Zorica removes her shoes at the door, instructing her son to take off his sneakers. She politely shakes hands with me, Eldin, and Dad. She isn't armed or eyeing our belongings — she already has Huso's place. What does she want from us?

"I'd offer coffee, but we don't have any left," Mom says, embarrassed.

"I heard the boys outside playing and recognized your son's name. Your father and my Uncle Novak were friends during World War Two," Zorica tells her.

"Kenan, why don't you go show Dejan your miniature cars?" Mom says.

"Okay." I want to hear more about my grandfather and the war so we play with my police van, the Mack truck, and my green American Sherman tank in the corner of the living room. That way I can listen to what they're saying.

Mom sits in the rocking chair while Eldin settles onto the floor in front of her. Dad and Zorica sit on opposites sides of the couch. In case of stray bullets, we've been avoiding the middle, since it's under the window.

"During the war, your father jumped out of a moving truck to escape from the Germans," Zorica says to Mom. "He ran to the village where Uncle Novak lived. Your father hid inside my uncle's house for three days."

Dad and Eldin listen closely as this stranger talks about my Djed Murat, who died before I was born. Majka Emina used to tell me all about him. She said he was a very handsome gentleman, well-dressed, and beloved by everyone and everything, especially the thirty parakeets and canaries he fed and cared for. Aunt Bisera got her love of animals from him.

"To thank my uncle, Murat promised to buy his milk from then on," Zorica says. "So for the next forty years, Novak visited him on his bike twice a week, bringing him fresh farm milk. Your dad could get milk anywhere, but Novak was poor and needed the income. He helped keep Novak in business. Your father was a good, loyal man."

"Oh, I remember your uncle!" Mom says, smiling.

I do, too — the milkman coming to Majka's door. He wore a dark suit and a hat just like Humphrey Bogart in *Casablanca*, Dad's favorite movie.

Zorica pats my mother's hand. "We know you're having a rough time, and we want to help you, however we can. Whatever my child eats, yours will eat as well."

Mom starts crying. But who is the *we* Zorica mentioned? If they're living in Huso's apartment, that means her husband is a Serb soldier, like the rest of the house-stealers.

She and Dejan don't stay long, but at midnight, she returns alone, holding a candle and a paper bag. There's no set bedtime or mealtime anymore, since we're woken up at all hours by gunfire and bombing, so we're awake to see the food she's brought us. Mom puts it away in the kitchen: meatloaf, a slice of chicken pâté, coffee beans, and two rolls that Eldin and I share on the spot. They're delicious.

"My father drives to Germany through Serbia, where he fills his car with groceries for us," she whispers as she and Mom sit on the couch. The candlelight casts shadows on the floor.

It seems Djed Murat's good karma from another war is saving us from starving now. But can we trust a lady whose husband is killing our people?

Every week, Zorica comes by with a bag for us — full of coffee, tea cookies, a can of sardines, more candles — always late at night, in secret. If someone like Petra sees and reports her, she'll get into big trouble for helping the enemy.

One night, she arrives with food, her son, and her tall husband, Miloš. He stoops over to say "nice to meet you" to me. Dad and Eldin are polite, so I am, too. But I don't trust him.

When they invite me over to play with Dejan, Mom pushes me to go. The next day, I take my fudbal cards and miniature cars with me and knock on the door of the apartment downstairs, just like I used to with Huso.

Yet it feels wrong to be back in my friend's two-bedroom flat. His family escaped in such a hurry, they just grabbed their clothes and left everything else. Dejan has claimed Huso's toys and World Cup trading cards. I don't want to touch anything of Huso's without his permission. I'm ashamed to even be in the bedroom where he and I once played video games. I would hate it if some Serb soldier's kid invaded my home when I was gone and played with my stuff.

"Give this eggplant to your mom," Zorica says after I've finished shooting marbles with Dejan in the kitchen.

"Thank you," I say, taking the oblong food. I haven't seen one in months. I vow to one day say I'm sorry to Huso, when he returns. I hope he'll forgive me for selling out our friendship for a purple fruit.

ELEVEN

AUGUST 1992

One late summer night, when I'm sitting on the steps of my building, Stevo's dad comes home carrying treats: Twix, Mars Bars, Milky Ways, and Mallomars, all with Bosnian labels. As he walks into the courtyard, kids swarm around him, and I can only see the top of his red beret as he bends down to hand out the sweets. My brother says that the Serbs who wear red hats belong to a paramilitary group that loots abandoned Muslim homes. They walk in with bags to take all the money and jewelry they can find, and then they raid the pantries.

I want chocolate so badly, my mouth waters. Stevo's dad knows my dad, so I think he'll give me a piece. But as I step forward, he looks at me and says, "No candy for your kind."

I turn away, wanting to disappear, knowing nothing I say will change his mind. It's bad enough getting picked on by my former friends, but now I'm also being bullied by men my father's age.

—

On mornings when the blasts aren't too close, I walk to the fountain on the hill to refill our two plastic canisters, a white one and a yellow one. The fountain is the only water supply for everyone in the neighborhood. Mom rations what I carry home for bathing and drinking.

One day while I'm at the well, I do a quick wash as usual —splash my face and under my arms—then drink up. My stomach growls from hunger, but the water makes it stop for a few hours. On the way home, I see Stevo and his dad walking behind me with Stevo's sister, Ana, and their scary Doberman. The jugs are so heavy, I have to stop to rest. They catch up to me.

"Hi," I say to Stevo, trying to act normal.

"Sic him," he tells his dog.

The pointy-eared Doberman barks, rushing forward. I jump back, but his paws scratch my legs beneath my shorts. Then he licks my toes. He's just a sweet puppy who doesn't understand the war and isn't taking sides. He spins around, barks happily, then runs back to his owner.

"Don't talk to my son anymore!" yells Stevo's dad. He's wearing his crooked red beret and camouflage pants with pockets everywhere. I can see that he's armed with two guns, a knife, grenades, and a stick. Before I know what's happening, he takes his handgun from the holster and shoots twice at my yellow plastic jug. The sound shudders through me, and I jerk. For a second I think he's shooting at my feet to make me dance, like

Yosemite Sam does to Bugs Bunny in the cartoons. I leap away from the canisters, covering my head with my hands. Water spews out from the bullet holes. They all laugh.

I'm shaking so hard, I can't feel my feet. "Nothing lasts forever!" I manage to yell as I run away, taking my white canister but leaving the ruined yellow jug on the side of the road. I pray for the day they'll get what they deserve. I wish their own bombs would blow away Stevo, Ana, and their dad, along with Petra, Mr. Miran, and my so-called friends who've turned on me. I spare only the puppy from my curse.

Coming home with one less jug, I keep thinking, *I should have pushed my father to leave.* We could have tried escaping by swimming across the river. Or I could have insisted we go with our cousins to Vienna. If we'd tried to go to Majka Emina's, we might have made it over the bridge with her before it was blown up. My head is filled with regrets.

"The yellow jug cracked, so I had to throw it out," I lie to Mom when I get home. But I can't stop myself from adding, "We can't stay here where everyone hates us. What are we going to do?"

"Hopefully the war will end soon," Mom says.

"Basically, we're screwed," Eldin clarifies.

As day after day of endless artillery fire passes, the sounds of gunshots and bombs start to feel almost soothing. At least it means my old gang will stay inside and can't beat me up.

During the most intense fighting, Mom makes Eldin and me sleep on the floor of the hallway outside our bedroom so the wall will protect us from the bullets whizzing outside the windows. If we hear whistling followed by a bang, we know the mortars have landed a safe distance away. If there's a one-second pause after a high-pitched whistle, I brace myself, leaning against Eldin or face-down on the floor, closing my eyes and holding my breath. Our home vibrates like a guitar string, walls absorbing the shock waves. Soon I can't fall asleep without the noise. The rare nights of silence keep me up.

One evening, Petra opens our door without even knocking. "What are you guys doing?" she asks. Before we answer, she comes in, sizing up our furniture, light fixtures, appliances, the artwork on our walls.

"I want your electric iron," she says. My mother stares at her blankly, handing it over.

The next day, Petra takes a denim skirt from Mom. I want to scream, *How dare you take advantage of us now, you disgusting thief!* But I glare silently, knowing not to speak. We have to give her whatever she asks for, so we won't be turned in.

Another time, Petra comes over wearing Mom's skirt. She brings coffee, which we know is just an excuse to case our place to see what else she can grab. We wait for the well water I've gathered to boil. Then she and Mom have their coffee in the kitchen.

I know Petra's wearing the skirt she stole just to rub it in. Before the war, she was a nobody. This is her only power now.

"Soon you won't be needing that rug. I may as well take it before someone else does," she says. I feel like crying as I watch my mom hand over her beloved black and white carpet, humiliated.

"Who cares about objects, as long as we're safe," Mom tells me later. But her bloodshot eyes give away how stressed and sad she is. "Her bad karma will catch up with her," she adds.

Mom isn't very religious, but she's superstitious, big on the idea that "you reap what you sow." If you do something bad, you get what you deserve. Majka Emina once told me that God doles out mercy or punishment, and if you don't get penalized for your sins in this world, you'll get yours in the afterlife.

I want Stevo and Petra to get what they deserve and for good to win over evil. But I'm losing hope.

When Petra invites my mother over to her place on Saturday, Mom takes me too. She feels safer with me there, hoping Petra will act with more decency in front of a kid. They sit at the table, drinking coffee, Mom's black and white carpet under their feet. I scan the boxes on the floor and the couch, stuffed with blenders, clothes on hangers, boxes of soap, china, wineglasses. So she hasn't just been taking our stuff. She's looted the homes of all the Muslim people in our building who fled.

Petra sees me eyeing the loot. "They're never coming back. I may as well fill up my summer home in Serbia," she tells us, smiling.

I hate her and her fake friendship game. I hate being surrounded by enemies, ex-friends and their dads bullying me. If I could enter my neighbors' homes and take anything, even without getting punished, I wouldn't do it. It's bad karma to cash in on someone else's misfortune. I think of the army equipment I swiped with Vik and the guys, and I console myself by recalling that Uncle Ahmet didn't mind me robbing the bad guys.

Mom has had a toothache for weeks, and the day after we go to Petra's, she runs out of painkillers. Her head is pounding so badly she says, "I'll use your dad's pliers to extract my own tooth."

Dad insists that she needs a dentist. We've heard the closest medical center is treating only wounded soldiers, with what little medication is left. We don't know if the smaller health clinics are still in service or will help us, but we decide to take the risk.

Since it's too dangerous for a woman to go outside alone and they throw Muslim men over eighteen into the camps, we decide I'll go with Mom. I'm small for a bodyguard, but accompanying her makes me feel useful. I want to protect her.

The town is empty as we pass roofless, demolished buildings. The streets smell like gunpowder and metal. Our shoes crunch through layers of glass and rubble. The sound of shooting echoes in the distance, and I notice bullet casings on the ground. I reach down and put one in my pocket, to remember.

The infirmary building is shot up from shells, like Swiss cheese. Inside are a receptionist and another patient waiting. We walk to the dental department, passing a doctor and a few nurses. Another doctor talks to a soldier who's being treated. From their calmness, I can tell they're all Serbs.

We sit in the same room where I once waited to be fitted for my retainer.

"What's your name?" the receptionist asks.

"Adisa Trebinčević," Mom says. "The entire side of my face hurts."

As we wait to be seen, I hear more fighting outside. I slouch against the wall as pebbles from the explosions ricochet off the infirmary's windows.

The dentist and a nurse step into the hallway. "Not that one. The other filling. The good stuff's for *our* people," I overhear him say.

I keep quiet. If I tell Mom, it will only upset her more. And if she complains, they might not fix her tooth at all.

After she's called in, she spends forty-five minutes in the office alone as I grow more nervous. I feel like I'm on guard. But when she finally comes out, she seems to feel better.

"They gave me novocaine before filling the cavity, so my mouth is numb," she says, rushing us home to Eldin and Dad. She's afraid they'll be taken away again if we're not there.

On the way home, a Serb soldier who looks like he's in his late teens tells us, "Don't hang around here. The mosque will be blown up in two hours. Open your windows."

Mom gasps. Does he know which side we're on? I look at the mosque, with its pointy wooden top, only two hundred yards before us. How can anyone ruin a holy building? We hardly ever prayed there, but Majka's father was once the imam, so this feels personal.

Back at our apartment, we tell Dad and Eldin what the soldier said, and we lift all our windows so the glass won't shatter. Mom unlocks the balcony door too, and I keep my bedroom door open to let the breeze through. We sit in silence, staring at the clock on the table.

At exactly four, loud explosions roar through the air. Though they are open, our windows still crack, shards flying everywhere. The mosque is more than a mile away from us, but it feels like we're being blown up too.

Through the open balcony door I hear cackling and cheering from Vik, Marko, Ivan, and their new best friend, Stevo. They whistle and yell that a parking lot will be built on our most sacred space.

"Why don't they fear God's wrath?" Mom asks. "Don't they know he's watching?"

"What God? He left us a long time ago," I say. I can feel my heart crying.

"No. Don't worry." She touches my shoulder, sounding like Majka Emina. "He's still here."

TWELVE

SEPTEMBER 1992

I don't want to trust Miloš or Zorica. But they're so nice to me, I feel safe at their place. I eat what they offer, bring my toys over, and teach their son games. Then, one September afternoon when we're sitting on the floor eating crackers, Miloš walks in the door, and Dejan jumps into his arms and asks, "Daddy, did you kill any Muslims today?"

Miloš has been away on a two-week tour, fighting in the nearby suburbs. He's in his green uniform, looking grimy and sweaty, his hair matted to his forehead. He removes the AK-47 from his shoulder strap and leans it against the wall as he takes off his muddy boots. My stomach tightens.

"How many Muslims did you get?" Dejan repeats. Miloš doesn't answer, just goes into the kitchen.

Zorica glances at me. "Dejan! Don't say that!" she scolds, her face red.

I finish the cracker Zorica has given me. Miloš comes back into the living room, and I stare up at him, my neck tingling.

He's six feet, taller than my dad, with huge shoulders. I'm afraid to speak in case I say something wrong. If he kills Muslims on the battlefield, he could easily shoot me here, then go upstairs to take out Dad and Eldin.

"Can I wear your jacket and gun?" begs Dejan.

"Okay," Miloš says, handing his coat to his son, who puts it on, sleeves reaching the floor. Miloš takes the clip off his assault rifle and gives it to Dejan with the bullets gone. Dejan holds it with both hands.

For a moment I feel like running home. But if I hang around, I'll get a piece of bread with chicken pâté and maybe candy or a Fig Newton.

"Want to hold the rifle?" Dejan pushes it my way.

I'm curious to see a gun this close and touch it. But now I'm afraid the warm barrel means Miloš has just been shooting Muslims like me. What if he killed my Uncle Ahmet, who's fighting in the Bosnian army a few hours away? Outside, mortars fire across the street. I picture bombs falling on roofs, turning walls to ashes.

"Can we play war now?" Dejan asks. His favorite game is taking on a different meaning for me today.

He gives the clipless AK-47 back to his dad, who puts it on the dining room table. As explosions ring outside, Dejan and I hide at different ends of Huso's apartment and search for each other. I aim my plastic Luger replica water pistol. Dejan puts his dad's holster around his waist. We use a pair of rolled-up socks as a grenade. I sneak behind Dejan's back and toss it in front of him, and we count to three out loud, yell "*boom!*" then "*ksssh.*" We cover our ears and throw ourselves onto the floor, the way they do in war movies, so we won't get hit by a second shock.

Dejan might be half my age, but I won't let him win. It's a thrill to pretend I'm a Bosnian commander conquering Serb bad guys to save my people. Make-believe is my only chance.

I'm still petrified of Miloš, but he never knocks bread out of my hand, points his gun at me, or calls me names. Whenever he sees me around the building, he says, "Hey, Kenan," and grins, patting my head. One day, when my old friends are taunting me as I walk back from the trash bins, he even tells Vik and Ivan to stop bullying me.

My dad calls Dejan "a good, well-behaved little boy." He teaches him chess. They play for three or four hours at a time. We have nothing else to do. Dejan is pretty good for being just six.

"Mr. Keka, can we play one more game?" he often begs.

Dejan also plays chess with Eldin, who Miloš calls "the Buddha" for his calmness and poker face.

Still, we're enemies, aren't we?

One night in October, I'm there when Miloš comes home.

He's smoking a cigarette and has dark lines under his eyes. "We lost a lot of men in Vučilovac," he tells Zorica, throwing his bag down. "The Bosnian and Croat forces burned the whole damn village. Our T-84 gunner was sliced in half."

I try to hide my elation and run upstairs. "Miloš said their army lost a battle and this guy in their tank got cut in half like a watermelon!" I tell Dad and Eldin, who pump their fists.

"Is Miloš okay?" Mom asks.

I nod, annoyed. "You should worry about *our* side. That's who his army is killing," I tell her.

"They've been good to us," she argues. "I don't want Miloš to die. Do you?"

"No," I admit. But the Vučilovac victory gives me hope.

Most days, Eldin spends hours lying on the floor. His ear is pressed to the radio so our neighbors won't hear the Bosnian station he listens to and think he's a collaborator. There's news of a cease-fire, and Eldin convinces me we have a chance of making it to safe territory, like Majka Emina — and soon Aunt Bisera and Halil, too, we've heard. But in the next broadcast, the radio announcer says a compromise can't be reached, and the battles resume.

One afternoon, as I'm returning from the well with a full jug, I pass Marko in the stairwell. He sticks out his foot to trip me, my water spills, and I fall down the stairs and land on my hands, scraping my palms.

It's not the first time one of my former friends has tripped me in the stairwell. But this time, I stand up and punch him. He spits and slaps me in the face. Then Vik sneaks behind me for a cheap kick, the coward.

From our terrace, Dad screams at my former friends, "What crawled out of your asses into your heads lately?"

Vik looks down, ashamed. He runs his sneaker over pebbles on the ground. Marko kicks a ball against the stairs. They've never heard Dad swear and sound so angry before.

"Go screw yourself!" Stevo yells back at him.

My mouth opens, and my heart falls as the guys chuckle.

I used to love having the coolest dad. He charmed all my pals, teaching us to play volleyball and swim in the river, talking about his days as a drummer in a jazz band, treating everyone to ice cream in town on summer afternoons. (My favorite is vanilla mint, and Vik likes chocolate with sprinkles.)

But there's no ice cream now, no swimming or stories. The war is changing my father. His face is harder, and he uses bad words all the time and wishes people dead.

Shaking his head, Dad turns and goes inside.

I'm used to their nastiness toward me. But I can't believe they're disrespecting my father.

—

On a windy morning that fall, a car pulls up in front of our building and two Serbs with red berets get out. Their faces are serious as they stop in front of Stevo, who is sitting on the steps.

"What's your name?" one asks.

Stevo answers.

The other soldier says, "Where's your mother?"

When they take off their caps, I know they've come to pay condolences. Stevo's father must have been killed in battle. Stevo runs up the stairwell crying, and I hear his mom shriek.

I rush into the living room, where Eldin, Dad, and Mom are sitting, to share the good news: she and Majka are right about people getting what they deserve. The mean man who shot my water jug got shot himself.

"Hey, I wished Stevo's dad dead. And now he is!" I announce. Eldin grins.

"Don't ever wish death on anyone, Kenan," Mom snaps, sounding angry. "We let God be the judge."

"Let them all rot," I mutter, like my father. He nods his head.

"Don't say that. They aren't all bad," Mom says. "There are good people who help us too, like Zorica."

"What do you think Miloš does all day?" I ask her. After all the horrors we've seen, I don't know how she still has faith.

"They're not all bad," my mom insists.

But I no longer believe her.

THIRTEEN

DECEMBER 1992

On my twelfth birthday Mom wakes me up with a cheerful "Happy birthday, Kenan!"

I'm the opposite of happy. I have no friends, cake, party, or gifts. Last year I had two celebrations — one with all my relatives and one with my pals. Dad bought me a remote-controlled Transformer. Majka Emina baked me a special apple cake and knitted me a blue sweater with a panda on it. She gave me money that I used to buy a new sports uniform and some miniature foreign cars. This year, I don't even know where my Majka is.

"I've saved you special chocolate, just for today," Mom says.

"Who cares?" I mumble. "The Muslims they murdered are better off than we are."

She stares at me, her eyes filling with tears. I don't want to make her cry, but I'm sick of pretending we're going to be okay. All I want for my birthday is to get out of here.

I go to wash, heating up water in a pot over the propane gas tank. In the cold bathroom tub I use the Red Cross soap Zorica gave us, rough like sandpaper, as I pour a cup of water over my head. I hate feeling hungry and dirty all the time.

That afternoon, Zorica brings me candles, a Milky Way bar, and a little money, which I immediately give to my parents.

"No cake, bro, but plenty of candles," Eldin teases.

He wants to stick a candle in the Milky Way and light it, but we don't dare waste a single match. I take out a ruler and measure the candy bar, breaking it evenly and giving Eldin half.

It's my worst birthday ever.

Nine months into the war, we're still stuck in our Bosnian apartment, with no electricity, running water, or heat, spending most of our time in the dark on the living room floor. We whisper and tiptoe, afraid soldiers might come for us at any moment.

"We need the right papers to get us out of here and go stay with Ahmet," I hear Dad whisper to Mom on a cold, foggy night before I go to bed. We've just learned that my uncle was wounded in the leg during battle and has escaped back to Vienna to reunite with my aunt and cousins and get medical treatment. He's eligible for resettlement with Aunt Maksida's sister and her husband, who they're staying with.

If only we could get to Uncle Ahmet, six hours away, we would be safe.

"I'm going to see Miran," Mom announces one day at the end of December.

"Mr. Miran?" I still haven't told her he held a gun to my head.

"No, a different Miran. He's a good guy who used to lift weights at Dad's gym," Eldin explains. "They just made him the new police chief."

Every day I see how two Serb women—Zorica and Petra—can behave in completely opposite ways. Still, I'm skeptical that two Serb men with the same name can be that different.

"Yes. He might be able to help us get out of here," Dad agrees.

"Going to the police station is dangerous," Eldin tells me later. "Women have been attacked there, like Ruža at Luka—and Larisa, from my high school, I heard."

My heart screams in my chest. That's Lena's sister! I thought her family had made it out of the country. I'm wrecked and angry, fearing they've taken Lena too.

"Wait, is Larisa okay? What about her sister?" I ask.

"That was months ago," my brother says. "Who knows where they ended up."

Anywhere is better than here.

Mom takes me to the police station to see if Good Miran, the new police chief, will help us leave the country. She hopes having me with her might get us sympathy, she says.

On the walk there, our town is unrecognizable. Dead dogs

and cats rot in alleyways, swarming with flies. Garbage is piled up on street corners, and black clouds of diesel exhaust blow out of the tanks and other military vehicles that have taken over the roads. Dark smoke swirls from the chimney of the rubber factory on the outskirts of town, where — a family friend told us — piles of Muslim corpses are brought in on meat trucks to be burned.

At the front door of the station, a guard stops us.

"What do you want?"

I'm terrified as Mom calmly says, "We're here to see Captain Miran."

"One second."

A minute later, a short, pale man, armed with two guns, bullets on his belt, comes out and shakes her hand. He's polite and clearly in charge. He brings us into his office.

"Yes. Let's get this going. I'll draw up papers in a hurry. Get me your passports to update. I'll personally call all the checkpoints in advance," he tells Mom in a quiet voice.

"My sons don't have passports or photos," she says.

"They need pictures fast," he says. "Here." He writes an address on a piece of paper and hands it to her.

The next day, Good Miran sends an elderly Serb man to our apartment. He drives Eldin and me five minutes away to a photography studio near our school to have our first passport photos taken.

When he drops us off back at home, he instructs us to re-trieve the papers and documents from a woman who works in the police station. We can leave on January 3, less than a week away.

It seems straightforward, but I doubt that this Miran will really call all the border checkpoints before our departure to make sure that our names are cleared. Even if he does come through, we have no idea who might turn on us, stop us, send us back, or shoot. I have little hope, but Eldin thinks this time it might work. He keeps saying, "We have a better chance with his help."

Last New Year's Eve, my buddies and I played with firecrackers out in the courtyard. This year, the explosions we hear are real weapons. Mortars are being fired from the army base next to school. We hear bullets hit the side of our building. My fam-ily welcomes the new year lying on our living room floor, face-down.

On January 2, Dad has to pick up our new papers. He doesn't want to go alone, so he decides to take me. We wear sweaters, raincoats, and rubber boots as we sneak out in a snowstorm before the sun comes up.

I feel like a spy on a secret assignment. Nobody has plowed the streets, and the snow is up to my waist. Trudging through it, we hope we won't run into soldiers who'll question us. It's cloudy, with no stars or moon, and we can't see much. The snow muffles our steps.

We walk for ten minutes without seeing anyone; then Dad opens the front gate of the house we were directed to. He knocks lightly with his fingertips. The door opens. A Serb woman I don't recognize slips us an envelope, saying, "Keka, here are the passports and the documents you need to leave the country. Good luck."

Zorica knows about our plan to get on a bus and join Uncle Ahmet's family in Vienna, and she comes to visit at midnight with hundreds of schillings — the money they use in Austria — tea cookies, and a bottle of moonshine "to bribe the bus driver." We all kiss her goodbye. I hold her tight, feeling guilty I doubted her loyalty.

None of us sleep well, awaiting our D-Day, the most important mission of our lives. We pray the snowstorms will worsen so soldiers will stay in their guardhouses at the checkpoints and not come onto the bus.

On Sunday, January 3, 1993, Mom gets up before dawn. She prepares the last pathetic food we have left — chopped onions on slices of bread — and sticks the sandwiches in her purse. I dress in layers: my Wrangler jeans, two shirts, and a sweater under my navy parka, and sneakers with two pairs of socks. Eldin wears two button-down shirts under his flight jacket, the kind Tom Cruise wore in *Top Gun*.

We don't know what will happen; we're winging it. We each hold a suitcase as we say goodbye to our home one more time and head out into the freezing, wet darkness. I don't know if I'm shaking from the cold, fear, or both.

"Lousy weather's on our side," Dad says. "Keeps everyone indoors."

We arrive at the deserted bus stop, and soon a white cross-country bus with gray stripes comes along, the kind I rode for an hour to visit my Uncle Ahmet last summer.

"Hi, Keka," the bald driver says as we board. It's Radivoj, a chubby Serb in his thirties who used to work out at Dad's gym. We give him money; he hands us blue tickets.

He's writing down all the passengers' names. At the checkpoints, a soldier will be looking at the list. For us, Radivoj writes "S. Trebinčević," then winks at Dad. I wonder if he thinks my father's first name, Senahid, is more Muslim-sounding than Trebinčević. If our names stand out, our trip ends—and possibly we end, too.

Dad smiles. The driver smiles back. He's on our side, even before Mom hands him Zorica's moonshine.

Walking up the aisle of the bus, I count thirty rows of double seats, but not all are filled. A few businessmen travel alone.

Three elderly couples with hardly any luggage look like they're going on short trips. These riders are older than my parents and better dressed than we are, in nice coats, scarves, and leather gloves. They don't look ratty or hungry. Clearly, they're all Serbian. Are they our enemies?

A lady with gray hair like Majka's is laughing at something her husband says. It seems heartless to me that they're going on holiday in the middle of a war when so many Bosnians are suffering. Eldin says that certain areas, far from the fighting, are hardly affected by the bombing. While thousands of our people are being massacred, Serbs visit Europe every weekend to shop and dine out with friends.

I fear it's obvious we're Muslim refugees, clearly terrified, trying to escape. In the middle of the bus, I take the window seat next to my father while my brother sits next to Mom right in front of us. We don't speak.

Eldin and I share the package of Zorica's tea cookies. We offer some to my parents, who shake their heads. I stare out the dirty window at the swirling snow. The fattest flakes fall sideways. I feel like I'm one of those snowflakes, being blown around, lost in the fog.

We ride in silence for three hours until we stop at the Bosnian-Serbian border. A soldier with a mustache, wearing a red beret, comes out of a little cabin. I guess he's about Eldin's age. I try not to tremble as he climbs the steps.

"Do I have reason to check this bus?" he asks Radivoj, snow dripping off his hat. He sounds bored, like he just wants to get back inside his warm kiosk. My pulse is racing. Will anyone turn us in?

"No, we're okay," Radivoj replies. They chat a bit about the storm conditions.

I hold my breath, praying the soldier won't notice us. He appears to only skim the passenger list. *Please God, let us leave this time.*

Seconds feel like hours. We wait for someone to give us up, but the other riders keep quiet. I don't know why. The flakes are falling faster now, and at last the soldier stomps back out and into his dry cabin.

Finally the bus takes off. Hot tears of relief pour out of my eyes. So far, the weather, Radivoj the friendly bus driver, and the silence of strangers are saving us.

At the second checkpoint, we stop on a bridge, where an iron gate lifts. Another soldier in camouflage and a red beret comes aboard. This one is older and taller than Eldin, maybe six foot four, with huge shoulders and a big belly. Strapped across his chest are two guns: an AK-47 and an Uzi, and a handgun hangs in the holster above his pants pocket. His cheeks are ruddy, like he's excited about shooting someone.

"Identification out," he bellows, marching down the aisle. I stare at my boots, leaning against Dad. I know Eldin is in more danger than I am, since he's eighteen. I wince as the red beret heads straight for us like a magnet drawn to our terror.

"Documents," he demands.

Mom hands him our new passports and Good Miran's letter. But the red beret is mad. "Get off the bus!" he yells.

Please, no, please, I pray. For someone who isn't religious, I'm sure praying a lot, though it isn't the technical kind. More like silently begging God to spare us.

Mom points to the letter again. "Captain Miran signed it," she says, hoping the soldier will recognize the name and leave us alone.

"Who the hell is he? You're not going anywhere," the red beret screams.

"Please, we have the required paperwork," Mom pleads.

Tears stream from my eyes. I can't help it, or stop.

"My young son has the flu," Mom tells him.

Dad stands up stoically but lets Mom speak for us.

"So take him to the doctor! What the hell do you want me to do about it?"

He orders us off the bus, telling Radivoj to continue on without us.

Radivoj salutes and turns on his engine as we lose our only chance to escape.

"But Captain Miran was supposed to call the checkpoint to leave our names with the guards. Can you call him, sir?" my mother begs as we step out into the cold. "Please."

We're hours from home, stuck in a no-man's-land during the worst winter storm in years. I'm trying to stay calm, but I can't stop crying. We have nowhere to go. Even if it's possible to catch another bus back, we have no money and hardly any friends there anymore; we'll be killed. As we walk out into the snowy fog, my whole body quivers, my teeth chattering.

"Come with me," the soldier yells, leading us to a room inside the bus terminal.

I eye the handgun on his holster and the nightstick hanging off his belt. Inside the office, I spot more pistols and rifles in an open closet. Will he shoot us here? If he tries, I decide I'll make a grab for one of the weapons, like in an action movie. But are they loaded? Maybe we'd be safer outside? He might not kill us while traffic passes by. As he rummages through a stack of papers on his desk, I'm desperate for an escape plan. We stand there, waiting for him to find whatever he's looking for. Eventually he grabs a note with several lines and a number scrawled on it in pen.

"What's your name?" he barks at Dad as I suck in my sobs.

"Trebinčević," my father answers, not saying his first name in case the driver was right and our last name sounds a little less Muslim.

The soldier picks up the phone and dials. "Is this Captain Miran?" he asks.

Please be there, Captain Miran, I say to myself over and over. *Please be there.*

"Huh. Yes, sir," the red beret says into the phone. "Trebinčevićs?"

Is Good Miran on the line? Will we be allowed to leave or forced to stay? Will this Serb kill us right here? Live or die? I'm numb, waiting for the verdict.

The soldier slams the phone back down.

"Get out!" He orders us outside and follows with his two guns still over his shoulder and the handgun in his holster. I don't know if we're being freed or led out to be shot.

As we stumble back into the snowstorm, we're stunned to find that the bus hasn't left. Radivoj is waiting for us! Miraculously, instead of following the soldier's order, he turned on his engine, then pulled off to the side of the road, where he's been sitting for the last ten minutes.

"Are they coming?" Radivoj asks. "I'm late, and it's freezing out here."

"Get the hell back on the bus!" the red beret shouts at us.

I let out a breath I didn't realize I was holding. As we scramble to reboard and return to our seats, I dry my eyes with my sleeve. The bus starts down the road again.

Captain Miran's connections worked. His letter and a call

have saved us. So has Radivoj's kindness. I can't believe it. Have my prayers helped? Is it karma?

We did it! I want to yell. But I know that even on a bus with a sympathetic driver, our ordeal isn't over. We'll have to pass at least one more border checkpoint before we reach Austria, hours away. I'm still terrified someone else could send us back.

I look around and count forty-two other people. Forty-two chances to be turned in. I'm sure some of these Serbs hate us. Now they'll be more resentful because we've kept them waiting. I imagine that a passenger gives us up to the next checkpoint soldier. My stomach twists.

We don't say a word for hours. I stare out the window, frightened, checking for roadblock ramps or military jeeps. The snow is tapering off to flurries. Every time we slow down, I peek over the seat in front of me to see what's going on.

Our final hurdle is the Serbian-Hungarian border, where the bus stops at a ramp before another iron gate. The guard who comes aboard is dressed in an olive green uniform with an ivory belt and visor. He speaks in a thick accent that sounds German.

The soldier skims our identification. "Why isn't your passport stamped?" he barks at Dad.

We all stop breathing. Did the guard at the first checkpoint forget, or did he intentionally cause us trouble?

"I don't know, sir," my father responds. "I guess the Serbian border patrolman forgot to stamp it."

The soldier shakes his head. We wait to see what he'll do. Finally, he just stamps our passports and walks off the bus.

The iron gate lifts. I'm afraid to react, and keep holding my breath until the bus is on its way again and we cross the border. Then Radivoj lets go of the steering wheel and stares at us in the rearview mirror. I don't know what's happening. A wide smile creeps across his face, and he claps his hands. Everyone on the bus is suddenly laughing and nodding their heads, bursting into applause, too.

We've made it! My mother lets out a huge sigh. Eldin and I both raise our arms over our heads, cheering and pumping our fists in the air.

"Thank you," Dad says to Radivoj and the other passengers, his eyes filling with tears.

I can't believe how wrong I'd been about the others on the bus. Now we know they've been secretly rooting for us all along, afraid to show that they're on our side. But their poker faces in front of the soldiers made our escape possible.

I wonder if my mother is right: if there really is bad and good in all kinds of people. I think of Zorica, Captain Miran, my mom's friend Ankica, and Radivoj. Yes, some of our friends, neighbors, and teachers turned into monsters, but the last Serbs we see leaving our country are kind.

Nobody says much for the rest of the six-hour ride through Hungary. The snow disappears, and the sun overtakes the fog.

As my fear subsides, I remember how hungry I am, and we pull the onion sandwiches from Mom's purse. Eldin and I eat quickly as the bus speeds through miles of farmland. To calm down, I count cows and roosters in the fields.

In the evening, we reach Austria, Uncle Ahmet's new country. The streets are filled with so many lamps and traffic signals, I have to squint. It's been nearly ten months since my eyes were exposed to electric light.

PART TWO

STUCK IN LIMBO

Vienna, Austria

FOURTEEN

JANUARY 1993

We pull into the Vienna station amid dozens of other buses parked side by side. Hundreds of passengers spill onto the sidewalk, many looking like us — confused, scared refugees, speaking Bosnian, carrying lots of luggage. Some seem to be searching for family members who escaped earlier. Next to us, a woman wearing a green parka and holding a baby calls out, "Sestro!" and embraces another woman who I guess is her sister, as they both weep hysterically.

I wish Uncle Ahmet were here to pick us up. He knows how to handle everything. But we haven't spoken to him, so he doesn't even know we escaped yet. We've had no way to reach him for the past nine months.

"Hurry. Let's get our bags," Mom says. But as we go to retrieve our luggage from the storage compartment under the coach, the door closes and the bus starts moving down the street. Diesel fumes blow in my face, making me cough.

"Keka, our suitcases!" Mom shouts. "He forgot us!"

Eldin runs alongside the bus, punching it with his fists, trying to get Radivoj's attention. Mom, Dad, and I join him, sprinting across the busy intersection, which is wider than my school's fudbal field. The streetlamps light up the darkness. I've never seen roads with so many car lanes.

As I chase my brother chasing the bus, I think of what's in my bag that can't be replaced, like my plaque for being the best reader in first grade, signed by Mr. Miran — my only school prize, which even his gun to my head can't erase — and the two stray bullets from my collection that I slipped in when Mom wasn't looking. Then I picture all the stuff that Mom wouldn't let me take: my marbles, sport cards, and Transformers. I can't believe that after our seventeen-hour journey, we're losing what little we have left. Radivoj is such an awesome driver, how can he take off with our stuff?

"Be careful of cars! Don't get run over," Mom yells at Eldin, who gets caught between two oncoming trucks that both screech to a stop. One of the drivers opens the window, screaming in German that sounds just like the guys from *The Dirty Dozen*. Eldin keeps running and I follow. We're both panting. It's the most exercise we've had since the war began.

Behind us, Mom is crying, thinking we've lost everything. The bus makes a sharp left U-turn, and we cut in front of it, waving our arms. Radivoj pulls over and opens the door.

"Didn't you hear me say there was no parking on that street?" he asks us. "That's why I had to move."

"No. We didn't hear that," Eldin says, breathless. "Sorry."

Dad looks relieved, but Mom is still crying. We retrieve our luggage, shake Radivoj's hand, and thank him once more. I look around, weary. We've been on the road since five a.m.

The dry air is so cold I can see my breath. But at least it's not snowing here. Though the lights still burn my eyes, all the shining streetlamps and blinking traffic signals make me smile. Trolleys zoom past with bells ringing. Noises and colors swirl around us. It's dazzling.

Mom fishes out of her purse the scrap of paper with Ahmet's address and phone number. Together we find a pay phone and stick a schilling in the slot. Mom dials as we wait nervously. What if he's moved? Or if she wrote down the number wrong? Or nobody picks up? It's eleven o'clock at night. Where will we go? We could ask the black-uniformed policeman on the corner, but he reminds me of the nasty Serb soldiers at the checkpoints. Could he deport or arrest us?

Mom nods, signaling that someone has answered. "This is Adisa Trebinčević, Ahmet's sister. Who is this?" she says in Bosnian. "Oh, thank God. Fadil! We're here in Vienna! Yes, we got out. Yes, we're safe. At the bus station. Is Ahmet there?" Mom asks. Then she says, "Yes. Okay," and hangs up.

"Ahmet's not home, but he'll meet us there," Mom says, excited. "Fadil said we should get a taxi."

We find a man in a gray Mercedes with a taxi sign. Dad shows him Uncle Ahmet's address. The driver nods, opening his car doors. Dad gets in front, the rest of us in back.

We haven't seen Uncle Ahmet, Aunt Maksida, or my cousins in so long. "Who is Fadil?" I ask Mom.

"Don't you remember? He's married to Raza, Aunt Maksida's sister."

I've never met them. They lived an hour away from Brčko, in Ahmet's town, but they've spent the last six years in Vienna. They moved here for work long before the war, so they're already citizens.

"When do I get to see my uncle?" I want to know.

Mom grins. "Soon."

Forty minutes later, I'm imagining eating Aunt Maksida's famous apricot jam when we finally come to a gated area and pull up to a fancy apartment building. We have no idea what the fare should be or how to count schillings. Exhausted and out of it, Dad shows the driver two of the big bills Zorica gave us the night before.

"Yes, two hundred," the driver says in our language, in what sounds like a Serbian accent that makes the hairs on my neck stand up. He takes it all. We get out and ring the bell as he speeds off.

"Think he's a Serb?" I ask Eldin. He nods.

"Remember to take off your shoes, and do not touch anything in their home," Mom warns.

A couple open the door. "Fadil! Raza!" Mom cries, rushing into their arms.

"You made it," they say, leading us into the foyer, shaking all our hands warmly, saying "Welcome" in Bosnian. Fadil has slicked-back hair and is wearing a crisp buttoned-up shirt and jacket — spiffy, like Al Pacino in *The Godfather*. He's the building superintendent here, we learn. Raza has on a silky dress, and her lipstick is very red against her white teeth. She has stylish braided hair. The only hint that she's an accountant is the glasses she wears on a chain around her neck.

The narrow foyer has white furniture and floors made of marble. The apartment's about the same size as our Brčko place, but I've never seen such an elegant home. When Mom's not looking, I kneel to touch the tiles. "Look, it's heated," I tell Eldin, sitting down to warm my butt.

"Let's put your bags here," Fadil says, storing our luggage in the hall closet.

A younger boy runs in. He's shorter than I am, wearing fudbal footie pajamas. "This is Enes. He's eight," Raza says.

"*Willkommen zuhause,*" he says. I don't understand the German words, but they sound friendly.

"I love fudbal too," I tell him in Bosnian, pointing to his PJs.

"Rapid," he says his team's name and asks for mine. I'm about to say *Outlaws,* since I follow Eldin's favorite team, but then I remember that Yugoslavia suspended our fudbal league because of the war.

I nod, then say, "My team is no more."

"Share all your toys with Kenan," Raza tells her son, leading us to the dimly lit kitchen. "Look, Kenan, honey, you can have anything you want," she says sweetly, opening the refrigerator.

It feels wonderful to be in a warm house filled with toys and food in a fridge with a light that works. Raza and Fadil set out a buffet of glittering dishes and platters.

"Don't eat too much too fast or your tummy will hurt," Mom cautions.

I'm too excited, though, and famished. I sit down on a stool at the counter and inhale the delicious food—beef salami on thick rye bread, fruit yogurt, and apple strudel—washing it down with a glass of milk. It's been so long since I've tasted anything fresh and cold. I put a spoon in the mayo and eat it like ice cream.

"Stop doing that. It's disgusting," Mom whispers. Enes cracks up.

"But I haven't had mayo in a year," I tell her, and everybody else laughs too.

"Why aren't you eating?" Dad asks Mom.

"I'm too tired," she says. "I had the sandwich on the bus."

Dad pushes over a bunch of purple grapes, and she eats a few. She always ate like a bird, but the war has wrecked her appetite. I hope her hunger comes back soon.

At last the doorbell rings, and Fadil says, "There's Ahmet."

"Uncle!" I yell as he walks into the kitchen slowly, using crutches. I'd forgotten that his leg was shattered fighting in the war. I hate watching him limp, his face twisted in pain.

But as soon as he sees me, he puts down the crutches, picks me up, and kisses my cheeks, which he's never done. Then he scruffs up my hair. I grab on to his neck, ecstatic to be safe here, with him.

"My leg's one big toolbox, full of screws and bolts holding the bones together," he jokes.

"You look good," Mom says, taking her turn to hold him close. Then he hugs Dad and Eldin.

"We finally made it out," my father tells him.

"So what'd ya pay for the taxi ride?" Uncle Ahmet asks.

"Two hundred of the schillings," Dad says.

"Jerk ripped you off." My uncle shakes his head. "It should've cost half what he charged."

"He had a Serbian accent," Eldin pipes up.

"Figures."

Dad looks ashamed he's been scammed. Being screwed over by another bad Serb pisses me off, even after the nice passengers on the bus.

"Where's Aunt Maksida and my cousins?" I ask. I've missed Minka, who is fourteen, and Almira, who's ten, two years younger than me. This is the longest we've ever been apart.

"You'll see them in the morning," Uncle Ahmet promises.

"Have you spoken to Mom?" my mother asks him.

"Yes. She's fine. In the suburbs with Bisera. We just got a letter from her," Ahmet says.

I'm glad they're safe, just an hour away from Brčko now.

"Thank God," Mom says, tearing up again. Over the past year, even with all we've been through, I've seen her cry only once or twice. But her eyes have been watery all day today. I guess she saved her tears until we were safe.

"Everyone's okay for now," my uncle assures us, putting his hand on hers. "So tell me what happened." He sits down at the kitchen table with my father and Fadil while my mother helps Raza take out more food. Eldin and I load up our plates with second and third helpings.

"Miran threw us out of our own apartment," Dad says angrily. "Then they put us in jail for two weeks."

"They killed thousands of civilians," Mom says.

"There are mass graves outside of town," Dad adds.

"Those bastards are war criminals who should all be shot," my uncle mutters.

Fadil nods sadly. "All the Bosnian refugees here have been filling us in on what's happening."

After we finish eating, Raza tells Enes it's late and he has to go to bed.

"*Gute Nacht*, Kenan," he says as his mom leads him upstairs.

"*Laku noč*," I tell him in Bosnian.

The rest of us move to the living room. It has beige leather couches, a huge television, and a fancy glass chandelier on the ceiling, with a lot of little bulbs. When I tell Fadil I'm not used to bright lights yet, he makes it darker with a dimmer switch. As everyone sits down on the couches and ottomans, I curl up in the corner of the sofa with a sudden terrible tummy ache.

"When you've been starving, your stomach shrinks," Uncle Ahmet tells me. "You have to take it easy with food." He turns to Dad. "You lost too much weight, Keka. You should go weigh yourself on the bathroom scale."

Dad does. When he comes back, he looks alarmed. "I'm down fifty pounds. How do I regain it?"

Mom bites her lip. We've seen Dad every day, so we didn't

notice how much he'd shrunk. "Well, I'm a fat pig now," Uncle Ahmet jokes, "since I've been eating well for six months." It's true, he's heavier now.

"There was no running water in Brčko for nine months." Dad fills everyone in on what we've endured. "We had to pour buckets of well water into the toilet to flush. Kenji had to go out to get us bread."

"You're safe now," my uncle reassures us again, then checks his watch. "But it's past midnight. I have to go."

"Go where?" I ask.

"We live twenty-five minutes away," he tells me. "I'll come get you guys tomorrow."

"Why not tonight?" I ask. My chest thumps. I'm confused— why doesn't he live here with his sister-in-law and Fadil? I don't want to lose my uncle again.

"We've been staying with a Viennese family, the Raths. One in the morning is too late to move you all in. We don't want to wake everyone up," he explains, hugging me goodbye.

"Why can't we all be together here?" I ask quietly.

"They only have two bedrooms, not enough to sleep eight more of us," he says, scruffing up my hair one more time before he leaves.

I wave from the front door as Fadil pulls two couches out into double beds. Raza comes back downstairs, holding sheets and pillows for us.

After they go upstairs to sleep, I check out the bathroom on the main floor. There's a big tub and two sinks. These past months, I've hated going to the bathroom in the dark, with only a candle. Now I keep flipping the light switch on and off.

"Stop that. And don't make a mess," Mom says. "Take a shower, but be quick. Don't use up too much hot water."

It's the first shower I've had in close to a year, and I don't want it to end. The water pressure tickles my skin. It feels so good to wash my hair with real shampoo instead of laundry detergent. My stomach is feeling better as I dry off in the big, fluffy white towel Raza left out, and I put on my sweats and T-shirt. I haven't brushed my teeth with anything but baking soda for so long, the peppermint toothpaste stings my gums.

"Go to the bathroom too," Mom instructs. "I don't want you making noise and disturbing the family by opening and closing the door in the middle of the night."

After I'm done, Eldin takes his turn, then Mom and Dad wash up.

"Let's sleep," Mom finally says. I'm so tired. Eldin and Dad take one of the sofa beds, and I crawl into the other with Mom, asleep before my head hits the pillow.

Early the next morning, Raza leaves for work, dropping Enes off at school on her way. I'm hungry again, so Mom makes us toast with strawberry jam, which I down with more fresh milk. Uncle

Ahmet returns, and he and Fadil carry our bags outside, hailing two cabs for the six of us. I go with my uncle and Eldin. As we head down the road, I stare back, thinking of Fadil and Raza's beautiful apartment, wishing we could stay.

"Where are we going now?" I ask.

"To the Raths, on Hauptstrasse, at the other end of town. They're very nice philanthropists who Fadil knows from work," Uncle Ahmet says. "They want to help refugees."

We all climb out, and Fadil pays for both taxis. Then he knocks on the door of a redbrick house. A smiling couple answers.

"This is Mr. Raimond and Agnes Rath," Fadil says.

Mr. Rath looks older than Agnes, like my parents. But they seem richer and much better dressed. We shake hands and say *"hallo"* and *"Danke,"* speaking an awkward mix of English, Bosnian, and the broken German we've picked up, with Fadil helping to translate. What do you say to total strangers who are taking your family into their home?

Fadil picks up Mom's bag, and we follow as he takes it through the kitchen and down some stairs to the basement. There we find my Aunt Maksida, Minka, and Almira.

"Auntie Ada! You're here!" Minka says to my mom as we all hug.

"You girls got so big and beautiful," Mom says, kissing their heads. They do look taller, rested and happy, and they're wearing pretty plaid outfits, earrings, and barrettes in their hair. I'm sure I look ratty in my worn-out T-shirt, sweats, and sneakers.

"I can teach you German," Minka offers in Bosnian to me and Eldin.

"Let's play Legos," Almira tells me.

We sit on the floor and build a castle together.

After Fadil leaves, Ahmet says he'll show us around town. He has to go pretty slowly on his crutches as we walk to the bottom of a hill to catch the trolley. He pays for our tickets and tells us where to stand. I can't help but stare at all the clean Austrian people in their pea coats, matching hats, and gloves. They're staring back at us. They can probably tell from our language and run-down clothes we don't belong here.

"Pull this wire when you want the bus to stop," Uncle says when it's time for us to get off. We're in a bustling area of stores and restaurants.

I'm delighted by how bright and shiny Vienna is, surrounded by snowy mountains, hills, and sculptures. "Eldin, that man on a horse is made of gold." I point to a statue in the middle of a square that's surrounded by regal estates that look like they're from a fairy tale.

Uncle Ahmet takes us to a toy store and buys me a miniature metal tank and two tiny green air force jets. They have no flags or insignia; they seem generic.

"*Hvala.*" I thank him in Bosnian.

"Don't throw your money away," Mom tells him.

"What can I get for you?" my uncle asks Eldin.

"I want a Bosnian newspaper," Eldin answers.

"Yes, let's get a paper," Dad says.

Aunt Maksida picks out a paper doll cutout book and fashion magazine for Minka and Almira. When we leave, I take my presents out of the package and play "Dogfight," with the planes.

Strolling through the elaborate Viennese gardens, I breathe in the crisp air. Their churches and museums are taller than the ones back home, magical. We see a building that resembles a medieval castle, and I imagine a king and queen walking out, waving grandly. It's all almost too much beauty to take in. Looking up at bronze eagles and plaster angels on the ornate buildings, I feel dizzy.

As the sun goes down, we find a newsstand to buy the Bosnian paper *Oslobodenje,* then stop at an ice-cream parlor, where Uncle Ahmet treats us to rainbow gelato, tangy and delicious.

"I'm tired. Why don't we go home?" I ask Eldin, forgetting we don't really have one.

"I bet he doesn't want us back at the Raths' too soon, bothering the family," my brother says.

We wait another hour before we return to the Raths' house. When we enter the kitchen, Agnes introduces us to their big, bubbly youngest daughter, Fani, who is fifteen. She has brown hair, cut in a bob with bangs, and she's wearing a buttoned plaid skirt and white shirt with a collar.

"*Hallo. Wie geht's dir?*" she says. We smile and nod, assuming it's some kind of greeting.

Then Uncle Ahmet takes us back to the basement. Slowly I understand that all eight of us will be staying down here in one long, slender room. It has wall-to-wall brown carpeting and wooden walls, beds on both sides. The small windows don't open, and you can see only the bottoms of trees. There's no bathroom here.

"Wait until Eldin has to go so both of you can sneak upstairs together," Mom tells us right before bedtime. "Don't disturb the family."

"I have to go now," Eldin says. We tiptoe upstairs, trying not to impose. There's no way I'm undressing in front of my girl cousins, so I bring my sweatpants and T-shirt with me to change.

When we come back downstairs, I sit on a twin-size bed and scan the room. It's dim and cramped, like a bomb shelter. Uncle Ahmet's family will sleep on one side, and they've made room for us on the other. They give us the trundle bed, and Eldin, the tallest, gets the top. Mom and I share the pull-out mattress below, feet to head for more room.

"Sorry you're sleeping in tiny matchboxes," my uncle jokes.

"It's just temporary." But he seems embarrassed that all of us have to bunk in such tight quarters.

Dad sleeps on a flimsy beach chair that keeps collapsing all night. I can't fall asleep, so I hear him snoring. Then he twists around, getting stuck and snapping awake, muttering swear words while untangling himself. It's pitch-dark, like it was in Brčko without electricity—but he doesn't want to disturb anybody else by turning on the lights. At least we're not afraid of being killed or taken to jail or a concentration camp. But I worry we'll be homeless. How long can two families live in someone's basement?

"Eldin, are you up?" I whisper.

"Shh, go back to sleep. You'll wake everyone."

Ahmet is the one keeping me up, with his snoring like a buzz saw. "How long will we be here?" I ask.

"Nobody knows," my brother tells me.

"Think we can play outside tomorrow?" I whisper.

"We'll ask Mom. But we don't want to disturb the rich people."

In the morning, we can hear the Rath family getting ready to leave the house. By nine a.m. they're gone, and we go upstairs to their kitchen.

"Auntie, when will you make me your apricot jam?" I ask Aunt Maksida. "When do we go home?"

"I don't know if we'll ever go home," she says sadly.

I join my cousins outside in the yard to play tag and jump rope, trying not to think about that.

In the evening, we go back downstairs to stay out of the Raths' way. As we're having beef salami sandwiches for dinner, there's a knock on the basement door.

"*Wollt ihr rodeln gehen?*" Fani Rath calls out. "*Mit meinen Freunden.*"

"Since it's snowing out, Fani wants you to come sledding with her friends," Minka translates.

"Can we, Mom?" I ask, excited to finally be able to play with a bunch of kids.

Mom looks at Aunt Maksida, who nods yes. The girls put on snowsuits, boots, mittens, and winter hats. All Eldin has is his flimsy black flight jacket. I don't have boots, so I put on extra socks, and I wear a sweater under my parka.

Outside, Fani and four other teens, two boys and two girls, are waiting. They're wearing warm down ski jackets with gloves and scarves. But they have the same type of wooden sleds we had in Brčko.

We walk with Minka and Almira's group a few blocks, past all the houses, to what seems like a huge public park, with the steepest hill I've ever seen. I'm out of breath as I climb up, grabbing on to Eldin to get my balance. Standing on top, we see how huge Vienna is, surrounded by mountains. We watch everyone winding down the slope with two or three kids on a sled, yelling and laughing.

My brother, the tallest and oldest, keeps quiet. We don't speak their language, so we stick together and share a ride, wind pushing against our faces.

For hours, we keep running up and speeding down until we're freezing and sopping wet. But it's the best time we've had in what feels like forever.

Three weeks later, we relocate with Uncle Ahmet's family to a two-bedroom on a street called Fleischmanngasse. The Raths own it, but they haven't rented it out yet. We're excited to have a place to ourselves, but we arrive to find no heat, no carpet, and little furniture. In the living room there's a couch and two coffee tables. In the kitchen is a small table and a tub with a shower hose. There's a bathroom out in the hallway, with just a tiny toilet, that we'll have to share with the other tenants on our floor. The larger bedroom is at the back of the apartment, and you have to walk through the other bedroom to get to it.

"We'll take the smaller bedroom," Mom says. "Your uncle needs more room to move around with his leg."

I nod. I've noticed that with his weight gain and injury, he's having trouble getting around.

Uncle Ahmet's family moves into their room. It's almost

completely filled with one bed and a pull-out sofa. Our bedroom, the smaller and colder one, has only two pull-out couches.

"Why is it all in a straight line?" I ask.

"It's called a railroad flat," Mom replies.

I think that's weird, since there are no wheels or tracks. And if anyone wants to bathe, we'll have to clear out of the kitchen, since there's no curtain. It's an awful setup, but we've heard thousands of other Bosnian refugees in camps here have it much worse. I don't complain. I don't want to seem ungrateful.

When I heard that Uncle Ahmet had escaped to Vienna, I didn't picture him, Aunt Maksida, Minka, and Almira all crammed into someone's basement or sharing a bathroom with strangers. Back home, he owned a thriving TV repair business, a fancy house, and a big car. He had lots of money, often treating us to dinner and buying us presents. I was so proud when he joined the resistance forces.

Now, Mom says, since he's been wounded, he can't work. Aunt Maksida is cleaning the houses of aristocrats in the area for cash under the table.

I feel horrible adding to their burden. Because of us, they're crammed into one room in this tiny apartment, Uncle Ahmet sleeping on the couch, his feet hanging over the armrest, while his wife and daughters have to share the bed. He has no car or job, hardly any money, and he can barely walk.

My big, strong uncle is a nobody now, just like my dad.

FIFTEEN

FEBRUARY–MAY 1993

One cold Wednesday in February, Uncle Ahmet wakes us, saying, "We have to apply for you to get temporary protected status today."

"What does that mean?" I ask, getting out of bed. Because it's freezing, Eldin and I have been sleeping in our sweatpants, long-sleeve shirts, and sweaters. Mom and Dad wear pajama bottoms with sweatshirts. Mom starts looking through our bags to find socks.

"It means they can kick us out anytime," Eldin says.

I guess it's good we haven't unpacked.

Fadil takes the day off to help us with our application. He leads Uncle Ahmet, me, Eldin, Mom, and Dad on two trains and a trolley to a big government building. Fadil has been in Vienna for seven years, is well-dressed, has a good job, and speaks German fluently, so he'll be able to vouch for us if there are any problems.

"Listen, Kenji," my uncle says, struggling to board the subway with his crutches. "This country is treating us nicer than our own people. They took in a hundred thousand Bosnians, and they give us cash each month. They're saving our lives."

When we arrive, there's a long line of refugees from Bosnia and Croatia. I hope I'll recognize someone. Everyone seems scared and helpless, like us. It makes me feel more normal to hear my language spoken all around me and to be with people who understand what we've been through. I realize how alone we were as the only Muslims in our Brčko apartment for so many months.

"Keka!" yells a tall man I vaguely recognize from Dad's gym.

"Jusuf! How are you, my friend?" My father hugs him.

Eldin nods, and Mom shakes his hand. We're all happy to see someone from our town.

"How long have you guys been here?" Jusuf wants to know.

"Just arrived last weekend," Dad says.

"How is your family?" my mother asks.

Jusuf breaks down in tears. "My Vehida didn't make it."

Dad puts his arms around him. Jusuf says his wife was killed by a bomb. Mom tears up as he describes the destruction, just a few miles from our home.

"We're the luckiest Bosnian Muslim family here," my uncle whispers in my ear. "We haven't lost any relatives."

The six of us stand in the line for hours. To get visas, Fadil says we'll have to show our passports and papers. At last we fill out forms that say our family of four can come here to pick up schillings each month, and my parents and Eldin sign an agreement promising not to get jobs. We're now officially exiles, not legally allowed to work, and we'll have to apply for new visas every three months to stay in Austria.

As they stamp our passports, I look down at mine, labeled YUGOSLAVIA, the name of the country that threw us out. But it's not my country anymore. It's nobody's. It ceased to exist when all the republics separated. My brother explains that all the Yugoslavians we knew are currently living in the separate nations of Bosnia, Croatia, or Serbia.

Uncle Ahmet gets his stipend right then. We have to wait until next time.

"Why don't they want us to work for our money?" I ask my uncle on the subway ride back.

"We'd take jobs from the locals," he says. "Though not that many Viennese want to clean toilets."

"They don't want to encourage refugees to move here permanently," Fadil explains. "It would drain Austria's resources for affordable housing, schools, and medical care."

"Well, it won't be for that long. We'll all go back after we win the war," I say.

Uncle Ahmet pats my head.

—

I'm regaining the weight I lost while we were in hiding, and I'm getting taller too. All my clothes feel too small. My corduroy pants are so short that my ankles get cold, so I pull my socks all the way up. I'm embarrassed by how shabby Eldin and I look next to the Viennese kids, who wear puffy down coats with fur collars, high boots, cashmere scarves, and sheepskin muffs. The only sneakers I have are so small, my toenail gets swollen.

When I complain, Mom says, "Have gratitude we're alive and safe. Other Muslim families in refugee camps here have to live in decrepit buildings with no windows or privacy. Or in tents in the middle of nowhere."

She stops putting our clothes in the dryer when she does the wash, so they won't shrink. Another Balkan boy Ahmet's family knows gives me his old pants and shirts.

I wish I could still wear the panda sweater Majka Emina made me, but it no longer fits at all. I hope she stays safe in Bosnia. Mom keeps trying to phone her, but there's no signal — the Bosnian phone towers are still screwed up.

I wonder if we'll ever reunite with our relatives or make new friends, or speak the right language. How will we pay rent and bills if we have no jobs? Aunt Maksida says Mom can babysit and Dad can shovel snow or work as a gardener to get extra cash.

"But Dad's not a gardener or a snow plower," I say. "And Mom's too old to be a babysitter."

"No work is beneath us," Mom tells me. "Whatever job you get, you must be the best at it."

I'm glad nobody is pushing me to work, or to go to school where they speak a different language, surrounded by strangers. After Vik and my friends betrayed me and Almir and Omar disappeared, I don't want to take a chance on new friends.

Though we aren't enrolled anywhere, Agnes Rath gets Eldin and me special student IDs so we can use public transportation for free. The red trolley cars are my favorite, a fun cross between a bus and the kind of trains we took back home. I'm impressed by how fast the underground trains go and how neat the Austrians are. I like the clean streets, with no shattered glass from broken windows crunching under my sneakers and no smelly, rotting garbage piled everywhere. But I wish I had something to do.

After a week, I can't believe I'm actually missing my old classes. Eldin and I are bored, so we just ride up and down the rails every day, picking up bits of German, memorizing each stop.

"Karlsplatz, Landstrasse, Längenfeldgasse, Praterstern, Schottenring, Schwedenplatz . . ." I recite the funny names. "What's the next transfer station?" I quiz Eldin, imitating the man calling out the names over the loudspeaker.

"You tell me, you weirdo!" my brother says.

One morning we get off at the Praterstern stop to check out

the enormous Ferris wheel at the Prater amusement park. Eldin has enough change for one ride for each of us, and decides on the roller coaster.

I'm scared of heights and fear I'll fall out, but I don't want to be left alone in the crowd either. So I go with him, keeping my eyes closed and my arm clutching his the whole time. When we get off, I feel dizzy and wobbly.

"Man, I wish we had enough money to do it again," Eldin says.

We spend another afternoon at a toy store, where there's no fee to try out video games, though the manager keeps an eye on us to make sure no one's hogging the machines. Austrian kids we meet there, waiting to play *Super Mario Land* and *Mortal Combat,* ask us questions I can't understand, but everyone's kind to me.

Still, I'm on edge. I keep reminding myself to be grateful that we're safe. But with no classes, sports, teammates, friends, or home of our own, I feel sad and restless.

A wealthy colleague of Fadil's recommends Eldin for a top-notch karate club, which allows him to enroll with no payment. He takes me along to the sports center, and they let me come in and watch as they do freestyle exercises. The sensei asks if I want to try, but everyone's older than me, and I'm too intimidated. Plus, it doesn't seem worth the effort to start anything new when I don't know where I'll be next week.

I adopt Eldin's radio obsession, checking constantly for war developments. At least we can listen to it at full volume here. The news isn't good, though, and it looks like we'll be staying in Vienna for a while. Everything's in limbo.

In March, we return to the big government office to pick up our first payment. It'll cover enough groceries until the next check. On the way back, I stop to drool over pastries in the window of a bakery: pyramids of muffins, tall cakes, different color tarts. Mom says I can pick one. I choose a sugar doughnut that makes my tongue do somersaults.

A few days later Agnes Rath stops by the apartment and tells my mother, "We just found out it's illegal for kids under eighteen not to be in school, even for refugees. So I'll enroll Kenan. It'll help him learn German."

I'm not happy to hear this. I wish I could go with Fani, but she attends a private all-girl's Catholic school, where my cousins Minka and Almira have also enrolled.

The next Monday, Mrs. Rath takes me to a public elementary just a three-minute walk from where we stay. It's a huge, five-story redbrick building. I'm worried about getting called on in class or picked on. I hope I can at least play fudbal at recess.

She brings me to the sixth-grade teacher she calls Herr Huber. He's tall, with combed-over red hair. Unlike Mr. Miran, who was serious in his brown suits, Mr. Huber wears jeans, with a colorful green button-down shirt. He makes the class laugh with jokes I don't get. I laugh anyway, covering my mouth so they won't see my teeth. They're all watching me, and I'm afraid they'll think I have no sense of humor.

I hate being here, stuck in a sea of strange kids speaking a language I don't understand. German is filled with short words, and after a while it sounds like a dog yapping. I've never seen so many people with red hair. I feel like a foreign freak. I keep my head down, wishing I could jump out the window.

At the break, Mr. Huber calls three classmates over to meet me. Their names are Ivo, Olivia, and Tarik. Mr. Huber explains that Ivo and Olivia were born here in Austria, but their families are from Croatia. Tarik is a refugee from Bosnia, like me.

"How bad was the war?" Ivo asks in my tongue. I'm so happy someone here understands me!

"Pretty bad. There were dead bodies on a meat truck right down my block."

"Wow, cool," he says, impressed.

"Sorry," says Olivia. They offer to be translators for me and Tarik until our German gets better.

"What town are you from?" Tarik asks me in Bosnian.

"Brčko."

He nods. "I was born in Orašje, half an hour from there. We escaped last month."

"I know your village," I tell him.

"I hope we're kicking some butt back home," he says.

I smile, high-fiving my new friend, the first kid my age I can relate to here. He's staying in Vienna with a bunch of extended relatives too. If I get picked on, Tarik will defend me.

"Yo, I have a lot of war songs on my Walkman," he adds. He shows me a cassette tape filled with patriotic Bosnian ballads I recognize from listening to Eldin's radio.

When the break is over and we go back to our lessons, I like knowing Tarik can't understand what the teacher or other kids are saying either. Being in the same boat with him makes me feel less alone. Plus, we have Ivo and Olivia to tell us what we missed. And Mr. Huber doesn't make us take notes or do homework.

Recess is great: Tarik and I listen to the music on his Walkman, and another kid lets us borrow his Game Boy. I've never played a handheld video game before. I want to get my own when we can afford it.

In the afternoon, we have gym class. An Austrian kid asks me, *"Fussball,* Kenan?"

I realize he means fudbal. Aha. That's my ticket! I can't wait to play, but I want Tarik on my team. "I'm with him," I tell Mr. Huber in broken German. He nods and puts Tarik and me together. We fly down the field, passing the ball to each other, and Tarik scores with my assist.

"Tor!" everyone yells, which must mean "goal" in German.

"Tor! Tor!" I cry, pumping my arms in the air. My heart pounds against my rib cage. I haven't felt this happy in nearly a year.

"Me and Tarik were the best fudbal players on the team," I tell Eldin that night.

"That's not saying much in Vienna," he jokes, since they're much better at skiing and sledding here than at fudbal.

The next day, Ivo and Olivia tell us that our class is going to take a fun field trip to a park later that week. Everybody's bringing their own lunches to eat outside, so on the morning of the trip, Mom packs me a tuna sandwich for the picnic.

When I return from school that afternoon, she gives me a special present: a notepad with black and white graphite pencils that she found at an art supply store. "This will keep you out of trouble," she says.

I love it, and I love having something new of my own. I draw for hours in my free time, making pictures of tanks, planes, and rifles, and of boats sailing under the blazing Balkan sunsets I miss.

SIXTEEN

APRIL–JUNE 1993

Everyone in our family reads *Oslobodenje,* the international Bosnian newspaper for refugees, filled with updates and pictures of the war. One day in April, before school, Mom cuts out an ad for a contest for young artists and shows it to me. I look over the rules while I eat breakfast at the small table — since we can't afford to get more furniture, we take turns eating there. You're supposed to submit two illustrations inspired by your current life.

"I want to enter this," I tell her.

"You should. You're a great artist," she says.

That evening, I do a drawing of a dove embedded in a broken missile. For my second entry I draw a boy sitting on a globe, yearning for his homeland. To his left, bombs drop on a cemetery filled with tombstones and crosses. I title it *Sad Days.* In a paragraph underneath, I write, *"My name is Kenan Trebinčević. I'm a 12-year-old born in Brčko. Last year, we were thrown out of our apartment. My dad and brother Eldin were put in a concentration*

camp. My Serb best friends beat me up. My favorite teacher betrayed
us. After nine months, my family of four escaped to Vienna, Austria,
on January 3, 1993, to live with my Uncle Ahmet and Aunt Maksida
on Fleischmanngasse Street."

Mom stamps the envelope for me, and we put it in the mailbox in the hallway outside our apartment, with plenty of time to make the deadline. Even though I know they're going to announce the winner in two weeks, I check the paper every time we pass a store that sells it, just in case the judges decide sooner.

Exactly fourteen days later, we're out for pizza — with mushrooms, our favorite, and the only topping everyone in my family can agree on — and Eldin finds a copy of *Oslobodenje* at a stand inside the subway station on the way home. I watch as he sits on a bench and scans the pages one by one.

"Ah, look, Chicken Arms, you won!" he yells suddenly, jumping up in the air. "Great job."

Dad picks me up and spins me around.

"You're a published artist now!" Mom says.

The last time I felt this proud was when I scored the winning goal during recess back in Brčko. I'm pumped to be recognized for something other than sports. We all crowd around to examine the paper carefully. There's my drawing, along with my paragraph about the Serbs who turned on us. The article also notes my full name and when we escaped, plus our new address.

A week later we get a letter from Dad's colleague Truly, who saw *Oslobodenje* in Germany. I didn't realize you could get this newspaper in a bunch of other countries! Truly sends his phone number, and that evening we call him from an outside pay phone to catch up and make sure his family's okay.

Mom kisses my forehead after they hang up. "I'm proud of you."

She keeps my drawing in her purse, showing it off wherever we go. I like letting people know what happened to us, and I'm awed that my art helped my folks find Truly.

In the days that follow, we hear from other friends who are dispersed. The whole world of displaced Bosnians has seen my story. It makes me feel important and powerful.

But my power doesn't help us feel at home in our tiny Viennese apartment. It becomes harder for eight of us to be crammed into a little two-bedroom. Something is going on with Uncle Ahmet. He's eating dinner late and refusing to leave the kitchen so we can shower, even when it's eight or nine p.m. on a school night.

He stops sharing the soups and meats that Maksida cooks, so we go out for cheap pizza to stay out of their way, or we have salami and cheese sandwiches in our bedroom. We try to sneak a shower in the afternoon while my uncle is napping. But if we wake him up, he yells, "Stop the damn noise!" If the door squeaks, he mutters, "Shut the hell up." We're clearly getting on his nerves.

I don't know who talks to the Raths about our troubles, but they find Mom, Dad, me, and Eldin a new apartment on Ungargasse, where we can live for a while before it's rented out. It's small, but has floor-to-ceiling windows overlooking a courtyard garden full of purple, blue, and pink flowers, and the wooden floors are shiny and smell like expensive polish. Everything echoes when we talk. I love how spotless and bright it is.

We get two used beds, an old sofa, and chests of drawers that someone donated for refugees, and Enes gives me a G.I. Joe and a miniature toy tank, which I immediately treasure. For the first time since arriving in Vienna months ago, we finally unpack our clothes.

My parents still don't have jobs, and Eldin doesn't work or go to school, but still, I almost feel normal again.

"I hear Sejo and Edita are here in Vienna," Dad says one day in May. "At the Bosnian refugee camps. Let's visit."

That Saturday, the four of us take the trolley and two subways to visit my parents' friends, who are living in the makeshift migrant quarters that have been set up in a cold, sterile former hospital. It's like an abandoned warehouse, with a broken elevator and only curtains for privacy. Even the hallways are used as rooms, separated by hanging bedsheets.

I can hear everyone's conversations around us as we walk up and down the halls looking for Sejo and Edita. Kids are yelling, shouts echoing. It's dirty and smells of cigarettes. I had no idea it could be this bad here for people like us.

"This place used to be a mental asylum," Eldin says quietly.

We finally find Sejo and Edita and their two kids, Elvira and Dino, in a tiny curtained-off space on the third floor. It seems like they're all sharing one twin bed. Mom hugs and kisses Edita, overjoyed to see someone from Brčko. Dad offers the juice and cookies we've brought, our meager housewarming gift.

"Did you see Kenan's story in the paper?" Mom asks, pulling it from her purse.

"Yes! Look, we bought it too." Edita pulls out her copy. "He was always a good artist. I remember."

"You're lucky Ahmet found those people to help you," Sejo tells us. "We're stuck here indefinitely."

"We can hear everyone breathe," adds Edita.

I realize how privileged we are to be living in a nice private home, even a temporary tiny one.

The next Saturday, Mom wants us out so she can scrub the floors. Eldin, Dad, and I go back to visit Sejo, Edita, Elvira, and Dino. When we return early that evening, we find Mom outside the apartment, screaming at a police officer.

"You can't do this to us!" she yells in Bosnian, which he

doesn't understand. "I can't handle this anymore! They threw us out of Brčko, and now they're kicking us out of here too?" I've never seen Mom so freaked out.

Two workers in overalls gesture at each other in confusion. The couch, beds, dressers, and our bags have been thrown out onto the sidewalk. We rush over to Mom, not understanding what's happened. Are we being driven from Vienna?

Dad's trying to speak with the officer in German, and Eldin goes to call the Raths from a pay phone. I stand by Mom, trying to comfort her. After a few tense moments my brother comes back. "Nobody's throwing us out," he tells us. "It was a mistake."

After speaking to the officer and workers in German, Eldin translates what's going on into Bosnian for us. The workmen accidentally came to the wrong apartment. They were supposed to evict the tenants right above us, on the third floor, who didn't pay their rent. The policeman radios back to his precinct and confirms this, then apologizes to us and leaves.

Eldin and Dad carry our belongings back inside, but Mom still sits on the sidewalk, sobbing.

"I was all alone when the men stormed in," she says. "One had a gun in his holster."

My mother has kept her calm all this time, even after losing Dad and Eldin, while we were forced to flee. She has always made sure we were fed and clean. But I can see the weight of it all is breaking her. She grew up a popular, pretty girl in a nice family, the youngest of three kids, protected by her older brother, Ahmet, her sweet sister, Bisera, her mom and dad. She lived in the same house for eighteen years, until she married Dad and moved ten minutes away. Before the war, they'd never had an enemy or been treated badly.

I sit down next to her on the concrete. "Mom, it was just a dumb slip-up. There's no war here," I tell her, patting her back. "Nobody's going to hurt us or throw us out."

"I'm just so tired of being degraded," she says, weeping.

I am too. It sucks having no money, no jobs, no home of our own. Dad and Eldin return to haul the couch back up the two flights of steep stairs. I stay with Mom, on the sidewalk.

"I can't handle being a nomad, moving from one place to the other," she goes on. "I hate not knowing how long we can stay anywhere. I'm afraid to unpack."

Even after we've resettled in the apartment, she cries all night. She turns the lights off and we use a candle, like we did in Brčko. I don't understand why she wants to be in the dark now that we have electricity. I wish I could take away her sadness, but I don't know how.

"We should go stay in the refugee camp with the rest of our people, where we belong," Mom keeps repeating.

I don't know if we belong anywhere anymore.

SEVENTEEN

JULY–OCTOBER 1993

"Are we going to stay in Vienna until we can go home?" I ask my brother.

"We don't have a home anymore, kid," he says.

"Then where will we go?" I'm frustrated that after six months in Vienna, we're still in limbo. School is finished for the year, and our time in this apartment is about to run out — it's been rented for July, so we have two weeks to find a new place to live.

Eldin just shrugs.

We can't go back to living with Uncle Ahmet. I fear we'll be forced into the crowded refugee camp. Worse, I'm afraid we'll be sent back to Bosnia while the war is still raging. Dad says we could be deported if we don't keep applying for updated short-term visas every three months. And from Eldin's radio, we hear the war is getting worse. Even if it ends, he says, we could be sent back to a hostile land with no home to return to.

We've gone from being a well-liked, successful family to beggars praying for somebody to take us in. It feels beyond humiliating to be poor and homeless, dependent on people we barely know for a roof over our heads. Whenever someone looks like they feel sorry for us, I want to shout, *My mother's really an office manager at a fancy clothing company, and Dad's the owner of the best gym in town!*

Mom still thinks we should go to the refugee camp, to be with Sejo and Edita and their kids. But a week before we have to move out, Mrs. Rath asks us to meet with her son-in-law, a guy named Siegfried. He's a businessman in his thirties, with pale blue eyes, red hair, and red eyelashes. He takes us to a pastry shop, where I get an apple turnover and juice.

"My wife, Theres, is a nurse. We have two little kids, and we work all day," Siegfried says as we all sit together at a little table. "Would you consider moving into our spare room in exchange for babysitting? For as long as you can? You'd be doing us a favor."

My parents agree. He seems nice, and he pays for my pastry, so I'm in.

We move to our fourth Vienna home in seven months. Our secondhand beds, sofa, and dressers are left behind. Siegfried's family lives in the heart of the city, next to a big cathedral, in a second-floor apartment with high ceilings and chandeliers. In their extra bedroom, we share two twin beds, me and Mom in one, Dad and Eldin in the other.

Once again, I don't drink water before bedtime because I'm afraid I'll wake everyone up if I have to go to the bathroom down the hall. My mother tosses around in our bed, mumbling in her sleep. Dad's snoring gets worse. It's hard to get rest here, in yet another place not big enough for two families.

Siegfried and Theres both leave for work at eight a.m. I stay out of their way in the morning, surfacing only after they're gone. I'm getting used to making myself scarce.

Mom babysits their two little redheaded boys all day and on weekend nights if they go out to dinner. Jacob is two, and Moritz is three. They have elaborate toys and a lot of miniature cars. I play cops with Moritz and give Jacob piggyback rides, pretending I'm an ambulance driver soaring across the Bosnian war fields to save our soldiers. They're sweet, well-behaved kids, and I love playing with them. Their smiles and giggles bring joy to Mom as they keep hugging and kissing her.

But I can never really relax or act natural here. Mom doesn't want to get their kitchen dirty, so we mostly eat soup and sandwiches, while she nervously cleans up every crumb. Soon I'm sick of not being able to touch anything, make a mess, or sit on any of their nice furniture. It's like I'm a guest visiting my own life.

—

Dad and Eldin get jobs working as gardeners at the Raths' neighbor's estate, cutting the hedges and trimming the roses.

"Hey, it turns out the guy we work for is an ambassador," Dad tells me one day.

"Really?" I'm amazed.

"I think all the rich Viennese people must know each other," Eldin says.

Since my parents can't get Austrian work visas, they apply for permanent residence in several different countries. The ambassador helps them get an appointment with an immigration official.

Two weeks later we're called to the United States Embassy for an interview. That morning, I comb my hair until my scalp stings and pull my cleanest jeans and denim jacket from my duffle bag.

"Make sure to call the diplomat 'sir.' Give him a firm handshake, and let us do the talking," Dad instructs us on the subway ride there. Nobody in my family is fluent in English, but Eldin did ace his high school English classes and Dad studied it in college. I try to remember my lessons with Huso's dad.

"We'll tell you everything he's saying," Dad promises Mom and me.

The diplomat leads us into his office, where a picture of U.S. president Bill Clinton hangs next to the American flag. He's tall and slim, with dirty blond hair and a blue suit. He speaks slowly, wanting to know exactly what happened to us. Dad answers in English, and Eldin translates for me and Mom.

"Do you know who put you in the concentration camp in June?" he asks. He names prisoners and guards who were at Luka with Dad and Eldin. I'm stunned by how much this guy already knows.

"Yes. Miran," my father says.

"He was the teacher who was in charge? When was this?" The diplomat is taking notes.

"Over a year ago. June sixteenth," Eldin answers quickly. It's a date he can never forget.

"Do you know anyone they hurt or killed?" the diplomat asks.

"Yes, my college friend Anto," Dad says, adding quietly, "and they attacked his wife, Ruža." Eldin doesn't translate that last part, but I understand it anyway.

Mom shows the diplomat Dad's and Eldin's release papers from Luka, and the form signed by her and Good Miran, transferring all our property to the government. She keeps the documents in her purse, next to the silver key to the Bosnian home that's no longer ours.

Inspecting the pages, the diplomat raises his pale eyebrows, nodding. He asks if he can keep our papers as evidence. I get the feeling he knows all about Mr. Miran and is trying to make a case against him.

Still, I'm scared to trust this guy, and my legs are fidgety. I stay quiet and try not to shake. If we flunk this meeting, maybe nobody will accept us. Then we'll be stuck living here in Vienna, where we're not wanted.

I watch as Mom hands over the documents. She looks pleased by the possibility that Mr. Miran and his circle of murdering Serbs could be convicted. Then it seems that the interview is over. With a thin smile the diplomat says, "Good luck," and he stands up.

Dad shakes his hand. "Thank you very much."

"Thank you, sir," I repeat in English.

"Think he's a CIA agent?" Eldin asks once we're out on the street.

Dad nods. "Seems like it, the way he interrogated us. Or maybe FBI?"

I hope he's a secret agent, though he doesn't look anything like James Bond. I like thinking I'm part of an international conspiracy.

One day Eldin and I climb a steep, spiraling staircase to get to the top of the cathedral next door to Siegfried and Theres's place. I'm out of breath and claustrophobic as we reach the top, but it's worth the steps to be able to look out and see all of Vienna. I've never seen so many high wavy mountains before. It's breathtaking.

We have fun with Siegfried on the weekends. He shows up

with McDonald's french fries and cheeseburgers for us. I love the fries, so salty and greasy. But I miss eating my favorite beef burek.

Siegfried kicks around a mini fudbal with me, Jacob, and Moritz. Watching their joyful young family reminds me how great we had it growing up. Like always, I try to be grateful that we're out of danger. But I still feel a big hole inside me where happy times used to be. I miss boating with my uncle, Majka's apple strudel, playing fudbal with my friends — even the smell of Dad's gym.

People escaping the war are still pouring in and out of Vienna every day. We go to the bus and train stations with letters addressed to Majka Emina, Aunt Bisera, and my cousins, hoping someone going back might agree to hand-deliver our news to our relatives. We search the crowds for old friends and ask anyone speaking Bosnian to give us updates on the fighting back home. I keep waiting to hear that the Serb army has fallen and we can go home.

When school starts again in September, Mom says I don't have to go. I think we all know we won't be in Vienna much longer. Sure enough, one day in late October my father and Eldin come home from their gardening job with an official-looking letter.

"We have incredible news," Dad says. My heart leaps, sure

the war is over and everything can go back to normal at last.

Then Dad shouts, "The United States is taking us. They said yes!"

"We're crossing the pond!" Eldin sings.

I wish I could be excited too. But we don't know any Americans. And the U.S. is so far away.

"Where will we live? What jobs will you be able to get there without any connections? We don't even speak English well!" I burst out. I just want to go home to Brčko, sleep in my own bed, and play with my marbles and G.I. Joe. I secretly pray that before we have to leave, the U.S. will rush in with marines to bomb the bad guys out of my country, like in *The Dirty Dozen,* Dad's favorite film.

"Kenji, it's okay," Dad says, putting his arm around me. "America has good schools. You'll get the best education."

"We'll be nobodies in the USA," Mom adds, "so you and Eldin can be somebodies one day."

EIGHTEEN

OCTOBER 1993

We spend the next couple of weeks preparing to move yet again. We visit Sejo and Edita and their kids at the crowded refugee camp one last time, say goodbye to Fadil and his family and to my cousins and Aunt Maksida and Uncle Ahmet.

When Dad writes to Truly to tell him where we're going, he wires us three hundred dollars in American bills. The U.S. consulate sends plane tickets to my parents, one for each of us. A few nights before our departure date, my mother cooks a big Bosnian feast of minced beef, rice, and potatoes for the Raths as a way to thank them for all their help.

Everyone's thrilled we're going to America. Not me. I feel lost. All I know about the United States is from TV. They play baseball and hockey and a dangerous fudbal I'll never try. They have stores that are as big as sports arenas. The guys Eldin's age drive fast convertibles, surf, and hang out with pretty blond girls in bikinis on the beach, like Jennie Garth on the show *Beverly Hills, 90210*. I have a huge crush on her.

But without good English, a car, or money, I know I won't fit in.

Mom worries too. "Where will we be? In a village? The mountains?" she asks Dad. "Will they stick us in a dirty refugee camp? Will we have our own place or live in somebody else's house? Can you find out?"

The diplomat at the consulate tells my father only "Connecticut." We've never heard of any place called Connecticut.

"Can't we at least go to New York or Beverly Hills?" I ask.

"Shut up. It's not our choice." Eldin swats my head. "It's a miracle they're taking us at all."

He looks in Sigfried's atlas and finds Connecticut, a tiny box bordering the Atlantic Ocean. "It's from the Native American name *Quinnehtukqut*," Eldin reads. "It means beside the long tidal river."

Good, it's on the water. I love the beach. "Is it warm — near California?" I ask.

"No, other side of the country," he answers. "Rural, and colder."

I imagine lonely cabins surrounded by sad-looking trees.

"How will we get around?" We've never had a car. In Brčko, you walk everywhere or take buses and trains. How will we afford a car without jobs or money? Who will teach us to drive?

—

On the cold morning of October 20, we wake up early and shower fast. Mom takes out my sweatpants and a loose sweatshirt, telling me to dress comfortably for the long flight. I'm feeling restless, hyper, not hungry at all.

"Have breakfast," she says, handing me toast with jam. "We don't know when we'll eat again."

Dad's flown before, back in his single days, but the rest of us have never been on a plane. The Vienna airport is a chaotic maze of lanes and counters, with travelers lined up everywhere. Luckily, Siegfried has come in with us and points us to the right gate. I hug his waist and say goodbye, trying not to cry.

After he leaves, I look around nervously, eyeing the badges and serious faces of the security guards, who remind me of soldiers. My back is tense, and I have to pee.

In the bathroom mirror I look pale, my bangs uneven. My front teeth seem like they've gotten bigger and more crooked without my retainer. Americans on TV and in the movies all have perfect teeth. I decide to just keep my mouth closed from now on.

Back in the waiting area, a woman from the International Organization for Migration finds us and gives us each a sharp-looking blue-and-white tote bag with the same globe emblem that's on her uniform. There's paperwork inside.

Mom thanks her and then sits quietly, clutching her bag, nervous about flying for the first time.

At last we're allowed to board. The inside of the plane is a long, steel tube filled with lounge chairs, like a huge spaceship. There must be hundreds of other refugees in our section, all speaking our language. They look as ragged and confused as we do, wearing layers of clothes, holding plastic bags filled with their belongings.

I grin and wave at everybody as we make our way to our seats, suddenly feeling less alone. If they're all going to Connecticut too, we'll be safe.

"Gruesome what's happening in the war," Dad says to the man behind us. "Where are you going?"

"Florida," he replies.

Next to him, a woman shows a ticket for St. Louis.

Another says, "Chicago."

Nobody else is going to Connecticut.

While we're waiting to take off, the flight attendants point at aircraft safety cards and demonstrate how to inflate a raft in case of an emergency water landing. That's when Mom loses it.

"The plane's going to come down," she whisper-shouts. "We'll fall into the ocean!"

"No. It's just regular procedure," Dad explains, holding her hand. Eldin holds her other hand. I'm stuck out on the aisle, wishing we would disappear into the sky.

As we take off, my stomach feels like it did on the roller

coaster, except we keep going faster and my ears are getting clogged. It's exciting to be up so high. When the wing tilts, I imagine I'm in a fighter jet like Tom Cruise in *Top Gun*. But then it gets quiet and we level off. I tilt my seat back and loosen the belt.

"How fast do you think we're going?" I ask my brother.

"At least five hundred kilometers an hour," he guesses.

An hour later, a stewardess hands me a pasta lunch on a tray.

"I didn't order this. I can't pay," I tell her, pointing to my empty pocket.

She laughs and says, "It's free, honey," in German, which I can finally understand. Though what good is it now that we're leaving Austria? She gives me delicious apple juice too.

After lunch, my brother and I walk to the bathroom together. I go into the tiny lavatory first. When I flush, it's so loud, my feet vibrate. I'm afraid I'll be vacuumed out into the sky. Nervous, I fumble with the latch. I can't open it, and worry I'll be stuck here for the rest of the flight.

I bang on the door, yelling, "Eldin, how do I get out of here? Where's the door handle?"

"I don't know. I've never been in one," he says. "Didn't you lock it?"

I don't remember, so I just keep pushing on the door until it finally opens.

I show Eldin where the latch is. "Don't get too close when you flush or you might get sucked into outer space," I warn, and he laughs.

I don't sleep for the whole nine-and-a-half-hour flight. I just keep going over plans in my head: how we'll stay in America a few months, until we win the war. Then we'll go back to our country and I'll get to play fudbal and see Lena again.

Will she still like me? I wonder.

I hope I don't have to repeat sixth grade.

Will Lena's hair be longer?

If Vik says he's sorry, should I forgive him?

PART THREE

SEARCHING FOR HOME

United States of America

NINETEEN

At 6:20 p.m. on Wednesday, October 20, 1993, Mom, Dad, Eldin, and I get off the plane.

"Welcome to New York," the flight attendant says as we walk out of the gate.

New York? How awesome, they switched us! As we follow the crowd from our plane toward customs, there seem to be millions of travelers swirling from every direction. I hear lots of different languages, which I try to decipher. Back home, everyone's white, speaks the same tongue, and looks pretty much alike. Here, there are people who remind me of Cheech and Chong's great movie *Born in East L.A.* and of the amazing Harlem Globetrotters (only shorter). I wonder where they're all coming from and going. I stare at the pizza, taco, and hotdog stands and realize how hungry I am. But Dad says we can't afford to buy anything.

Then six men in blazers and badges make a beeline for us. They look like the guys in Jackie Chan films. They herd us and the other refugees to the side, putting their hands on our shoulders and pushing us into the corner, forming a human barrier to contain us. "Get over there!" one yells in English. I don't understand what's going on, and I feel dizzy, scared that they're rounding us up to be quarantined or killed.

"Are they foreign soldiers?" I ask my brother, tugging at his shirtsleeve.

"No. Just U.S. airport employees," he explains. "Look, their tags say they're security."

"They look Chinese," a confused refugee says in Bosnian. "Are they taking us to Beijing?"

I don't know where Beijing is, but I remember Dad telling me that Jackie Chan is from Hong Kong. Is that farther from Bosnia than New York is?

We don't even know who's coming to meet us here or where we're going. What if they forget — or change their minds? I want to go home, but we don't have one.

As the security guards lead us through the busy terminal, I hear someone say we're in Queens. "Hey, like Eddie Murphy in *Coming to America*!" I tell Eldin. "When he landed in New York, he went to the Queens McDowell's. But it was really Mc-Donald's, like Siegfried got for us. We should go."

But there's no time for french fries. Another team of men and women from the International Organization for Migration come to get us. I know who they are because their badges match the tote bags we're all holding.

"That's what they're really for," Eldin mutters. The bags aren't a nice present after all—they're to identify us as refugees. Two men hand my parents pieces of paper and point toward a nearby counter.

"Are they arresting us?" I ask, frightened.

"No. Don't worry. They just need their signatures on the paper," Eldin explains.

"Why? To make us Americans?"

"To promise we'll pay back the three-thousand-dollar cost of the airfare," Dad says.

At customs, we wait in line for eons until the immigration officials stamp our passports. Then I try to find our luggage on the merry-go-round at the baggage claim. My brother snaps to attention, using his long arms to grab all four of our bags, which hold everything we own. When we finally get ushered out into another hallway, I see a tall man holding a sign that says TREBINCEVIC.

"Senahid and Adisa, I'm so glad to meet you," the man says as Mom and Dad approach him, smiling as he shakes our hands. "Welcome to America, Kenan and Eldin." He's pale, and his brown hair is gray on the sides; he looks older than Dad. He wears khakis and a sweater, with a blue blazer over it.

"Thank you, sir," I say in English, hoping to sound American so he'll like me.

"I'm Donald Hodges, a Methodist minister. Just call me Don."

I've never met a Methodist before.

"I'm from the Interfaith Council, the group of churches and synagogues sponsoring you. You're our first refugees, though at my last church, we took in a great Cambodian family." He speaks slowly, drawing out his words, like John Wayne in *Rio Bravo*.

"Are you hungry? Thirsty?" he asks, taking Mom's bag and leading us through the doors to the parking lot.

It's dark, cold, and raining outside. Mom shakes her head at the weather. "This can't be good."

"Hey, Eldin, I have a Matchbox car just like this in Bosnia," I tell my brother when I see Don's huge burgundy Ford SUV.

Eldin and I get in back, and Don gives us apple juice cartons (my new favorite drink), turkey sandwiches, and Chips Ahoy cookies that are crunchy and sweet. Then we zoom out onto the giant highway.

I've never been in such a fast car! Mom looks scared and buckles her seat belt tight, but I love it. "I had one like that too," I remind Eldin as we pass a Mack truck. I stare at a splashy billboard of a girl in a green bikini. Taxis whiz by, honking as drivers cut each other off, cursing out their windows. It feels badass, like we're in a car chase. I look out the window for the skyscrapers, gangsters, and police vans I've seen in the movies.

Is Connecticut part of Queens? "Why didn't they tell us we'd be living in New York?" I ask. Eldin translates my question into English.

"You're not. We're going to Westport, Connecticut," Don says. "Not too far."

As the ride continues, we fall into silence, exhausted from our trip. Outside, it gets quieter and slower too, with more bridges and trees but less people, especially when we leave the highway. Soon there are no other cars around, just rows of long houses with big windows.

I don't see a single kid, bike, or toy. There aren't any sidewalks. Through the rainy darkness I think I see a ghost in the trees and what looks like a skeleton on a porch bench. There are strings of lights on a few houses, but it's too early for Christmas. When I spot tombstones on a lawn, I worry we're going to a graveyard.

After a two-hour drive, Don turns left and stops in front of a beige shingled house surrounded by a big green lawn that's spotted with thick oaks and pines, like the kind in Aunt Bisera's backyard. A lady with short, curly, gray-streaked brown hair comes out to greet us.

"I'm Reverend Don Hodges. Nice to meet you," he tells her, shaking her hand. "This is your host, Barbara Lane," he says to us, as Eldin translates.

I'm confused that Don's never met this lady before. Barbara

is Mom's height, around five foot six, but not as thin. She's wearing a long skirt, a pink blouse, a gold pendant, and bright lipstick, and she's holding a fluffy, tan-colored cat. There are spiderwebs across her windows. A paper skeleton hangs on her door. On the porch, there's a round orange blob the size of a basketball, with eyes and a spooky grin carved into it and a burning candle in the center. Inside, another cat, a black one, stares at us from the couch as we all stand around awkwardly. It feels like we just stepped into a haunted summer cottage.

"Who is this? Why do we have to be here?" Mom speaks to Dad in our language. "For how long?"

A limping mutt wobbles over to Dad, sniffing his feet. My father pets the dog, who wags its tail.

"This is my Lynn and Lonnie, and my doggy is Penny," Barbara says, introducing her pets like they're one big family.

"It's like the house of horrors at the amusement park," Eldin says quietly in Bosnian.

"I'm sleeping with the lights on," I reply.

We thank Don and I watch him get back into his SUV and drive away. I'm afraid we'll never see him again, that his job was just to give us a ride from the airport and leave us with this weird lady he doesn't even know, who lives in the boonies with her scary decorations and girl animals.

TWENTY

"Sit down, don't be shy." Barbara speaks faster than Don, and her voice is squeakier.

We'd taken off our shoes on the porch, but Barbara told us to bring them inside. Mom never lets us wear our dirty shoes in the house, but Barbara leaves her flats on. Americans must allow footwear indoors.

Even with shoes on, though, her house is very clean, like our Brčko apartment. The living room has wall-to-wall beige carpeting. I'm blown away by the huge television.

"You have CNN?" Eldin asks her in English. "Can we see war updates?"

"Sure," Barbara says, and turns to the channel. I recognize the anchor, Wolf Blitzer of *World News,* which we watched regularly at Siegfried's. With his bearded, scruffy face, he really looks like a wolf, and he sounds mad at the bad guys.

I'm feeling so lonely, like we're on the other side of the universe, I imagine Wolf is my new buddy. But the report changes to show a guy in a turban and pictures of an earthquake in India.

Meanwhile, Barbara keeps talking to us. "I'm divorced, with two grown-up sons now on their own. So there's plenty of room here. I don't have to go back to work until next week, so I can show you around." Eldin is translating. "Do you want to go upstairs to see your rooms?"

Reluctantly, I leave the giant TV and follow Barbara and my family up the steps. She points out her bedroom on the right. The next room down the hallway is for Mom and Dad.

"There's the bathroom, which we'll share. There's another half bath downstairs. You boys will sleep in the attic," she says, showing us another staircase. We pass one more room, the door shut. "Don't ever go in there," she says firmly. I picture a dead body inside.

"Are you hungry?" she asks, leading us back downstairs. "I'll make you something." The word *hungry* I know, and I give her a thumbs-up.

In the kitchen, a big, airy space that looks out onto her yard, she takes out turkey, lettuce, and tomato from the refrigerator. She makes us each a sandwich with brown bread that's thick and tasty. I'm thankful she's feeding us and giving us a place to stay.

"Orange juice, cranberry juice, ginger ale, Pepsi, Coke, milk, water?" she asks.

So many good choices! I've never had ginger ale.

"Orange juice, please," Mom pipes in.

"Barbara pours us each a big glass, calling it Tropicana. It's sweet, pulpier than the kind we're used to.

After we eat, my brother and I climb up to the attic. I'm glad he's with me—I'd be too frightened to sleep here alone. It's a big room, with a beige carpet that smells like wet leaves and wood. There's a double mattress on the floor, made up with sheets and blankets, and a dresser with pictures of two teens in baseball uniforms, obviously Barbara's sons, on top. In the corner is a rugby ball and a baseball filled with autographs. I've never held either kind of ball, and I run my fingers over the baseball's stitches.

"Don't touch it, you'll smudge the signatures," Eldin warns.

Lying on the mattress that night, I hear Mom and Dad arguing in their bedroom below us.

"At least in Europe, we had relatives and friends," Mom says. "Here, the streets are dark, we're far from everything, no car or subway. How will we get jobs?"

"Don't worry. I'm sure someone will come help us with all this tomorrow," says my father, the optimist.

In Vienna, Mom liked being in the bustling city, taking Siegfried's boys to the park, window-shopping, and buying groceries with the government stipend. Every weekend she'd visit Edita in the refugee camp. I understand why she doesn't like it here. But I don't mind. In fact, I sleep better sharing the big bed with just Eldin, without Dad's snoring and Mom tossing around.

Early the next morning, it's sunny. From the attic window, I can just make out a large body of water only a few blocks away. I want to run out to explore.

"Let's go to the beach," I beg Eldin, picturing sand, bikinis, surfing, and ice-cream cones.

"I told you, we're far from California or Florida. We're closer to Canada, and it's cold here in October. That's the Atlantic Ocean."

I run downstairs. The news is on the enormous TV, showing the weather is 40 degrees outside. Why is it so scorching hot, like the middle of August? Then I remember that in Bosnia we use Celsius, but in America they use something different.

In the kitchen, all the appliances are silver — the fridge, a microwave, even the electric can opener. Barbara's not awake yet. Mom hands me toast with butter and jam and a box of cereal called Cheerios. I pour some into a bowl with milk. It tastes like cardboard. I eat fast, then pace around, feeling hyper and cooped up. "Let's go to the beach," I tell Mom.

"You're not going anywhere. The last thing I need is to lose you," she answers.

"But it's right down the hill." I want to get outside and see America already.

"We don't know what's happening to our lives, and you want to go swimming?"

I frown and go find the bathroom, where I pee sitting down to avoid sprinkling the toilet rim. I know we're lucky to be safe, but it's hard, always feeling like a visitor on my best behavior who can't even take a normal whiz.

I go outside and play catch with Barbara's old dog, Penny, in the front yard. It's cold, so I run back inside to get my jacket. When I come back in a few hours later, I stare at the TV, looking for Wolf. Eldin helps me find him on CNN, then Barbara and my parents watch it with us as we have more turkey sandwiches in the living room. I play with the dog on the carpet while Mom and Dad sit next to each other on the couch, hoping for good news from the Balkans that never comes.

After lunch, we hear cars in the driveway. From the window, Eldin helps me read their makes: Honda Civic, Chevy, Toyota, Jeep Cherokee. Four women get out, carrying overflowing shopping bags — a good sign.

"People from our group are coming by to meet you," Barbara says.

The church ladies walk in, smiling. They all look like Barbara, with gray hair, beige clothes, and lots of jewelry. They're really into beige here. One carries a bag filled with linens and towels, another a vase. Barbara takes the gifts upstairs.

"How do you like America so far?" one lady asks my father, slowly.

"Fine, thank you," Dad says in English, nodding. I nod too as we stand around awkwardly.

"Do you know how to work a washing machine?" another lady asks Mom.

"She thinks we're from Mars," Eldin whispers to me in Bosnian.

"Can't Dad ask them how to get jobs and our own place?" I whisper back.

"He doesn't want to seem rude or impatient," my brother explains.

"What are they saying to each other now?"

"One's telling Barbara, *It's nice of you to take them in,*" he translates. "And Barbara is saying, *It's just for a week until they get settled.*"

Eldin and I look at each other. "What happens in a week?" I ask. He shrugs.

"They have no idea what to do with us," Mom says to Dad in our language as the ladies chat among themselves.

"These Americans saved us. They didn't fly us across the globe to get rid of us," he reasons.

"Don't worry. We won't get deported or thrown out on the street," Eldin assures Mom. "It'll just take time."

"I bet they want us out of here already," she mutters.

We don't tell her that Barbara expects us to stay for only a week. "What's up with Mom?" I whisper to Eldin when she turns her attention back to Barbara's friends.

"She can't sleep," he tells me. "She's exhausted, stressed. And her tooth is hurting her again."

I'm worried about my mother, glad Barbara can't understand what she's saying. I know this is hard for her. How long will it take for her and Dad to find jobs and make money? We don't know if work is outlawed for refugees here, like in Vienna, or if Dad can still be an athletic trainer and Mom an office manager. Do they even have those jobs in Connecticut? Or will they have to garden and babysit again?

We need work, green cards, a car, and a place to live, but I don't know the order or who is taking care of all that. Is Dad supposed to?

My parents are drained and tired, and too many questions will stress them out more, so I keep quiet and try new desserts the church ladies have brought. The apple pie tastes like Grandma's strudel; the one called *pumpkin* is squishy. I wash it down with a clear, fizzy soda called Sprite that's like Fanta from home.

After Barbara shows her friends out, Mom brings their empty plates and glasses into the kitchen. Dad and Eldin turn the TV back on.

"Do you want to go to the beach?" Barbara asks us.

"Is Atlantic Ocean?" I try in English. Though it's cold out, I want to play in the sand.

"Long Island Sound," she corrects. "Eighteen miles wide." She points in the direction of the water I saw from the attic window. "Go to the end of the street, make a left, down the hill," she instructs, making it clear she won't be coming with us.

The four of us walk there, unsteady on the gravel road. The beach is dark and muddy, nobody else around. My feet crunch on rocks and broken seashells. It's low tide, and smells like seaweed and rotting fish — nothing like the beaches on *Baywatch* and *Beverly Hills, 90210.* I dip my hand into the ocean and my fingers feel like icicles.

"Told you so," Eldin taunts as Mom and Dad look at the houses lining the shore, their huge glass windows facing the sea.

It's already dark when we trek back at six p.m. In the kitchen, Barbara's cooking. I smell liquor on her breath, but she doesn't seem drunk or anything.

When we sit down together at the dining room table, she serves us lettuce and tomato first, which feels odd, since we usually have salad *during* dinner. Then she puts out soup, fried chicken, string beans, and mashed potatoes, and Chips Ahoy chocolate chip cookies for dessert. Don's were crunchy hard. I'm surprised these are soft and chewy. How many kinds are there?

It's wonderful to have a four-course meal in comfortable chairs in a dining room instead of eating on stools or the bed, or standing for a pizza slice.

Over the next few days, more Americans come from local churches and synagogues to visit us, but nobody from mosques. Eldin figures there must not be any Muslim houses of worship in Westport. They bring us fruit baskets, cider, toiletries, pots and pans. Once again, Barbara takes the gifts upstairs. I listen to her footsteps overhead as we sit in the living room. It seems like she's putting everything in the room that's off-limits. I try to smile without showing my crooked teeth and say "Thank you" to each one. I'm amazed that members of other religions are helping us.

A lady with short blond hair and glasses, named Ellie Lowenstein, shakes our hands with a powerful grip, looking into our eyes. She gives us a radio that Eldin immediately fiddles with.

"You'll need to go to the immigration office for green cards to get Social Security numbers," she tells my parents and Eldin, our translator. I like this take-charge woman.

"Ellie heads Westport's Zoning Commission and the League of Women Voters," Barbara fills us in.

I don't know what those groups are, but it's clear that people follow Ellie. I'm bummed when she says goodbye without mentioning if she'll return.

On Monday, Barbara leaves the house before eight a.m., but first she gives Mom some cash in case we need it.

"Where is she going? We can't drive anywhere," I whine.

"She has to work. She's a secretary at the high school," Mom explains. "She took time off to stay home and welcome us last week."

So we're stuck in Barbara's house. During the long days that week, we stay mostly in the living room, trying not to take up too much space. Mom cleans and does our laundry, using only the tiniest bit of detergent and fabric softener. I'm embarrassed that we still can't even afford our own food and cleaning supplies.

Eldin's new radio won't pick up international stations, but from watching TV all day we eventually learn that CNN's *World News* runs updates on our war at ten a.m., noon, three p.m., six, six thirty, and eight. Then ABC's *International News* is on at ten. The reports are all we look forward to, structuring our days. Crammed together on the couch, we wait to see the latest on how ravaged our homeland is. There's footage of explosions, peace talks, and cease-fires that don't take. I'm scared that Brčko will be totally gone by the time we get back. It's already been twenty months since the fighting started.

"*Šta kažu?* *Šta kažu?*" Mom always asks Eldin what Wolf Blitzer is saying, and Eldin translates.

When Barbara comes home, she pulls up a chair to watch with us, bringing popcorn, which she shares, like it's a movie. "What's happening now?" she asks.

"Wolf will tell us," I say in Bosnian, pointing to him on the giant screen.

Wolf cuts to a dark-haired lady named Christiane Amanpour, reporting from Sarajevo, our capital. She has a British accent and is translating the words of a Bosnian Muslim girl my age who can't leave her house because of sniper fire. Then, in a voice-over, Amanpour says something about the U.S. president, sounding angry.

"She's asking why Clinton won't bomb Serb supply lines and lift the embargo that's preventing arms shipments to our people, like he promised to do," Eldin says, nodding, impressed.

In that moment I decide I'm trading my crush on *Beverly Hills, 90210*'s Jennie Garth for the smarter, tougher Christiane.

"We gotta get you guys away from the TV set for an hour," Barbara says on Saturday. At last, she takes us on our first outing: to a grocery store called Stop & Shop.

But this is more than just a food shop. The place is enormous. I'm awed by the mountain of endless apples. The cookie and candy sections span two aisles! There are chocolates I've never heard of, stuffed with caramel, marshmallow, peanuts.

Back home, supermarkets don't have meat — you go to the butcher to buy steak, lamb, or chicken. Here, in the deli, they cut slices of different cold cuts and slabs of poultry for each customer. In the fish section, I stare at lobsters, shrimp, crabmeat, and tuna. But it's the dairy section that excites me most: there are fruit yogurts in rainbow flavors that make my mouth water. Who knew there were so many different kinds of milk in so many different size bottles and cartons?

"Wow. I've never seen a supermarket with so many aisles," Eldin says as Mom stares at all the different kinds of plums, pears, and peaches stacked in pyramids in the fruit section.

People around us pack their carts with food. I watch two kids grabbing whatever they want off the shelves as their mom nods, agreeing to buy everything. Then I wait to see what Barbara chooses, hoping for something I like. I linger in the cookie aisle near the Chips Ahoy, and she puts two packages in the cart. *Yes!*

After she's done shopping, we go to an outdoor market across the street, where a man gives us free hot, spicy cider. Barbara buys another orange blob like the one she has on her porch, saying it's a pumpkin. I think of the squishy pie the church ladies brought, and hope she's planning to make more.

"You'll love Halloween tomorrow night," Barbara promises on the way back. When she explains it's a night for ghosts and goblins, I picture real corpses coming back to life, but Barbara insists it's just a fun holiday. Now I understand all the weird decorations.

On her front porch, she teaches Eldin and me how to scoop out the goopy insides of the pumpkin and carve a face in the shell, with triangular eyes and jagged teeth. I ace it—my "jack-o'-lantern" looks awesome. Eldin speaks more English, but I'm better than my brother at arts and crafts. Barbara says we can cook the seeds to eat, and that other kids will come over tomorrow, dressed in costumes.

The next day at sundown, I'm stationed on Barbara's porch, holding a tray of candy. First a little kid dressed as Spider-Man comes by with his parents. Barbara introduces me, and I say "Hi" and give him a Snickers and a Kit Kat. He waves as he leaves. Next I greet a group dressed as Superman, Batman, and an alien creature. Then a princess, a butterfly, and a ladybug. Where are the ghosts and goblins Barbara mentioned?

There are tons of costumed neighbors out, and they keep coming. There must be fifty in a row. So this town does have lots of kids my age. *Where have they been hiding?* I wonder. I hope they'll remember me as the one who gave out candy.

I love handing out treats, and the handmade outfits are my favorite — one kid comes as a shower, with his brother as a bar of soap. We don't have anything like this holiday in Bosnia. I wish I had a costume, too. I decide that next year I'll be a soldier with a bayonet and an AK-47, the kind Mr. Miran held against my head.

While Dad and Eldin watch TV, Mom looks at the costumes through the window, smiling and waving.

When nobody's watching, I feast on sweets from the tray I'm holding. It's candy I haven't had before: Reese's Pieces, Twizzlers, Skittles, and Sour Worms. I shove more into my pockets for later, and I save a mini Snickers, a 3 Musketeers, and some SweeTarts to give to Dad on his birthday next week.

I sneak candies in between meals every chance I get. A couple days after Halloween, some of the church ladies return with Ellie Lowenstein to talk about enrolling me in the local public school.

"What grade are you in?" asks Ellie.

"I'm in seventh. I finished sixth grade when we were abroad," I lie, telling Eldin to repeat it in English, which he does. The truth is, between the war and moving around, I missed half a year, and barely understood anything at school in Vienna. But I really don't want the Americans to put me in sixth again, where I'd be the oldest kid in class. Everybody will think it's because I'm dumb, foreign, and can't speak the language.

Mom, Dad, and Eldin agree I shouldn't be held back. I hold up seven fingers to make sure Ellie and the church ladies get it.

On the morning of my first day of school in the U.S., Barbara gives me a notebook and pencil before leaving for work. Mom says I should wear my gray sweater and the Wrangler jeans I've outgrown. I worry that my ratty clothes will make me an easy target for bullies. I'm nervous and excited all at once. And I feel guilty leaving my parents and brother stranded at Barbara's house.

"Go to school, learn English, make something of yourself — for all of us," Mom says.

"Yeah, that's what we came here for," echoes Dad, making me even more nervous.

If I fail, I'll be letting my whole family down.

TWENTY-ONE

NOVEMBER 1993

At 8:30 a.m. sharp, Ellie Lowenstein shows up at Barbara's house in her silver Honda to drive me to school. "Are you ready for your first day?" she asks. I nod and try to smile.

After a seven-minute drive (I time it on her car clock), Ellie parks outside a blue brick single-story building that has wide windows and a sign that says BEDFORD MIDDLE SCHOOL in block letters. Ellie says it's grades six to eight, which she calls "junior high." There's elaborate landscaping, with shrubs and wide lawns, like the schools in Vienna. When we enter through the main door, I see that the floors are covered in blue carpeting, like someone's house — it's much fancier than my school in Bosnia.

Suddenly bells ring, and dozens of kids pour into the hallway, talking and laughing, opening and closing lockers. I wonder if I'll get one too. I don't even have a backpack. Everyone here looks taller and better dressed than me. The boys' pants are baggier and longer than mine. Some of the girls wear leggings under shorts, which confuses me because aren't shorts for summer and tights for winter? They all joke around with one another, using English words I can't grasp. I look down at my worn, ratty clothes.

As we walk down the hall, a few students glance at me curiously. I wish I knew someone. These good-looking rich Americans probably won't like a poor, short foreigner with choppy bangs and bad teeth who can barely communicate in English. Why should they even be nice to me? They haven't known me since kindergarten like they probably all know each other. Nobody here shares my religion, my language, or my background.

"The principal is Dr. Glenn Hightower," Ellie tells me as we step into the school's main office. A tall man with glasses is there waiting for us.

"Welcome, Kenan. We're pleased to have you here," he says.

He bows his head, shaking my hand with both of his, treating me like I'm his special honored guest. He's dressed in a suit, like Mr. Miran. I want to like this Dr. Hightower, but for years, Mr. Miran was nice to me too. How can I know this man won't turn on me and my family one day?

"Let me show you to your classroom," he says.

Ellie smiles at me encouragingly, then leaves. The principal takes me down the hall, which is quiet and empty again, and into a room where about twenty boys and girls my age are sitting at desks. The teacher standing at the blackboard looks older than my father, maybe in his sixties. He's chubby and balding, with gray hair on the sides. He wears a button-down shirt, a green V-neck sweater vest, dress pants, and leather shoes.

"Mr. Sullivan, this is Kenan," says Dr. Hightower, leading me up front.

"Oh, welcome, welcome, Kenan. We're so happy to have you here," Mr. Sullivan says in a chirpy, warm voice, like we're old buddies.

After Dr. Hightower leaves, I can't make out what Mr. Sullivan is telling the class about me, but I imagine a humiliating announcement, like *Kenan is our new foreign student. He's poor, doesn't speak English, and he's a basket case. Please help him.*

Everyone stares. I smile with my mouth closed so they won't see my bad teeth. Looking down at the floor, I feel like a stray mutt waiting to be adopted. I miss my home, my relatives, my clothes, my old school, and my friends — that is, before they wanted me to die. I pretend not to care about that, but I do. I can't stop thinking about Vik and Mr. Miran turning on me.

"He can sit here," says a small kid in front, pointing to an empty desk to his right. I feel relieved, even though I'm not at all psyched about sitting in the front row near the teacher.

"That's nice of you, Miguel," Mr. Sullivan says as I take my seat.

Miguel is even shorter and skinnier than me, with long blond hair and bangs parted down the middle, like one of the

Baywatch surfer guys I saw on television. When he speaks, I hear that he has an accent too. He has a kind of braces I've never seen, with a square hook on each tooth. His teeth are uneven, but they don't jut out as much as mine. I bet nobody calls him Bugs.

For the rest of the hour, everybody takes turns reading the papers they've written out loud to the class. I make out a few verbs like *talk* and *walk*, but I have no idea what their essays are about. I just hope the teacher won't ask me questions. Then the bell rings, and everybody gets up. Miguel packs his things into a green book bag.

"Vat class this?" I try to ask. He seems to understand.

"This was Mr. Sullivan's seventh-grade English," he answers.

I don't know where I'm supposed to go next, but Dr. Hightower appears in the doorway and beckons to me, asking questions too fast for me to decipher.

So I just nod and say, "Thank you."

He hands me a schedule, then says something else to the rest of the students. He must be asking if anybody will assist me, because Miguel glances at my class list and says, "Come," gesturing for me to follow. I nod, relieved that I won't be lost for the next hour at least.

I trail Miguel to his locker, where he switches books. Some kids he knows come up to me and say "Hi." A few shake my hand.

"Thank you," I keep saying.

I'm stunned by everybody being so kind to me, especially Miguel. Why is he being so helpful? Has someone assigned him to be my guide?

He shows me where our next class is, and for the next hour a chubby teacher with a long mustache makes jokes in different voices as he scribbles math numbers on the chalkboard. The class laughs a lot, and I gather he's popular. I open my notebook and copy every equation the teacher writes, pretending I know what he's doing. My country has the same numbers as the U.S., but I've fallen behind in school, and I've never been good at mathematics. I'm completely lost, and I wish I knew what everyone was laughing at.

When the bell rings, I'm relieved. I get up to follow Miguel to the next class.

"No," he says. "I have history now, but you're in art."

I don't know the word *art*. I must look clueless, because Miguel walks me there, giving me a thumbs-up before I go into the room. I'm afraid I'll mistakenly take someone's chair, so I wait until all the students sit down, then sit at an empty desk. I look around at the collages and paintings on the walls and supplies on the shelves, happy I'm in a drawing class. Something I'm good at! I might not even have to speak or try to interpret fast foreign talk this period.

"Oh, you're Kenan. I'm Miss Jones," the teacher says. She's young, with dark curly hair.

"Thank you," I say.

She gives out charcoal pencils and lets us draw whatever we want, and I'm elated. I try a battlefield, with a tank and missiles dropping from the sky. Miss Jones looks at my work and nods. I hope my drawing skills will get me an A, so at least I won't fail *every* class.

When the bell rings, I understand it's lunchtime. I follow the crowd to a big room filled with long tables and plastic chairs, where everyone is chomping away. In my Bosnian school, I'd buy minced beef *ćevape* from the meat truck lady or bring a salami and cheese sandwich, apple, and chocolate bar in a brown bag to eat with my pals on picnic tables outside. Now I glance around the crowded, noisy cafeteria, my heart pounding.

I don't want to sit by myself. I close my eyes to hold in tears. If I survived a war, I should be able to handle a lunchroom. But I don't know how it works here, if they'll make fun of the food Mom prepared or of how I chew with my big front teeth.

I see Miguel joshing with his pals, who crack up at something he says. He's a prankster, I can tell. For a minute I fear they're laughing at me, but then Miguel catches my eye, waves me over. "Hey, Kenan, come sit over here, with us!" he yells.

I rush to take the seat next to him. He introduces his gang. Kyle, on Miguel's other side, says hi. He's smaller than me and Miguel, with really long light-blond hair. That must be the style here. Across from me, Darren and John nod, and I nod back.

I'm starving, so I pull out the turkey sandwich Mom packed and eat it quickly. I turn to watch Miguel, who has a feast going on in front of him: a cheeseburger that looks juicy and delicious, chocolate milk, an apple, and a brown vegetable on the side that he dips in ketchup. His lunch is so much better than mine. The other guys eat hotdogs and burgers from Styrofoam trays too, and I realize they've all bought their lunches. I feel stupid.

Miguel catches me watching, pushes his tray toward me, and says, "Take."

Wanting to know what the brown stuff is, I pick one up and inspect it. I dip it in ketchup, the way he did, and take a tiny bite. It's great. I finish it off.

"Vat is dis?" I ask.

"Tater tots." He chuckles, amused that I don't know, gesturing for me to take more. I eat another, then stop. I don't want him to know I'm still hungry. But tater tots are now officially my new favorite American food.

After lunch, I follow Miguel out the back door to the playground. I'm ready for recess — a place I can connect with other kids without talking. Some boys are playing basketball on a paved court. I'm surprised to see girls kicking around a ball; in my country, they stick to jumping rope and hopscotch. As Miguel and I stand surveying the scene, he asks, "What do you like to play?"

"I vas best at fudbal," I tell him.

"Here we say *soccer*," he reminds me. "What's your favorite team?"

"Sports stop in var," I try to explain. "My team no more."

"Oh, sorry, man," he says as a bunch of guys gather around, adding, "You're on my team now."

Everyone splits into two groups of five for an impromptu soccer game on the other side of the concrete. Our team is me, Miguel, and his posse from lunch: John, Darren, and Kyle. The roles are pretty loose, but as a new kid, I figure I'll play defense. I'm insecure that I'm out of practice.

Yet from the minute Kyle kicks the ball to me, I'm rolling.

I know Americans have never won a major soccer/fudbal tournament. They're better at basketball, baseball, and hockey. So I figure this is my shot to stand out here, in my sport. The ball hits my foot, and I masterfully spin around, tapping it back and forth. I can feel everyone's eyes on me. I'm determined not to make a mistake. I dribble down the court, showing off how fast I am, replaying the victory I won at recess right before the war that ruined my life.

I pass the ball to Kyle, who kicks it into the goal. Man, he's a great player, like Vik times five. I notice a group of girls watching him and giggling. The next time I get the ball, I pass to Miguel, who scores too. We win the game, and they both give me fist pumps and say "Good game."

"Vat *your* favorite team?" I ask Miguel as we walk back inside.

"Mine is Real Madrid," he says.

I remember from geography class that Madrid is in Spain. "No USA?"

"Madrid, where I'm from," he says. "My home."

So that explains his accent. What's he doing here? Do they have a war in Spain too? I'm frustrated that I don't know his language well enough to ask him.

"Kyle is good player," I tell him.

"Oh yeah, Kyle's gonna go pro one day, I bet," he says.

I don't know what "go pro" means.

"You're a great soccer player too," Miguel adds.

"Thank you," I say, getting the change clear in my head: my game isn't fudbal, it's *soccer* now.

After recess, Miguel walks me to my social studies class, then meets me in the hall again at the end of the period to take me to science.

At 2:40 p.m. the final bell rings, and I rush out into the hallway with everyone, with no idea where I'm going. I never asked Ellie how to get home, and I have a sudden vision of myself standing out in the parking lot all night. I'm relieved to see her in the lobby, waiting for me.

"Hi, Kenan," Ellie calls, waving. "Did you like school? Were they nice? How was the teacher?"

I'm glad she's come to take me home, but she sure asks a lot of questions. I nod, smile, and say, "Thank you."

When we get back to Barbara's, Mom, Dad, and Eldin are sitting on the couch. They turn off CNN as soon as I walk in.

"We've been waiting for you to get back," Mom says, leaping up to give me a hug. "So how did it go at school today?"

"What were your teachers and the kids like?" Dad jumps in.

I'm surprised by all their questions. "So far, it's okay. The principal introduced me around. He was very respectful, and you could tell everybody listened to him," I say, happy to finally be able to relax and speak in my own language.

"You figured everything out?" Eldin asks.

"Did you make any new friends yet?" Dad wants to know.

"I think so. A kid named Miguel walked me to my classes." I show Dad my schedule. "At recess, we played fudbal, and he chose me for his team. Americans aren't as good as we are, except for this one kid, Kyle, who had dangerous moves."

"That's nice," Mom says.

"Good boy." Dad messes up my hair. "You already made a new friend."

"How was it different from back home?" Eldin asks.

In Bosnia, nobody asked about my school day. They weren't very interested in my schooling in Austria, either. But here, I'm the first one in our family to be out in the world. I feel important, yet pressured to report on the Americans.

"They were nice; almost everyone looked rich. Each student had their own desk. The classes are smaller here than in Brčko, and the rooms were carpeted. They have lockers lining the hallway, like at the gym," I say, talking faster than usual. "They eat lunch inside at a restaurant where they sell hamburgers, hotdogs, and cheeseburgers, like McDonald's."

"I'm sorry we can't afford to buy lunch," Mom says. She tells me to go change out of my Wrangler jeans and gray sweater so she can hand wash and lay them out to dry for school the next day.

Just thinking about doing it all over again is exhausting. But it's better than being claustrophobic in a Connecticut house, watching Wolf on CNN all day.

"Any change in the news?" I ask, hoping to hear *We won. We can go home now.*

"It's escalating." Eldin looks bummed. "Far from over."

The next morning, Ellie shows up with a blue backpack for me.

"Thank you," I say, looking it over eagerly. I had one in Bosnia, but the American kind is much sharper, with more pockets. I place my notebook and pen in the zippered pouch and put it on my back, smiling.

She drives to the bottom of the hill, then pulls over. "You'll take the school bus number one that stops here," she explains, then waits with me to make sure I understand. "From now on, you'll take the bus every day." I nod and look for it in the distance nervously. I've always walked to school, and I don't know what to expect.

When the yellow bus finally comes, I wave goodbye to Ellie, then climb up the high steps. As I reach the top, I realize I don't have any money to pay the fare. But the driver lets me on anyway, gesturing that I should go sit.

I don't know if the seats are assigned, and I choose an empty one up front, waiting for somebody to get mad at me and tell me to get up. But nobody does. I sit alone, studying my schedule. Which word is *Tuesday*?

When we arrive at the school building, I recall how to get to my first class. Turn left, then right. Okay, I'm ready. I can do this. I'm pumped.

Then I walk into the classroom, and a boy points at my clothes. "Hey, didn't you have that on yesterday?"

That, I understand. I look down at the Wrangler jeans and sweater I've carried with me almost five thousand miles. They've been washed so many times, the elastic in my collar is limp.

I want to disappear. I don't have the words to explain that, like him, I used to be well-dressed. I walk quickly to my seat, paranoid the other kids will notice I've repeated my outfit too. How will I ever afford new pants?

Luckily, Miguel doesn't mention it. After English, he takes me to the gymnasium, where kids are playing something they call dodge ball. Everyone throws orange balls, trying to hit each other. If a ball touches you, you're out.

It's the dumbest game ever: there are no real teams, you're basically just in it for yourself. Still, I want to win, so I dive, jump, slide, anything to avoid getting hit. It's like dodging bullets and shrapnel from Serbs back home. If I can survive gunfire, this is nothing.

Miguel and I are on the same side of the room, so we don't have to throw the balls at each other. We're the smallest and fastest, and we outlast everyone. Eventually we're the only ones still standing. The teacher blows his whistle. We win!

At the end of gym I pull the schedule out of my pocket to see the room number of my next class. Miguel reads from the paper and says, "Shop." Doesn't that mean going to stores? We're in this class together too, and I follow him into a room filled with wooden tables, pieces of plywood, and big cutting machines that look dangerous. The students all go to the shelves along one wall, which they call cubbies, and pull out projects they've been working on, small sculptures made of wood and glue.

I stand in the middle of the room, not knowing what to do. I want to go sit next to Miguel, who's already cutting wood with an electric table saw. But the teacher leads me to another table saw and gives me a small, blank slab the size of a hardcover book along with a pair of goggles.

I've never carved anything before, and I'm scared I'll cut my finger off and no American hospital will treat a foreigner who can't pay. I picture getting sent home with a bloody bandage, and I think about how Mom will kill me for ruining my chance in America.

I glance around to see what the others make: a tiny baseball bat, a picture frame, a treasure chest. I look down at the slab of wood, and for some reason I remember the day our mosque was blown up. I can still hear Viktor laughing. I decide to make a replica of what we lost.

First I take a black Sharpie pen to draw it on the wood. I outline the entrance door, windows, and a minaret high above the roof, then add the small balcony where the imam stands to say a prayer over the loudspeaker during the holy month of Ramadan. Next I maneuver the saw attached to the table to carve out the shape. To smooth out the rough edges, I use sandpaper. I color the entrance doors and windows black. It feels like my hands are making it without my brain even telling them what to do.

When I'm done, I place my mosque upright, proud of my work. Then I look up, glance around, and see that everyone is staring at me.

"What is that?" asks a kid in a skateboard T-shirt. The teacher comes over to my table, also wanting to know.

I don't know the English word for *mosque,* so I say, "House."

"Oh, that looks more like a church," says a nerdy-looking boy with glasses who's sitting next to me.

Church? I wonder if there is only one English word for all of God's houses.

"Before var," I try. But I can't explain the complicated story behind my mosque. How, after World War II, my Majka Emina donated money to rebuild the Christian Orthodox church in our town that was damaged by bombs. And how the Serbs repaid it by bombing the place where we prayed. How, when Eldin and I went there with our uncle on Ramadan, I was in awe of all the believers. And now the mosque is gone. Our home is gone. Our people, gone.

Miguel walks over with his own masterpiece — a painted wooden mask that looks scary. As he inspects my sculpture, the room goes silent, awaiting his verdict.

"Hey, that's pretty cool, dude." He high-fives me.

I'm not sure what *dude* means, but I high-five him back.

The teacher gives me a plastic bag to wrap my mini mosque in, and I carefully place it in my backpack and carry it with me for the rest of the day. On the bus, I hold it in front of me to make sure the narrow minaret doesn't break off.

"How was your second day?" Mom asks the minute I walk into Barbara's house.

"Look what I made in shop class." I hold it up to show my family.

"Oh, our mosque!" Dad says, delighted, recognizing it immediately and clapping his hands like he does when I win a sports game.

"Majka would be so proud." Mom kisses my forehead as everyone examines my creation. "You're an artist. You should stop chasing after balls and keep drawing and sculpting."

"Yes, that's really something!" Barbara agrees when she comes home later. "The kid's got talent."

That night, I stare up at the attic ceiling, thinking. I can't dress well, speak English, figure out math, or recite any American history. But I won a prize for my art once, and I can ace sports and shop. So maybe that's how I can be somebody here.

TWENTY-TWO

On Dad's birthday, I sing "Happy fifty-four" during breakfast and give him the treats I'd saved for him. I wish I had money to buy him real gifts, a fishing rod or a new woolen sweater, since it's getting colder outside. But he says all he wants is a hug, so we all hold him close. Mom kisses him on the forehead, pretending everything is fine. But we've been at Barbara's for almost three weeks now, and we're afraid she'll throw us out.

Instead she surprises us that night with a wonderful birthday dinner for Dad, sautéed chicken and rice, and then announces that a dentist named Dick Sands is coming by. I assume he's just another church member who'll shake our hands and maybe offer us gifts or cookies. Sure enough, after Mom clears the table, a frumpy old man shows up, smelling of cigarettes, like Mr. Miran. But he doesn't have any food or gifts.

"I'd like to help you with any dental problems you have," he tells us. He says he's heard about us through Don Hodges.

"We really need to get Kenan braces, Dr. Sands," Mom jumps in, with Eldin translating.

But wait, she's the one with tooth pain. The cavity she had filled during the war has been keeping her up at night again.

"You can call me Dick," the dentist says, smiling. He has very white and very even teeth — a good sign. "Open your mouth so I can examine you." He gestures that I should stand under the light in the kitchen.

I do as he says, ashamed of how much my front teeth stick out. I don't want him to think I don't take care of myself. Before the war, I wore my retainer every night at home.

Half the kids at my new school wear braces, but I don't know how we'll ever get enough money to fix my buckteeth. Mom smiles, but still doesn't say anything about her own toothache.

After his examination Dick says, "I know just the person who is going to make him look perfect."

Eldin translates, and we all laugh.

"And don't worry," he adds. "It will all be free of charge."

I can't believe my ears. I want to hug him! I can't wait to not look like Bugs Bunny anymore.

The next day, Dick picks me up after school. He's friendly, talking through the entire half-hour drive while he chain-smokes Camel cigarettes. I open the window and nod, pretending I understand what he's saying. I wonder why this stranger is willing to help without charging us, even though he doesn't know me, while back home, our supposed friends and neighbors betrayed and stole from us. Maybe he's another nice American man, like Reverend Hodges, who feels bad that he's rich while we're refugees with nothing.

Dick takes me to a modern office with impressive sci-fi video games in the waiting room that they let me play. Then a man in a white coat appears, and Dick introduces me. He's the orthodontist, Dr. Sanford, and he shows me "before" and "after" pictures on the wall. Pointing to the photo of a smiling boy my age, he says, "Your teeth are going to look that good."

I grin, following him into the examination room.

Two weeks later I have braces like Miguel. Goodbye, Bugs Bunny!

But the day after Dr. Sanford puts the metal on, I wake up with a throbbing ache in my gums. Mom says that means my teeth are already shifting to where they belong. It hurts way more than my retainer did. In the bathroom mirror at Barbara's, I stare at the wires, looking for progress. Then I examine the little blue rubber bands Dr. Sanford attached to each side of my mouth. They're supposed to pull my teeth in more when I speak or eat. I keep opening and closing my jaw to get the process rolling. It feels like I have a slingshot in there. Mom kisses and hugs me, overjoyed that my teeth will be fixed.

At school, when Miguel sees that the wires in my mouth match his, he high-fives me again. In the cafeteria, I intentionally talk more around Miguel's posse to show off my metal, even though I'm not sure I'm making sense. A bunch of kids come up and say, "Oh, you got braces too." I'm pleased to be part of the crowd and not made fun of.

By the time the war ends, my teeth will be all fixed. I'm excited for my classmates back home to see the special present from the Americans that I'll always carry with me — my new smile.

That weekend, Barbara drops us off at the office of Ronald Silverman, yet another kind dentist who takes care of us. It seems like we have three magic musketeers out to fix our mouths for free. Dad breezes through magazines in the waiting room. Eldin and I stay with Mom as the dentist examines her.

"Good golly, what is this?" he asks. He gives her Novocain and tries to take out her filling, but the needle breaks off his tool, forcing him to extract the entire tooth. Once it's out of her mouth, he separates the filling, which looks like a small rock.

"Didn't they have any better material?" he asks Mom. "This looks like cement."

"Tell him I overheard the dentist say they saved the good stuff for their own people," I whisper to Eldin.

After my brother explains, Dr. Silverman shakes his head, looking disgusted.

"As a Jew, I'll never forget how Nazis slaughtered my relatives in the Holocaust," he tells us through my brother. "I can't believe they're letting the monsters in your country get away with another mass murder."

All our eyes are wet now. I feel like Dr. Silverman somehow knows the hell we've lived through. We didn't know any people from his religion back home. All the Jewish people we've met in Connecticut are so nice, I wonder why Hitler hated them. Then again, I don't know why my own people hate us, either.

Dr. Silverman spends a whole Saturday treating Eldin, Mom, and Dad. He cleans and X-rays their teeth and fills their cavities with a mix of copper and silver. Then we wait for him to close up the office.

"You like to sail?" Dad asks, looking at framed photos of Dr. Silverman on a boat.

"Yes. Stay in touch. I'll take you on my sailboat in the spring," he promises, handing Dad his business card.

I'm still hoping we'll be back home by spring, but it feels good that someone wants us here.

—

That someone is not Barbara, though. When Dr. Silverman drops us off at her house, the door is locked. We ring the bell. Barbara comes down, her hair disheveled, looking annoyed. We've woken her from a nap.

We do our best to stay out of her way and be helpful. Mom pulls out place mats and silverware to set the table for dinner.

"Not those spoons!" Barbara snaps at her. "Get out of my way. I'll do it. You just don't understand." She grabs a tray from my mother's hand.

What's happening? Barbara's like a different person. It scares me a little bit.

"She gets testy when she drinks," Mom says later in Bosnian. We're in the living room now, and she looks tired and sad. "She doesn't want us here anymore. We've overstayed our welcome. She probably thought it would just be for a week or two, but it's already been almost a month. I wouldn't like four strangers living at our house for a month either. It's too long."

I feel terrible, like we're bad people. I think about how our old neighbors hated us and wished us dead. And how then Uncle Ahmet's new country didn't want us to stay. And now the first American putting us up is hoping we'll leave too. I hate this feeling of being a worthless burden. It's even worse now than when we were in Vienna. Here there's no migrant camp to go to, no government programs that we know of, no fellow refugees to talk to who understand how hard it is. Without any connections or relatives to take us in, I'm scared we'll wind up penniless on the streets of our new country.

I try hard to not get on Barbara's nerves. I smile and act polite around her. I tiptoe around in the morning so I don't wake her up. I don't make a mess or sit in her chair or get in her way in the kitchen. I'm never noisy, and I don't have friends over.

More church and synagogue people continue to come by to bring us presents and fruit baskets. Barbara puts out the food, then stashes the rest of the bags and boxes in her secret room. One afternoon, before she gets home from work, my curiosity gets the best of me and I sneak upstairs to try to open the door, but it's double-locked.

I wish someone would help us get what we really need — jobs for Mom and Dad, our own apartment, a car. But I don't know who to ask.

One night in November, after Barbara has gone to bed, Eldin says, "Reverend Don stopped by today."

I'm surprised he came back. I thought his job was just to pick us up from the airport.

"We're going to move in with him and his wife until they find us our own place and we can get jobs," Dad says. "We can't stay with Barbara anymore. It's been thirty-five days." He shakes his head. "That's too much."

Eldin says that along with the drinking, there have been "issues" with Barbara when I was at school that I didn't know about. Mom explains how they annoyed her by interrupting when she had company, depleting her laundry detergent, and using up all the hot water in the shower. Five people sharing only one full bathroom isn't working. Dad explains that we're overcrowding her, like we did with Uncle Ahmet.

Everyone seems relieved that Don is coming. But we need our own home so we won't screw up anyone else's routine.

We have little to pack, since we never really unpacked. When Don pulls up in his burgundy Ford Explorer that Saturday afternoon, we hurry out to load our bags into the back of his car.

Barbara hugs us each goodbye. "I'll visit you guys soon," she says.

I feel bad about how happy I am to go with Don. I climb into the back seat eagerly, but as we pull out into the street, it hits me that I might have to switch schools. I didn't even have a chance to say goodbye to Miguel, my only friend.

As Don drives, I scan the streets, hoping we're going to a city like Brčko or Vienna, where people walk and kids ride bikes on the sidewalks. But this town looks even quieter than Barbara's. It's practically deserted.

When we arrive at Don's house just twelve minutes later, their big dog comes right up to sniff me. I back away quickly.

"This is Cary, our golden retriever. He's very friendly," Don says. "I think he likes you."

I don't know this kind of dog and flash to Stevo's dad's Doberman. Then I think of Almir and his sweet dog instead, and I reach out cautiously to pet Cary. He wags his tail, and I can tell that he's friendly and trustworthy, like his owner.

"And this is my wife, Katie." Don points to a woman coming out of the house to greet us. She's tall, wearing orange lipstick, and has short, curly reddish hair. "She's a schoolteacher."

"Welcome to our home," she says, speaking slowly so we understand. "Let me give you a tour." We follow her inside, taking our shoes off at the door. The Hodges' house is bigger than Barbara's, and there are three extra rooms upstairs, filled with antiques and old furniture.

"Our congregation gives us this place. We use these rooms when visiting church dignitaries stay over," Don says, and Eldin translates. I smile when he adds, "You'll be our dignitaries now."

"I went shopping and bought you chicken and steak," Katie goes on. "Don said you guys don't eat pork, right?"

Mom nods. "Yes, thank you."

"I got bacon for Don, but don't worry, I won't mix it with your eggs." She seems to understand that Muslims never eat meat from pigs. "And there's cookies, rice pudding, and Jell-O," she adds, taking us into the kitchen. "Whatever you see, it's yours. Sit anywhere. Eat anything."

I try the red Jell-O, which melts in my mouth.

Later, when we sit down for dinner, Don says, "First, we pray." We all hold hands, and he continues, "Thank you, Lord, for bringing Kenan, Eldin, Keka, and Adisa here and keeping them safe with us."

I try to sneak a look at Eldin to see what he thinks of this, but he keeps his eyes on his plate. No Muslims we know pray at the table. They do prayers privately or at the mosque, like Majka. I hope Don's not trying to convert us. Maybe he's just trying to be welcoming.

Katie serves the salad first, like Barbara did, then meatballs and mashed potatoes. Dessert is vanilla ice cream on apple pie, which is very interesting mixed together. "It's Don's favorite, à la mode," Katie says. With my belly full of the delicious food, I finally feel relaxed enough to ask about school. When Eldin translates, Don says I'm allowed to keep going to Bedford with Miguel. I'm so happy.

Don and Katie's TV isn't as big as Barbara's, but it has just as many channels. Before bed, I turn on CNN to watch Wolf and Christiane, who show footage of enemy tanks rolling into a town near Brčko.

That night, I have my own room for the first time ever. I've never slept alone. It's eerie being in a new place, in the middle of nowhere, without Eldin, even though I know he's asleep in the room next door. Cary must know I'm scared and lonely because he comes in to sleep on the floor by my bed. I dream I'm caught in a shootout in my old schoolyard, where I'm the hero, shielding Lena and her sister, who are hiding behind me as I fire a rifle, killing the soldiers in our path.

In the morning, Cary sticks his face on my pillow. I scratch behind his ears. He licks my fingers, then nudges his nose under my hand so I'll pet him more. I like having a big, friendly boy dog in the house.

Later that day, walking Cary around the neighborhood on his leash, I feel protected. We play fetch and tag, with him chasing after me. It's like I have a sidekick who understands me without words.

On Monday morning, Dad and Cary go with me to the bus stop. It's a thirty-five minute walk from Don's house. Aside from the driver, the bus is completely empty when I get on — I'm the first kid on and the last one off. But when the bus driver drops me off after school, I can't remember how to get back to Don's. His neighborhood has hardly any street signs, and it's easy to get all turned around.

Lost at an unfamiliar intersection, I panic, shivering, not knowing which way to go. It's freezing outside. During Bosnian winters I wore long johns, a coat, gloves, boots, a hat, and a scarf. Now my short pants leave me with bare ankles, and my too-small parka sleeves don't reach my wrists. What if the cops pick me up and I don't have the words to explain what I'm doing here and they put me in jail? Or worse, I'll freeze to death out here alone. I keep walking, and at last I recognize a mansion with a silver gate on a corner. I turn left and find Don's street at last: Bushy Ridge Road.

"Why are you late?" Mom asks when I walk in.

"Got a little turned around," I say, acting like I wasn't scared to death. My parents have enough stress.

The next afternoon, I'm the last kid on the bus again. I sit in the front, near the driver, worrying that I'll get lost again and it's already almost dark.

"What's your name?" the driver asks in an accent I don't recognize. It's clear he's not from the United States either.

"Kenan. I stay Bushy Ridge Road vif Reverend Don. Since the var," I struggle to explain.

"Where you from?" When I tell him Bosnia, he says, "I am Offir, from Israel. I follow news. We root for your people. Where you stay?"

I give him Don's address. He drives me miles farther, right to Don's driveway, saying that from then on, he'll take me all the way there every day.

After that, I always sit up front, near Offir. I'm the only student he speaks to. It makes me feel really special.

—

One night, as we sit around the dinner table. Don asks my parents about getting jobs and putting down two months' rent and a security deposit for an apartment.

"We don't have that kind of money," Dad explains, looking depressed.

"What happened to all the donations everyone brought over for you?" Don asks.

"What donations?" Dad says. "We don't have any." He asks Mom if she knows what happened to everything that was donated, and she shrugs.

"Everyone who came over handed the bags, envelopes, and boxes to Barbara," Eldin explains to Don.

Aha. That solves the mystery of why she kept locking the door of her secret room: she was hiding the gifts to keep for herself!

Eldin tells Don about the locked bedroom, and his eyebrows furrow and he shakes his head, looking alarmed. He tells us that in addition to the towels and toiletries we saw, there was money, a dining room set, a washing machine, and a dryer, all bought on behalf of our family for when we get our own place. Where would she have put the washer and dryer? In her garage? Was that why she wanted us gone? I'm surprised Don doesn't say he's going to call her or go get our stuff.

"It's like Petra all over again," Mom says in Bosnian, scratching her neck until it turns red.

I don't understand. Americans are supposed to be helping us, not looting us. Then again, our own neighbor did this, so it doesn't surprise me that some lady we just met did too. It just makes me more wary. Like with Petra, we feel we can't really complain to the authorities about the theft. We're still scared of the police. We have no power. We have to keep quiet to survive.

"Why would she be generous and take us in, but then steal stuff?" I ask.

"*Sjedi s guzicom na dvije stolice.*" Dad mumbles a Bosnian saying that means "She's sitting on two chairs with one ass."

"Maybe she felt she deserved to be paid for boarding us?" I wonder. "Or she was jealous that everyone came to see us with presents, but not to see her?"

"No wonder her best friends are her cats," Eldin grumbles.

"You will find good and bad people everywhere. Let's just be thankful for Don," Mom says to us, suddenly calm and forgiving.

On Saturday, Don and Katie take us to the home of someone from their church. In the basement are clothes that members of the congregation have donated for us. Most of the garments look ratty and kind of gross. Not wanting to seem ungrateful, Eldin and I take sweatpants. Dad finds a sweater that isn't too worn out. I grab a Mickey Mouse shirt, and then I see a pair of cool camouflage pants in my size. I hold them up. Mom grabs them from my hand.

"No! You're not taking army pants. What are you, a guerrilla soldier?" she asks.

I wish I were. I'd get rid of our enemies so we can go home, where our real clothes are.

Though we try to seem grateful, I think Katie picks up on our disappointment with the donations. On the way back, she stops at a huge store called Marshalls. Instead of food, there are racks and racks of clothes, shoes, kitchen supplies, and furniture. Everything in America is gigantic; I'll miss these huge stores when we move back to my country. She buys Eldin and me each brand-new Levi's jeans with wide legs that go over my sneakers, and I also get a leather belt and a cozy red and black flannel shirt.

"They look so nice on you," Mom says, smiling. "I don't know how to thank you, Katie."

I've never been so excited to wear pants that fit, so I'll be like all the other kids.

TWENTY-THREE

Don explains that there's no school on Thursday and Friday because of a holiday called Thanksgiving. Eldin looks it up in the encyclopedia set on the bookshelves in Don and Katie's parlor. "It commemorates the Plymouth feast between the Pilgrims and the Indians," he says. "Turkey is the traditional dish . . . What an odd holiday." He closes the big book and puts it back on the shelf. "On CNN, one of the commentators said that Americans celebrate their friendship with the Indians they killed and stole land from. And now, to make up for it, they let them run the casinos and not pay taxes." This is very different from our holy days, which are about national pride or sacrifices.

"Why do they name so many sports teams after them?" I ask, thinking of the ones I've seen on television: Braves, Chiefs, Indians, Blackhawks, and Redskins. "Is that an apology too? We took your land, but we'll name our teams after you?"

Eldin shrugs.

—

On Thanksgiving, Mom helps Katie cook a huge meal for ten. She chops vegetables, peels and mashes the potatoes. Don and Katie's sons, Drew and Brad, arrive with their pretty girlfriends. They're friendly and good-looking, all in their twenties. Drew tells us he works at MTV, the music channel, and Brad's in computers. They're both very tall and warm, like young versions of Don. They sit with us in the living room, where the TV is showing an American football game. Soon they're asking questions about our homeland, eager to hear war stories.

"We heard you guys were taken away at gunpoint?" Drew says.

Eldin nods. "Our neighbors turned on us. They're butchering innocent civilians."

"I don't know much about your country's history. Why is this happening?" Brad asks.

"Because every fifty years, some nationalistic politician comes to power and decides his group is better than everyone else, so we should all hate and kill each other," my father says in Bosnian, frowning. Eldin does his best to translate, as Dad's English isn't as good as his.

"Miloščević, the Serb president, is modeling himself after Hitler," Eldin adds. "I read that his favorite book is *Mein Kampf.*"

"But even before that, during World War II, our region was so divided that we had four relatives fighting on four different sides," Dad adds.

Eldin nods. "It goes all the way back to the thirteen hundreds."

I'm excited to hear Dad and Eldin being smart and honest, explaining what's going on with the war. We want these educated Americans on our side.

Don comes in from his office and sits down on the couch next to Brad. He's surprised that I don't know the rules of the game we're watching. He tells us that he played football on his high school team, that we'll watch the New York Giants together on TV and he'll teach me.

At last the meal is ready, and we all sit down together around the long table in the dining room. Before we eat, Don says, "Let's all join in on a special blessing today."

I put my head down and stay quiet, hoping he won't call on me to say anything. I'm still mad at God for hurting my parents and my people and taking our home away. I have nothing to say to him. When the prayer is over, Dad and Eldin say "Amen" out of respect for Don, but I don't.

I've had turkey sandwiches, but I've never tried what Don calls "our roasted bird." It looks like a mutated chicken and tastes bland and dry. Salt, pepper, and even mustard don't help. There's a vegetable called asparagus that looks like green claws. But baked with olive oil and lemon, it's better than broccoli. There are also mashed potatoes and a delicious dish made of seasoned bread pieces that they call *stuffing*. When Katie passes us cranberry sauce and yams with marshmallows on top, we each take some and put it aside for later.

"You don't like the sweet potatoes and sauce?" Katie says.

"Isn't it for dessert?" Eldin asks.

"No, no. We'll have desserts later," Don says, smiling.

This is the first holiday we've celebrated in two years. It reminds me of the Muslim festival of Eid, when we feasted with our relatives in Bosnia.

"We're running out of ice cream and apple cider," Katie says to Drew when the meal is over. "Want to run to the store?"

"Sure. Kenan, want to drive with me?" Drew asks.

I nod, psyched to ride in his red sports car. I feel snazzy, like I have a rich American pal I cruise around with. He drives to the Stop & Shop really fast.

"Want anything?" he asks.

I shake my head, completely stuffed.

Back at Don and Katie's, a bunch of their church friends have stopped by for dessert, bringing candy, cookies, and incredible pies filled with custard, fruit, nuts. Barbara shows up and rushes over to embrace us, like we're best friends. She obviously doesn't know we've discovered what she did. It feels uncomfortable, but to be polite, I pretend nothing's wrong.

Don glances at her, then looks away without a word. I want him to confront her, to ask where our donations are, but he avoids her completely. Is he waiting until they're alone?

"Why isn't he calling Barbara out?" I ask Eldin in Bosnian. "Can't he threaten to throw her out of church or call the police if she doesn't return our stolen presents?"

"She goes to a different church," he explains. "Don's not her reverend."

"How many churches and reverends are there here?" I ask.

"Don said there are five in town," Eldin says. "He barely knows her. He's only met her twice — when he dropped us off and then when he picked us up."

"But don't they all have to listen to each other's leaders?"

He shrugs. "Don's a peaceful man of God. He doesn't like confrontation. Maybe ignoring her is his way of showing disrespect."

He's passive, like my father, who also avoids fighting. Eldin says Dad's mild nature is the reason we're still alive, but I'm not so sure staying quiet is the way to handle injustice.

I wish Ellie Lowenstein was here. I picture her getting in Barbara's face, demanding answers. I imagine calling the police myself, but I don't have the words to explain what's happened. Plus, the presents are at Barbara's house and were never in our possession. There's no way to prove anything's ours. We don't even know the names of the people who brought the gifts. She could say that she was just storing everything for us, keeping it safe until we had our own home.

Before she leaves, Barbara gives me another hug. Her old-lady perfume is too sweet. I don't trust her anymore, but I decide that as people go, she isn't so bad. She fed and sheltered us for four weeks. She never beat me up, called me names, or pointed a gun at my head. We hardly know anybody here, and we want everyone on our team. We might need her again. I hug her back.

At school on Monday, Miguel invites me to spend the night at his place over the weekend. I'm excited to go to my first American friend's house. I'm not sure why he asks for Don's phone number, but I give it to him.

That night, Miguel's mother, Nancie, calls Don and Katie to ask permission to have me over. Then they ask Mom and Dad. It's like an international summit just to get me a sleepover.

On Saturday, Nancie arrives in a green Jeep Cherokee to pick me up. She's blond, in khaki pants and a sweater. She seems younger than all the church ladies. She shakes Mom's and Katie's hands, tosses my duffle bag into the back of the Jeep, then drives us to their huge house.

It's incredible. It looks like a villa in a foreign movie, with a swimming pool in the gated backyard. The garage is filled with balls, bats, skates, and games. Each room has a big TV, and the place is full of books. There's even a woman named Emily, from a city called Liverpool in England, who takes care of Miguel's younger sister while Nancie works at a bank all day.

His family is obviously very well-off. Everyone is friendly and welcoming, but I'm still wondering why Miguel is being so nice to me.

Looking at photos and asking questions, I learn that Miguel's father is Spanish and Nancie is an American Catholic. Miguel recently moved to Westport from Spain after his parents divorced. So that's why he understands how it feels to be alone in a new country. Now I see that even with a big house, a nanny, and a garage full of high-end athletic equipment, Miguel has a sadness I don't know—from missing his father. I'd rather have my dad around than spiffy sports stuff and toys any day.

"What would you like to eat?" Nancie asks me as Miguel and I join her, his sister, and Emily in the kitchen at lunchtime.

"Vhatever Miguel eats," I say, and they all laugh.

She makes us cheeseburgers—another of my new favorite American foods—and chopped vegetables on the grill, but no tater tots. Dessert is pudding and cookies. It's delicious, and as we eat, I notice that they have chips, cashews, and even candy-coated pretzels in jars and bowls around the room. I hope to try them later.

In the playroom, Miguel teaches me to play a hockey game on his video console. He wins every time. While we're playing, Nancie brings us a tray of grapes, cheese, and dried fruit. Boy, does she have a lot of snacks. Everywhere!

At Don and Katie's, I'm always on my best behavior. Since

they're older than my parents and he's a minister and she's a teacher, they're authority figures. At Miguel's, there's a different vibe entirely. His mom and Emily are lenient, and it seems like he runs the show. It's playtime all the time, and I figure whatever he does without getting into trouble, I can too.

Out in the backyard, Miguel teaches me American football, showing me how to hold the "pigskin" and throw a perfect spiral. Then we try a pickup basketball game in his driveway. "Two out of three wins," he says. But I win the first two games, so he changes it to three out of five.

When I make the next basket, he calls out-of-bounds, saying I stepped over the line.

"Vrong, I vas not!" I yell, stepping on his foot. For our next round, when he goes for a layup, I stick my knee into his thigh to slow down his streak.

"What the hell, dude?" he yells, cracking up. Then he steps on *my* foot. I haven't had so much fun in two years.

No wonder we get along! Aside from me, Miguel is the most competitive kid I've ever known. This makes me trust him completely. It's a tossup which one of us is more of a sore loser, but it doesn't matter, because we understand each other.

To me, second place just means you're the first to lose. Playing sports is the only time I feel confident, in control. I hate losing more than I love to win. I've lost too much already.

TWENTY-FOUR

DECEMBER 1993

"Happy thirteenth birthday," Mom says as I sit down to eat my oatmeal. It's thicker than the hot cereal we're used to in Bosnia, and flavored with maple sugar. She kisses me on the cheek. I try to look happy, as if I don't care that I won't be getting any presents, since we have no money. I remind myself that last year we were marooned in a war-torn country with no electricity or water, that we're lucky to be staying at Don's. But I still miss the excitement I used to feel on birthdays when my *majka*, aunt, and cousins all came over to celebrate with desserts, cash, and toys for me.

At school, none of my teachers or classmates know. I don't want to draw any more attention to myself, so I don't tell anyone it's my birthday, which feels lonely.

After dinner that night, Katie goes into the kitchen and surprises me by coming out holding a big cake. It has vanilla frosting and my name written in blue icing, and there are thirteen candles on top. "Happy Birthday, Big Guy," Don says, giving me a hug as Eldin leaps up to turn off the lights. Katie sings a birthday song to me.

"Blow them out and make a wish, Kenan," she says.

I extinguish them all in one try, wishing the war would get over soon so we can go home.

As Katie carves out a slice for me, she tells us it's carrot cake. I don't expect a dessert made from a vegetable to be so good —I eat two big pieces. Then Katie and Don bring out a pile of presents wrapped in bright-colored paper. I can't believe they're all for me! The first gift I tear into contains two turtleneck sweaters—one black, the other gray.

"Go try them on," Don says, smiling.

They smell fresh, new and clean, as I slide into them, thrilled with the longer sleeves that fit my longer arms. I can't wait to wear them to school.

I also get pajamas, a Wiffle ball, and a plastic baseball bat. Though I've never played this game, I've watched it on TV with Don. In another box is a real leather football, made in the States. It does look like a dinosaur egg.

I treasure each gift, for different reasons. Though my parents have no money or car to get presents for me themselves, I bet they told Don and Katie what to get me, knowing exactly what I'd want.

—

On Saturday, Don and I toss around my new football. He's wearing his suit pants, a buttoned-up shirt, and loafers, which seems funny to me. But he has meetings at the church every day. For an old guy, he isn't in bad shape, though he's not as athletic as my father, who comes out to the back yard and joins in. Dad's quicker than Don, but he can't throw a spiral. Cary's the fastest of us all, running and barking alongside us.

"Would you and Eldin go with Don to pick out a tree?" Katie calls out the back door to me. "He needs help."

Don drives us to a lot in the next town, which is full of Christmas trees for sale. I've never seen anything like this. We choose one he calls a "wide eight-foot-tall Scotch pine" that has big, pointy branches and carry it to his SUV. We have to put the back seat down so the long trunk will fit.

Back at the house, Eldin and I carry the tree inside and stand it up in a base Don has assembled in the corner of the living room, next to the fireplace. Then we go out to the garage and help him carry in boxes of ornaments.

"Be careful not to break them," Mom warns.

Katie unwraps the decorations carefully. There's a painted heart, an angel, a bird, a star, and a snowflake. "This porcelain bulb plays music," she says, gently handing me another ornament. "My Grandma Lilly saved it from her childhood." I help hang her special ornaments on the tree as she rearranges the framed pictures on the mantel to make room for all her delicate-looking holiday figurines.

Although it's not our holiday, they're excited to celebrate our first Christmas in the USA with us. Back home, I'd buy fireworks and sparklers to set off with Vik, Ivan, and Marko for New Year's Eve. Just two years ago, Mom had screamed to me from the balcony, "You're going to lose your fingers!" When we visited Christian friends, I'd play with their train sets and toys under the tree and eat the peppermint candy canes they gave me. And every year, Santa Claus came to Mom's office, a treat for the employees' kids. I sat on his lap and got chocolates and lollipops. I'm hoping we'll get candy here too.

I'm understanding more English words now, interpreting for Mom and having long talks with Don, who tells me about his old parish in Virginia, where his family is from. When the church bigwigs transferred him to Connecticut, he didn't want to leave *his* home, either.

At ten thirty every night, Don invites me to take a ride with him "to lock up at work." My parents don't mind me being up late. Cary loves jumping into the back of the SUV, and Don speeds the five miles to his church, driving fast, like Drew. Maybe daredevil drivers run in their family. The streets are narrow, with no lights, so I put on my seat belt. At the church, Don calls the security company to say, "I'm closing down now," and then locks up his office. Then we zoom back to his house while Cary sticks his head between us in the front seat and I pet his wet nose.

"You and Cary are my protection," Don always says. "It's too dark in there. I'm scared to go alone."

My two grandfathers died before I was born, so being with Don is like getting a second chance at having a grandpa. He and Katie are becoming family.

One night at the dinner table Don tells us all about his church's preparations for their special midnight Christmas service. I'm glad he says we don't have to go, since we aren't Christian.

"But it's Don's big night, and Katie's singing in the choir," Mom says later. "Let's be there to show our support."

"No. We don't belong," I complain.

"We should all go," Eldin agrees. "Come on. Look what they're doing for us."

"I don't want to be in a church. It'll be too weird," I argue. I don't know how to act or say their prayers. I'm afraid the congregation members will stare at me, knowing I'm an outsider.

"It would mean a lot to Don and Katie. We're going," Dad says, overruling me.

Back in Brčko, when my parents went out somewhere nice, Mom would wear a fancy dress, high heels, and jewelry. Now she makes do with a long denim skirt, a red sweater, and flats, and she puts on eye shadow and lipstick. Dad doesn't have a blazer or a tie, but he does his best with dark dress pants, a button-down shirt, and a zippered jacket. Eldin and I wear the nicest sweaters and pants we have. We haven't gone out socially in two years, since before the war.

At 9:45 that night we drive with Katie and Don to his Westport church. It looks different all lit up. I'm startled to see hundreds of members out so late: men in suits and ties, women in dresses, with silk scarves and necklaces, like they're at a swanky wedding. There are a lot of kids in spiffy clothes too — I recognize many classmates from school. I've never seen so many people so dressed up for a religious service.

The inside of the building is modern, nothing like the churches we saw in Vienna. There's no tower, beams, or stained glass windows with heavenly angels. I've been in a mosque with Uncle Ahmet. Now I'm in a church with Don. Will they cancel each other out? What will my uncle and Majka Emina think? Am I a traitor for being here?

Don goes into his office and comes back out in a silk robe, with purple scarves hanging from his shoulders. He looks powerful and grand, like an American pope. Everybody rushes up to him, crowding around to shake his hand. I didn't know he was *that* important. I stand next to him so my classmates will see, and he puts his hand on my shoulder. If they know I'm connected to Westport's pope, maybe it won't matter that I look scruffy and poor.

Jill, a shy girl from my class who has blond hair and light blue eyes, walks up to me. "I didn't expect to see you here," she says.

"Mr. Don is my close friend," I brag.

She looks impressed. I'm too embarrassed to admit my family stays with him because we can't afford our own place.

Katie tells my parents she has to prepare to sing in the choir and we should find a place to sit before it gets too crowded. As we walk down the aisle, everybody is holding their Bibles, ready to pray, eyes closed. I'm definitely not doing that. I feel guilty being at a ceremony in Connecticut with rich Methodists and not at a mosque, trying to save my people.

As we find seats in the middle of a row toward the front of the church, I stare up at the cross above us.

"Where is Jesus?" I whisper to Eldin.

"They're not Catholics," he whispers back.

I once asked Majka Emina about the difference between our beliefs and Vik's, whose family celebrated Christmas. "Our holy text is the Koran, not the Bible, Kenan," she explained. "We believe Jesus was a messenger of God, not the son of God who was resurrected. And we have only one higher power, not the Holy Trinity." I didn't know what the Holy Trinity was, but I sure wished we had their chocolate Santas, lollipops, and peppermint sticks.

"Only Catholics have him hanging from the cross?" I ask Eldin now.

"Shhh. They're starting."

Katie comes through a doorway at the front of the church with fifteen other women, all in long blue robes. They sing "Silent Night" and other Christmas songs I recognize from the movie *Home Alone*. Katie stands in the front and has a beautiful operatic voice. She seems like an accomplished star up there.

Then Don speaks into his microphone. He greets the congregation and talks about the holiness of the holiday. Then he says, "We all know that Jesus, Mary, and Joseph had to travel a long and dangerous road from Nazareth to Bethlehem, migrants forced to flee their land to escape the violence of a local tyrant. For the sake of their child's safety, they became refugees.

"This year, I'm so proud that our community has sponsored a wonderful family who are seeking refuge from war. They were persecuted and forced to leave everything they had. They're living with Katie and me for a while, until they find their own home. They're already changing our lives for the better, and we hope you'll open your hearts to accept them into our fold. Kenan, Eldin, Adisa, and Keka, would you please stand up so we can applaud you?"

The last time someone called out our names in public, we were getting thrown off a bus. We slowly stand up. Mom's cheeks turn red as she stares at the floor. She's never liked having a spotlight on her. Dad, on the other hand, smiles widely and waves to everyone, like he's running for mayor. Eldin puts his hands in his pockets and grins. I keep my eyes down and don't stand up all the way, humiliated that now Jill and everyone from my school knows that I'm a penniless charity case without my own house.

I'm relieved when they take out coral-colored books from pockets behind the seats and start to sing. The lady to our left pulls one out for us and says, "We're on page thirty-two of the hymnal." I don't know what a *hymnal* is; I assume it's a Bible. Don didn't mention that we were Muslim, so I guess she's just trying to be nice. But none of us take the book. I'm afraid that touching it would be a sin.

After the service, we gather in another room, where they give out vanilla cookies and a selection of drinks. As I sip apple juice, Ryan, a kid from my class, walks by and says, "Pretty rad, dude."

Another guy, Matt, says, "Catch you in school, man."

As Jill leaves with her parents, she says, "Nice seeing you."

They don't make fun of me for being homeless — in fact, they seem to think I'm cooler now!

A younger woman from the choir puts her hand on Mom's shoulder. "Don and Katie say you're a wonderful family. We're sorry for all you've been through."

"We're here if you need anything," an older man tells Dad.

When another lady says, "Welcome to our congregation," I'm afraid they're going to make us come to church again.

"They're not converting us, are they?" I whisper to my brother.

"No," he says. "It's not like home, where they try to change your religion. They're just being nice."

A lady named Leah tells Eldin, "I'm Dutch, and I teach English to foreign students. If you want to talk about applying to colleges, call me." She gives him her card, and he thanks her.

Laszlo, a short, gray-haired man, shakes my father's hand. "I escaped to America from Hungary forty years ago. I'm a retired computer engineer. I worked for IBM," he says in a thick accent. "Once you get your driver's license, I'll help you get a car."

Late that night, after Don and Katie go to bed, the four of us sit in the living room. I pour myself a glass of milk and bring out a plate of Chips Ahoy cookies from the kitchen.

"Wasn't that swell, the way Don introduced us to the community and asked them to help us?" Dad says.

"We're not beggars. I don't want everyone feeling sorry for me," Mom replies.

"Well, I could use help applying to colleges, and Dad really needs a job," Eldin reasons.

I agree. We need to make money if we're going to afford the plane fare home after the war. We haven't even paid back the International Organization for Migration for the tickets to fly here.

The next morning, Katie calls, "Kenan, Eldin. Come open your presents." I go downstairs in the green and yellow pajamas Katie and Don gave me for my birthday. Holiday music's on the radio, and Cary's barking. My parents are already there in the living room. Katie and Don pull gifts from beneath the tree and give them to us. They're wrapped in metallic paper and tied with red and green bows. It's like in American movies, where kids rush downstairs to open their Christmas presents right after Santa visits.

Katie and Don watch as I open one box containing an orange basketball and another that holds a red, white, and blue soccer ball. I've never seen one in the American colors. I wonder if it's special made. They also get me a big navy parka and gloves. They give Eldin a bottle of men's Brut cologne, a green bomber jacket, and an atlas of American maps that Don says he can share with me. Mom smiles shyly as she opens her presents: a sweater, hat, and gloves. Dad gets a jacket, a small radio alarm clock, and an Old Spice men's aftershave and cologne set. And we each get our own red stocking, filled with chocolate Santas and candy canes!

I feel bad we have no presents to give in return. All we can offer is ourselves. Mom's always cleaning up while they're at work and preparing meals to show our gratitude. Dad and Eldin rake the leaves and shovel snow from the driveway. But that's everyday stuff, not something special for the holiday. Then I remember that in art class, I drew Don and Katie a Christmas card. It has a picture of their house on it and a Santa Claus sled on the lawn. I run upstairs to get it from my backpack and give it to them proudly.

"Beautiful work, Kenan. You're a real artist," Don says, and he hangs it on the refrigerator with a magnet for everyone to admire.

The last week in December, there's no school. I wait for snow, but there are only flurries. When I finally wake up to a frosted lawn, Eldin says he's too cold to make a snowman or throw snowballs with me. There are a lot of hills around the neighborhood, but when I go outside, I don't see any kids sledding. So I just hang out in the yard for a while in my new parka, feeling alone and out of place.

On New Year's Eve, Katie, Don, and my parents all go to bed around ten. My brother and I stay up to watch the ball drop in Times Square on TV, drinking milk and eating candy canes. I love seeing the lights and noise of New York City on the screen. I can't believe how many different people are gathered just an hour away from us, practically neighbors.

"When we landed at the airport, they should have taken us to Manhattan," I tell Eldin. "I bet there are lots of Muslims and refugees like us there."

"When we get older, we'll live anywhere we want," he tells me. "For now, we're just lucky to be alive."

He's right. Last New Year's we were lying on the floor in the dark, listening to guns go off. I picture what we'll be doing next year: celebrating our war victory at home with Majka Emina, Aunt Bisera, Uncle Ahmet, and my cousins, telling them about Don, Katie, Miguel, and all the other kind friends we'll miss in the United States.

TWENTY-FIVE

JANUARY–MARCH 1994

When Don tells Dad he can get government help called "welfare" until we "get on our feet," Dad refuses.

"I'll never take a handout when I can work. I'll do anything," he says.

"Me too," Eldin chimes in. "We need to get our own place."

"Eldin is nineteen," Dad continues. "He can work until he figures out how to enroll in some college classes."

"I need to save money for tuition and books first," Eldin agrees.

"I know I can't be an athletic trainer without an American certificate," Dad says. "But I'm tired of sitting at home. I'll do anything," he repeats. "I can do manual labor. I'm not ashamed."

"Okay." Don nods. "I'll make some calls to get you both jobs in town."

I wish I could work too. On CNN, my old pals Wolf and Christiane say this second year of the war has been worse than the first, with more Bosnians dead. A million refugees like us have fled for safety. It looks like we'll be staying in Connecticut for a while.

On Monday, when I get home from school, Dad, Mom, and Eldin are in the kitchen, looking excited.

"We both have jobs!" Eldin tells me.

"How did you get hired so quickly?" I ask.

"First Ellie drove us to Pancho Villa's, this Mexican restaurant just ten minutes from here," my brother explains. "She brought our papers and said Reverend Don recommended us, so they hired me as a part-time busboy. Then she took us over to Boston Chicken, where I'll be taking orders at the front while Dad roasts chickens in the back. Twenty hours a week. Minimum wage."

They show me their uniforms proudly. Dad has a white hat and overalls that say BOSTON CHICKEN. Eldin has a matching blue shirt with the same logo.

"Why isn't it called Connecticut Chicken?" I ask, and we all laugh.

The following evening, Dad and Eldin return to the house in their uniforms, bringing macaroni and cheese, a roasted chicken, and delicious, sweet cornbread that I smother with butter, eating two pieces. I'm overjoyed their manager gives them leftovers to take home. Don and Katie have more than enough food, but eating what Dad and Eldin bring home is a triumph. We're finally fending for ourselves, not just relying on others.

Four nights a week, they return from work with thrilling American delicacies: baked potatoes with sour cream, string beans, sweet potato casserole, chicken salad, creamed spinach (my new favorite vegetable), and chocolate brownies.

Don and Katie leave for their jobs each morning, but my father and brother work afternoons, so members of the church make a schedule to help drive them. When Eldin has the late shift at the Mexican restaurant, Don goes to get him at midnight.

On a day they both have off, Ellie Lowenstein drives us to the Social Security office in Bridgeport and then to the United States Citizenship and Immigration Services center to apply for green cards. "In five years, you can apply for citizenship to be Americans," Ellie explains.

Five years? We'll be long gone by then. Still, it'd be major to have an American passport. Nobody would be able to kick us off buses, planes, or trains. I picture going back to our country and showing off my official U.S. documents to my friends, who'll be so jealous. Then I'll come back to visit Don, Katie, and Miguel on vacation someday.

Ellie also helps Dad and Eldin open bank accounts. They only take home two hundred dollars each every other week, but they're proud they're earning paychecks to get us back on our feet. At Bedford, most of the kids' dads—and some of the moms—are lawyers, doctors, or businesspeople. I feel pride that Dad and Eldin are making American dollars and getting us free dinners too. But I don't tell my classmates they work at a fast-food joint.

I'm staying over at Miguel's house on the weekends more and more often, and soon Nancie is picking me up nearly every single Friday. Miguel and I play video games and run around his huge yard. I want him to teach me how to improve at American baseball and football.

One cold Saturday in February, after we finish a video game in the playroom, which Miguel wins, I take the remote and turn to CNN to see if there's any breaking news. Christiane says that enemy soldiers have bombed our capital. I get up and stand close to the television, staring at the footage of the destruction.

Miguel wants me to explain. "What's going on there?" he asks.

"Var getting vorse," I say, my neck turning warm and itchy.

"Are you okay, Kenan?" Nancie asks as she walks in. "Your face is all red."

Miguel points to the screen.

"Nobody cares my people die. Vee have very few veapons, not allowed to defend ourselves," I say.

"It's so terrible." Nancie looks concerned. "Maybe you boys should go out to play."

Miguel grabs the basketball. "Quick game of one-on-one? I'll cream you," he taunts.

"Vait, I cream you this time," I threaten, following him outside. We play basketball for a while, then he puts on Rollerblades to show me a new game in his driveway. He hits a tennis ball with his hockey stick and has me try to block the shot with mine. I wish I had Rollerblades so I could fly around like him. He runs upstairs to ask Nancie something and comes rushing back.

"Come on, we have to go," he says.

"Where?"

"It's a surprise." He grins as Nancie comes out of the house with her keys in her hand and tells us to hop into the car.

She drives us to the sporting goods store. "What size shoe are you?" she asks me as we walk in.

I'm not sure of American sizes, so I take off my sneaker to show her. She speaks to a salesman, and he brings out several different styles of Rollerblades in size seven and a half. I like the gray ones, but the price tag is $69, way too much for me.

"Vee don't have money," I whisper to Miguel.

"I know. We're getting them for you," he says.

"That's okay," I say. "Vee'll take turns vearing yours."

"Mine are too small for you. You need your own to be my goalie." He's determined.

"Thank you," I say, hugging the big box, holding my gray blades, feeling embarrassed but so happy I can now skate with him. On the way back to their house, we stop at Toys "R" Us, and Nancie also buys me a Mighty Ducks hockey helmet that Miguel picks out, along with a goalie stick, knee pads, and gloves. I can't believe how lucky I am to have such a nice best friend who has such a generous mom.

Back in Miguel's driveway, he suits me up with the helmet, gloves, kneepads, and a long-sleeved sweatshirt. I'm cold until I start playing. He shows me how to hold the stick to block a shot. He whacks the tennis ball right at me. For an hour, he takes wrist and slap shots at me, over and over, teaching me to control the ball and stop breakaways. The ball hits me everywhere as I move quickly to intercept each shot, but because of the pads, it doesn't hurt.

"You have fast reflexes," Miguel says.

"I vas good at dodging bullets," I tell him. He laughs, but I'm not really joking.

On Sunday morning Nancie drives us to an abandoned parking lot on a dead-end street in town, where we meet John, Darren, and Kyle, who I know from school, and a bunch of other guys.

They wave to me and say hi as we all put on our Rollerblades. I'm happy to have my own, glad they don't know Miguel's mom had to buy them for me.

We play street hockey for hours. I'm the goalie for Miguel's team, catching the tennis ball the other team shoots at me with the glove on my left hand or hitting it back with the stick in my right. I feel important, and I want to impress everyone so they'll let me play again.

"Isn't he quick?" Miguel brags to our teammate Pete, a tall, athletic kid with short brown hair. "It's from dodging bullets and bombs during his war."

"Really cool," Pete says. "He's wicked insane for someone who never played hockey before."

I beam. But Miguel talks so highly of my skills, it's also a little stressful. I don't want to let him down.

"I hope you stay in this country to play high school hockey," he says. "You're that good."

I feel popular, one of the guys, the way I did with my old buddies. Except now I have a new best friend who compliments me and treats me like I'm a special guest. It's like I traded up.

At school, my history class is putting on a play about America's Revolutionary War. Miguel is cast as Paul Revere. The teacher asks me to be a minuteman. I have to walk back and forth across the stage holding a wooden rifle. I like being in the play, but it's about a war that happened in America a long time ago. In my mind, I'm really practicing how to be a soldier to protect my people when we go back to Bosnia.

One Friday night, Don comes home and tells my father, "I've been talking to my church member, Donald Roth, who has a Polystar bottle cap factory in Norwalk. He wants to meet with you and Eldin."

Don drives them to the plant. When they return, Eldin says, "He offered us both full-time jobs on the assembly line. They make tops for fruit cups."

"Cool! What will you be doing there?" I ask.

"Dad is in charge of the plastic lid machine. If it gets jammed, he opens it up to clear it and get it working again," Eldin explains. "I'll work in quality control of the lids."

"It's much better pay. Plus we get full benefits with health insurance!" Dad adds.

They start their new jobs on Monday, getting a ride early in the morning, coming home at six at night. Everyone's pleased with this step up, so I am too. Though I really miss the different foods they were bringing home.

Then, in the middle of March, Dad comes home with news.

"We can't keep up this long commute to work without a car. And Westport is too expensive for us," he tells Don and Katie at dinner. "Ellie found us a two-bedroom on Clinton Avenue. A rental near the factory in Norwalk that we can afford. It's eight hundred and seventy-five a month. We just need to save up enough for the security deposit."

"You know what?" Don says. "I think we have a new church fund to help you out with that."

"We can't take any more from you," Dad tells him.

"That's what the money is for," Don insists. "For a worthy cause, to help those in need. I couldn't get back what Barbara stole from you. But this fund is my domain, and I insist you take it."

"Are you sure?" my father asks.

Don nods.

My mother jumps in. "That's so wonderful. We'll never be able to repay you."

The grownups and Eldin are all smiling now, but I'm worried about what this means. "Wait. We can't move now! I'll have to switch schools. I won't be in Miguel's class!" I yell. It feels like I've swallowed a rock and it's caught in my throat. "I can't start all over now! It's not fair."

"Get a grip, bro. It's only like twelve miles away," Eldin tells me. "We're going to have our own place."

"We'll be able to pay rent for the first time in two years," Dad says. "We can sign a year's lease."

"But what if the war finishes sooner?"

Eldin shrugs. "Then we'll just break the agreement and forfeit the security deposit."

"I'll skip my classes and flunk out until they put me back at Bedford," I mutter, fuming.

"Who'll drive you every day?" Eldin asks me. "There's no school bus that goes from Bedford Middle School to Norwalk. We don't have a car or a license."

My brother always has an easy answer when it's not *his* problem. He thinks he knows everything.

The next weekend, while Miguel and I are playing street hockey with the guys, I break the news. "I have to move. Different school. I don't vant to." I try not to cry when I tell him.

"Norwalk's really close. Just four exits on the highway," Miguel says, like it's no big deal.

"I hope it's not near the train station," Pete says. "It's dangerous over there."

I picture American gangsters, with cops chasing the bad guys.

"I take tennis lessons at a really nice place on Post Road in Norwalk," Miguel counters. "You'll still stay over on weekends." He puts his hand on my shoulder. "We'll come and get you. I promise. Don't worry, dude. It'll be fine."

I nod and try to smile, but I know he's just being nice. Everything's changing again.

TWENTY-SIX

APRIL 1994

It's my last day at Bedford Middle School and I never even had my own locker, or textbooks to keep in it. Only the principal, my teachers, and Miguel, Darren, and Kyle know I'll be moving on Friday, with less than two months left in the school year. I plan to quietly say goodbye to my classmates at recess.

I'm in a lousy mood as I shuffle to Mr. Sullivan's English class, sad that I'm leaving, sure nobody but me cares.

Miguel is waiting for me outside the classroom door. "We can't go inside yet," he says.

"Vhy not?" I ask, confused.

"Just wait," Miguel tells me.

A few minutes later two of the girls from the class open the door and stick their heads out, ponytails swinging. "You can come in now."

As we enter, I see that everybody's wearing silly cone-shaped paper hats. The word *Goodbye* is written on the blackboard in different colored chalk, in German, Italian, Spanish, English, and Bosnian, with *See you later, Kenan* underneath. Mr. Sullivan sits at the table behind a cake shaped like a cheeseburger. There are two vanilla layers for the bun, chocolate in the middle for the meat, and yellow frosting in between as the cheese.

"The cake was Miguel's idea," Mr. Sullivan says. "For your favorite American food."

I don't understand what's going on.

"We're throwing you a going-away party," Miguel whispers.

I feel my mouth hanging open in shock. I've been a student here for only five months. I wasn't sure they even liked me. Jill and a bunch of other girls from my class put their arms around me as Mr. Sullivan snaps photographs. "Say cheeseburger," he says, adding, "I'll get copies made for Miguel to give to you."

He assumes I'll be staying in touch with Miguel, but I'm not so sure.

"Why are you moving?" Jill wants to know.

"And where are you going?" asks another girl, Anne.

"Dad vorking new job," I explain. I leave out that it's on the assembly line of a fruit cup factory in Norwalk, afraid she'll know how poor we are.

I wish they had asked me questions and stood this close before. Then again, I should have had more courage to speak, especially to the girls, instead of hiding behind Miguel. But I was afraid my raggedy English and clothes wouldn't measure up.

The celebration lasts the entire period. My classmates and I eat slices of the cheeseburger cake, which is rich and delicious, along with Coke and nacho chips. They present me with an empty book, so each page can be signed by a different classmate. Everyone crowds around me, waiting to write me a goodbye note in bright-colored markers and asking, "So what do you think of our country?" "Did you like Bedford?" "How is it different from your old school?" "Will you visit us?"

For a while, I'm as popular as I was in my old fifth-grade class in Bosnia. Even more. I feel honored and special, like a foreign diplomat. I know it's only for one hour, but I don't want it to end.

Then Mr. Sullivan stands up and takes a letter from his folder. He holds the page carefully and slowly reads aloud, like he's reciting a poem:

Dear Kenan,

When you came here last November, I had no idea what a wonderful student would be joining our class. You turned out to be a teacher as well, showing us how a person survives a courageous journey and starts over with integrity and grace. On behalf of everyone at Bedford, thank you. If English is a difficult tongue to learn, you've encouraged us to speak more carefully. Time is all you need, the other strengths are already within you — your sense of goodness in a troubled world, your wish to understand and be under-

stood, your love for your family and country. Someday, if you return to your former home across the ocean, I hope you will bring with you inspiring stories of how people can help each other. If you need anything, I'm always here for you.

He hands me the paper. It's signed *Cordially, Mr. Sullivan.*

"Thank you," I say, my voice cracking. Nobody's ever written or said anything that's made me feel so valued. I'm so choked up, I can barely tuck the letter into my pocket.

As I walk out of this classroom for the last time, I shake Mr. Sullivan's hand, blinking so no tears will escape. It's so unfair that I'll never see Bedford Middle School again.

The worst part is leaving Miguel. I'm sure he's going to just forget about me. After all, friends I knew my whole life forgot and betrayed me, and I've known Miguel for only five months.

"I'll talk to you in a few weeks," he says as we walk outside to get on our separate buses.

I want to believe him when he says he'll visit me, or that his mother will pick me up to take me to his house on weekends. He doesn't have my new phone number — I don't even have it yet — but I know his by heart. If I'm understanding him correctly, he doesn't want me to use it for *a few weeks.* That's a bad sign. He's already drifting away.

As I board the bus for my final ride to Don's, I try to keep the tears from blurring my vision. When I sit down in my usual spot in the front row, Offir turns around and asks, "What's wrong? Why do you look so sad today?"

"Last day of school. Vee move to Norvalk," I mumble, staring out the window.

"Smile. Sometimes change is good," he tells me.

"But I like it here. Don't vant to leave. Made friends."

"Try to think positive. You have to move on, like me. I'm going to become an engineer in the city. I'm not driving this bus forever," Offir says. "It's just a steppingstone."

I picture a frog jumping from a small rock to a big rock. I know my problems are nothing compared with the kids who can't escape Bosnia's war zone, getting shot at for being on the wrong side of a battle that doesn't even make sense. I know I'm lucky we're safe in a country where nobody tries to kill us. But I'm mad at God again for making me move.

At Don and Katie's, I show everyone the letter Mr. Sullivan wrote and the scrapbook all the kids signed. Don asks me to read it aloud.

"'*Make sure you come visit.*' That's my classmate Doug," I say. "And Jill vrote, '*Ve'll all really miss you.*'"

"Look, she drew a red heart," Eldin teases. "She likes you."

I feel my cheeks getting hot. Jill's the prettiest girl in the class.

"'*We're still going to play hockey and football, dude.*' That's from

Miguel." I continue reading. "*It was great meeting you and fun to have you at Bedford.*"

"What a lovely memento," Katie says.

"We're so glad you made good friends here," Don tells me.

"Yeah, but I vish I could see them again," I say sadly. "And I heard Norvalk isn't as nice."

"That's not true. There are good people everywhere," Don says. But I'm not convinced.

Mom goes upstairs to finish packing.

The next morning, we carry our stuff out to Don's burgundy Ford Explorer. We don't have much — only our four suitcases and a couple of Marshalls tote bags. As we're getting into the SUV, Katie pulls her spiffy red Mazda out of the garage. Ellie Lowenstein drives up in her Honda, and her husband, Richard, follows in a big, boxy, yellow Ryder rental truck.

Dick opens the rear of the truck to reveal secondhand furniture donated by members of the Westport Interfaith Council: There are three mattresses with three metal bed frames, along with an oak coffee table, a tall lamp with a lopsided gray shade, a small television, a beige recliner, and a desk. I also see a plaid orange couch that smells like someone's musty basement. An oval brown kitchen table leans against the truck's side, with four chairs stacked on top of one another. I even spot four skinny, rusty silver Schwinn bicycles way in the back. They look like the bikes elderly men in my country ride, but at least we'll have wheels.

We need a whole caravan to move us this time. Eldin goes in the Honda with Ellie, Dad rides in the truck with Dick, and Mom drives with Katie. I rush to sit next to Don in the front seat of the Explorer. He talks the whole way, passing four highway exits before he turns off the interstate. It's a 7.4-mile ride, I clock it.

"Connecticut Avenue is another name for Route 1. It's one of the first roads in America. In olden days, it was for horses and carriages," Don says, trying to cheer me up. "If you stay on it, you can drive all the way to Florida." I picture orange trees, beaches, and Disney World at the end of the highway.

We pull into a parking lot next to a three-story redbrick building. There's a big chestnut tree on the front lawn, the kind we had at school in Brčko. I count the buzzers by the front door —twelve units. Mom points to a window on the second floor and says, "That's ours."

I wonder if all the people who live here are renting their apartments, like us. The neighborhood seems deserted. Across the street there's a factory surrounded by a big fence, but it's not the one where my father and brother work—the Polystar factory is a few blocks away. There aren't any kids playing outdoors. At Don's, I had a lawn where I could throw a ball around.

"Tell Cary I said goodbye again," I tell Don.

"You'll come over for dinner and visit him," he assures me. "And when we go on vacation this summer, I hope you'll take care of him for me."

"Of course," I promise.

We go inside and walk up a flight of stairs. The hallway smells like foreign spices. Ellie gives Mom the key and she unlocks our door.

The walls are white, and the shiny wooden floors smell of varnish. It looks like a shoebox with sliding windows. Though there's two bedrooms, it's half the size of our Bosnian apartment, with no balcony, views, or matching furniture. *This is only temporary*, I remind myself. Our old place will be there waiting for us after we win the war.

Eldin, Dad, and I unload the furniture from the truck, doing the heavy lifting while Dick and Don carry in our bags. Mom, Katie, and Ellie go to Stop & Shop to buy groceries and cleaning supplies with the $100 gift certificate the church donated, plus another $150 from Dad's and Eldin's factory checks. After paying the first month's rent, we have hardly anything left in the bank until their next paychecks, Mom says.

I help my brother carry two of the mattresses and frames into our bedroom. I don't tell him I'm secretly glad we'll be sharing a room again. But I wish Cary could still wake me up every morning.

"My bed looks saggy," I complain. "I miss Don's already." I'm so tired of moving. Just as I start to learn my way around a place, we have to leave. I feel like Robinson Crusoe from Eldin's book that I'd loved reading as a kid: a prisoner shipwrecked on the Island of Despair. Except my journey's more disaster than brave adventure. "At least in Westport, if I got lost, all I'd have to say is 'Don Hodges' Methodist Church' and someone would take me there."

"We'll figure out Norwalk," Eldin assures me. "We won't have to walk on eggshells here anymore. We can eat anything we want and make noise. It's small, but it's our own."

Now that I've lost Miguel and the guys, I need my brother as my friend again. "Want to see if there's a playground?" I ask.

"I'll explore with you later," he says, and heads back out to the parking lot.

We carry everything else from the truck into the apartment and put the bicycles in the laundry room downstairs. After Mom unpacks the groceries, Don announces, "I'm taking you out to lunch to commemorate this historic day." We drive the different cars to a nearby Pizza Hut, where Don orders appetizers and two kinds of pizza pies I've never had, the cheese-filled crust rich and gooey. I dip chicken wings in blue cheese sauce and drink two cans of fizzy A&W root beer. There are always new treats to try in America.

"Congratulations on your new beginning!" Don holds up his

glass, and we all toast with our sodas, as if we're celebrating something joyous. But it doesn't feel that way to me.

After lunch, Don drives me back to our Norwalk place in silence. He walks me to the door of the building and gives me a big bear hug. "I'll see you real soon, buddy, when you come to visit."

When? I'm afraid to ask, in case he's just being polite. I don't want to seem too desperate.

"The electricity is already turned on. Your phone will work tomorrow, and the cable company will come as soon as they can," says Ellie, ever the organizer.

"Will you take me to fill out an application at the Nivea cream factory?" my mother asks her.

Wait. If everyone's working, who will be here for me when I get home from school every afternoon?

"And I need to buy hair dye," she adds. I can see gray strands at her roots.

"We'll do that on Monday morning, right after I take Kenan to his new school," Ellie says.

My heart aches as our Westport friends turn to leave, waving goodbye as they get into their cars and drive away. We go inside, up the stairs, and into our new apartment, filled with unfamiliar furniture and smells.

Our door is still open when a short, dark-haired lady peeks in, surprising us. She's carrying a little Yorkie. "Hi. I'm Betsy. I live across the hall with my husband, José," she says quickly, in a squeaky accent I don't recognize. I bet the spices we smelled were hers. She looks like she's in her twenties, a little older than Eldin. "Where are you guys from?" she wants to know.

After we tell her, Betsy says she's a nurse from Puerto Rico and José works as a garbageman but is really a boxer. I'm psyched to meet another immigrant in our building. I reach out to pet her dog, but he yaps, and I jump back.

"Tiny tries to be a tough guy, but he's a sweetie," she says. "Don't show him you're scared." She puts Tiny down, and he rushes up to my leg, sniffing, then barking. Cary is older and mellower than this hyper mini puppy. I wish I were playing catch with Cary on Don's lawn right now.

When Betsy and Tiny leave, I ask my brother, "Where's her country?"

"Puerto Rico's part of the U.S., in the Caribbean," he says. So she's not an immigrant after all. I'm bummed. I was hoping we wouldn't be the only foreigners on our floor.

Mom takes out new sheets and pillowcases from their plastic wrappings and makes our beds, which she covers with scratchy hand-me-down wool blankets. In our bedroom, Eldin and I test out our mattresses. The springs in mine squeak and feel unsturdy.

"There's room for your clothes in here," Mom says, pointing to the dresser drawers.

I put away my underwear, shirts, socks, and the stuff Katie and Don gave me.

Mom takes the plastic mop, sprays, and sponges she just bought and goes at it until the entire place smells like detergent. "Don't sit on the toilet until I scour it," she says, scrubbing everything before putting away our new shampoo, toothpaste, soap, and deodorants. She rushes around the kitchen, washing the refrigerator and cabinets before putting away the pots and pans. She uses newspaper to wipe the windows. She's cleaning like crazy, the way she did in Bosnia. I can tell she's excited that we aren't guests anymore, and she wants every inch of countertop here to be spotless now that it's hers.

"Who knows what the previous tenants kept in there," she says, wiping the inside of the microwave. I'm glad she's energized, but I know this is just another temporary layover.

For dinner Mom makes meatballs in tomato sauce and rice, with slices of Italian bread that I dip into the red gravy the way I used to. We eat slowly in our new kitchen. It tastes good and salty, but everyone's quiet. I think we're all a bit shell-shocked. It's sinking in: this is where we live now. I look around at the mismatched furniture, worn out, like us.

"When are they coming to turn on the cable?" I ask Dad.

"Ellie said probably on Monday."

Without the TV, I don't have Wolf and Christiane to keep me company. All the nice people who have befriended us are miles away. We don't even have a phone hooked up to call anyone. As the sky darkens, there's no traffic noise, cricket sounds, or even dogs barking. I feel abandoned again. Through the curtainless windows, I stare at the sagging house next door. Next to it, there's a dumpster overflowing with black garbage bags.

We're alone. We barely speak the language. We have thirteen dollars in the bank. All I keep thinking is *When do I get to go home?*

TWENTY-SEVEN

"The next time I move, it's back to our country," I tell Mom on Monday morning as I sit with her, eating toast with grape jam for breakfast. This kitchen is wider than ours was in Bosnia and lighter, with white cabinets and counters. I'm wearing one of the turtleneck sweaters Don and Katie gave me and my best jeans, which are still a little too big. It's better than my too-small old Wranglers and gray sweater, but I still wish my clothes fit right for a change. I'm bummed that I have to start all over now, at practically the end of the school year, in yet another place where everybody knows everybody else, but not me.

"Just do well in your classes," Mom says. "That's your job now."

At seven thirty Ellie's silver Honda pulls into the apartment complex parking lot. Ponus Ridge Middle School is only a fifteen-minute drive, in a residential part of town that has bigger houses separated by more trees. It's brown brick and

looks larger and more rectangular than Bedford Middle School
— there's a bigger playground in the front and I see outdoor
basketball courts and a baseball field — a good sign.

Students are streaming in through the front doors, and we
follow. The halls are more crowded than at Bedford, and I'm
stoked to see that some of the Norwalk kids have black and
brown skin and look like they're from many different backgrounds. Some wear baggy ripped jeans and neon shirts and
socks. What a relief, after being surrounded by mostly rich
white kids who all wore the same preppy-looking polo shirts
and beige pants. A few guys we pass on the way to the office
have cool Knicks, Nets, and Yankees jerseys with matching caps
that they wear sideways. I want one that says Giants, Don's favorite team.

I overhear two girls talking in what I think is Spanish, like
my new neighbor Betsy. I'm so glad I'm not the only one here
who speaks another language. I hope I can figure out where I fit
in. I'll be happy if I can just find somebody to eat lunch and kick
a ball around with.

In the office, we meet the principal, Mrs. Vatelli, who says,
"Welcome to our school, Kenan." I guess she's Dad's age, and she
seems serious, in a navy dress with matching shoes. I've never
seen a female principal before. I bet she's strict, like Mom.

"At the end of the day, take school bus number three," Ellie
tells me as she turns to leave. "The third stop will let you off two

blocks from your street. You'll recognize it." I hope she's right, and that I don't get lost again.

Principal Vatelli takes me to a guidance counselor, who gives me my schedule. Homeroom has ended, so he escorts me to my first class, American history.

The teacher, Mr. Bauer, beckons me to stand with him in front of the class. "Everyone, say hello to our new student, Kenan," he says, putting his arm on my shoulder. His voice is calm, like Mr. Sullivan's, but the students clearly don't care about meeting me. Half of them don't even stop talking to each other or bother to look up from whatever they're doing when the teacher speaks. In the back of the room, two boys are teasing a scrawny kid with short hair who's wearing oversize Coke-bottle glasses.

"Fat Specs, you nerd," the taller guy yells, pointing to the kid.

"For real, you tool," the shorter one adds, cracking up.

"Jimmy and Andre, that's enough," Mr. Bauer says. "We treat each other with respect here."

Andre is the shorter one, about five foot six and skinny like me, with an Afro and a jean jacket collar popped up like John Travolta in *Saturday Night Fever*. Jimmy is muscular and at least six three, taller than Eldin. He's wearing dark jeans, a Knicks jersey, and impressive high-tops with untied shoelaces. He has a badass haircut, called a "fade," that I've seen on American athletes, with the bottom half of his head shaved.

I feel bad for Specs, but I'm relieved *I'm* not their target. Mr. Bauer is taking attendance as I find a seat. At Bedford, most of my classmates had short, American-sounding names, like John, Kyle, Lisa, Anne, Jill, Paul, and Matt. Here they're much more interesting: Juan José, Santiago, Alejandro, DeShawn, Jendayi, Kalifa, Malika, Demetrius, and Nakeisha. I'm hopeful I'm not the only one who wasn't born here.

But nobody speaks to me. I figure out my schedule on my own, thankful that at least I can understand it and I'm not completely lost this time. I sit alone at lunch, eating the beef salami sandwich and apple Mom packed, missing Miguel and the guys, twenty minutes away.

On the bus home, I find an empty seat in the middle and count the stops. At the third one, I stand to get off per Ellie's instructions, and five other boys stand up with me. I recognize Jimmy and Andre from American history, plus two guys who were speaking Spanish to each other earlier and a scrawny white kid with spiky dark hair and a gold chain. Do they get off here too?

"Vhere you live? Near me?" I ask the one with spiky hair, thinking I might make new friends in my neighborhood to play sports with. He doesn't answer. As I walk off the bus, they follow but still don't speak, just trail behind me, walking too close, like Vik, Marko, and Ivan in bully mode.

I go faster, my palms turning clammy. My chest is thumping. I'm fifty yards from my building, and I search for an adult on the street to help, but nobody's around. I wonder if I should run for it.

Too late. Someone kicks my legs from behind. I topple over onto my hands and knees, palms scraping against the pavement. As I try to get up, Andre grabs me by my shirt collar and pushes me back down. Jimmy kicks my side. Another sharp kick lands on my rib cage.

"Vhy you do this?" I yell, panting, the wind knocked out of me.

"Because you took our seat," Andre answers.

"You veren't sitting there!" I shout, struggling to get up, bicycling my legs in a circle to block their fists and feet.

"You talkin' shit about us," Jimmy says, ramming his foot onto my hip. I yelp in pain.

"Didn't talk vith anyone," I argue, rolling to the side to avoid more blows.

I scramble to my feet, push Andre away, sprint to my building, and go inside. Once I'm safe in the hallway upstairs, I cry from frustration as I dust the dirt and pebbles from my pants.

When I step inside our apartment, I'm embarrassed to find Ellie sitting in the kitchen with Mom.

Ellie's eyes dart from my ripped shirt to my dirty knees to my messy hair. "What happened?"

"Oh my God, are you okay, Kenji?" Mom rushes over, horrified. "Who did this? Where?"

"Five boys from school followed me off the bus," I say in Bosnian, sobbing. I feel spineless and ashamed that I barely fought back. "I want to go back to Bedford. I hate this place."

"Let me clean you up." Mom pulls off my shirt and puts ice on my scraped legs and burning cheek.

"I'm calling the principal right now!" Ellie grabs the phone. "We're going there to speak to her about this tomorrow."

At least I have one American on my side who knows what to do to stand up for me.

"Tell me their names," Dad says when he gets home and Mom tells him what happened.

"I'm going after them," my brother snarls. "Where do they live?"

"I have no idea." I shrug, wishing they would all just leave me alone. "I barely remember where I live."

The next day, Mom and Ellie take me to school late in Ellie's car. I feel protected by her authority. Some classmates playing outside at recess stare as we walk into the building. I see the guys who'd jumped me laughing on the playground.

"What a sissy," Andre calls.

"Momma's boy," Jimmy hisses as one of his buddies makes kissing noises.

I'm suddenly embarrassed that I'm bringing my mom and Ellie to the fight, my armpits sweating.

"Don't pay any attention to them," Ellie says.

Mom mutters under her breath in Bosnian, glaring at the kids making fun of me.

In the principal's office, Mrs. Vatelli takes out a yearbook and asks me to show her who beat me up. When I do, she goes out, and after we wait in silence for what seems like hours, she comes back with all five, asking each one, "Did you attack Kenan after school yesterday?"

"No." They all lie in unison.

"Kenan, are these the boys who did it to you?" she asks.

"Yes, this vas who jump me."

"Snitch," Jimmy mutters.

"I'm calling your parents," Mrs. Vatelli tells the boys. "You're all suspended for a week. You'd better apologize, now."

"Sorry," they mumble, staring at the floor.

"But he was trash-talkin' us," Andre jumps in.

"Vas first day of school. Don't know you enough to talk about. I vasn't talking to anyone," I tell him.

I'm relieved that the principal believes me. She sends me to class while my bullies stay and wait for their parents to be called.

Mr. Bauer sees me in the hallway. "If anyone hurts or threatens you again," he says, "you tell me. They'll be punished." I nod, grateful to have a teacher looking out for me.

But as soon as he's gone, a kid calls me a tattletale as I walk past. Others laugh and whisper. Yesterday I hated being invisible. Today I'm famous — for the wrong thing.

I keep quiet, with my head down. I want to disappear. At least I'll have five days without the suspended boys harassing me. Only two more months of school to go.

Later that week, I'm having a snack at home and watching CNN by myself when Wolf shows footage of the children's hospital in Sarajevo. It's in flames. I stop eating, walk over to the TV, and crank up the volume, sweating. I want to grab the chair and smash it through the screen.

"Can't we do anything?" I ask Mom when she comes in to see what the racket is. "Do you think Grandma and Auntie are safe? Did they get your letters?"

"I don't know. I haven't heard back," she tells me, turning down the volume. "I'm sure the phone lines are still cut, and the post offices are closed indefinitely. Getting mail during the war is almost impossible."

I feel helpless, five thousand miles away from my family and home. I wish I could do something to save my people. But we're barely saving ourselves.

The next Tuesday, the gang who hates me is back. Andre glares at me as I walk into shop class.

"There's the rat," Jimmy says.

I look to the teacher, Mr. Williams, but he pretends not to hear.

"'Vas my first day school. I vasn't talk to anyone,'" Jimmy says, imitating my accent, cracking up. "We'll be waiting for you at your bus stop again, Kenan."

I ignore him and try to focus on my woodworking project: a miniature soccer goal I plan to give to Miguel, if I ever see him again. But I forget to turn off the saw after making a cut, and a piece of wood flies across the room.

"Jesus Christ! How dumb are you?" Mr. Williams screams, rushing over to turn it off. "You stupid immigrant."

The class breaks out in laughter.

I freeze, my skin heating up, not knowing how to respond. He already hates me, like Mr. Miran did.

"Right, how dumb are you?" Jimmy laughs, as if Mr. Williams's slur is the funniest thing ever. He and the others gather around me.

My face is hot, sweaty. I feel trapped.

"Go back to your own country, you stupid immigrant." Jimmy gets into my face, and the room goes blurry. I see Mr. Miran holding his gun to my temple and hear Vik, Marko, and Ivan calling me traitor. I'm boiling over, thrown into a war zone of rage.

Exploding, I spin around, wind my right arm back, and

punch Jimmy hard in the face. He falls over a bench, clutching his cheek, then stares at me from the floor, astonished. The other kids are amazed. I am too. I've never clocked anyone like that.

"Oooh, it's a knockout," Juan José says, counting one-two-three, like a boxing referee.

"Ha-ha, little white boy's only half your size," Andre taunts. "You got skills, son," he tells me.

"Need some ice?" Demetrius teases as Jimmy stumbles to his feet.

I put my fists up, heart racing, ready to keep fighting.

"What the hell are you doing?" Mr. Williams grabs me and holds me back.

"Jimmy jumped me last veek, and now he make fun of me because of you," I spit out.

"You're going to the principal's office right now!" Mr. Williams says. "Jimmy too."

"Good. I vill report both of you," I say, outraged. I've had enough bullies lording their strength over me for one lifetime.

But as we sit waiting to be called into Principal Vatelli's office, some of my anger is replaced by worry. If I'm suspended, Mom will kill me. Dad will be disappointed. Ellie and Katie and Don won't respect me. I hope they'll see my side.

"What happened?" the principal asks Jimmy and me as we walk in.

"He threatened to beat me up again and said I vas a 'stupid immigrant' after Mr. Villiams called me that," I say. "I phone my mother and Reverend Hodges and Ellie Lovenstein."

"Oh good, call your mommy," Jimmy jumps in. "We're not even yet." He spits at me, right in front of the principal. He's fearless, like Ivan was.

"Jimmy, if you do this one more time, you're suspended for the rest of the year," Principal Vatelli warns.

"Yeah, tough guy, next time don't be a covard and jump me vith four other kids," I add.

The principal lets Jimmy go back to class and summons Mr. Williams. "Did you call Kenan a stupid immigrant?" she asks him right in front of me.

Mr. Williams defends himself. "He could have taken someone's eye out."

Mrs. Vatelli turns to me. "I'm sorry, Kenan. They were both wrong to say that. I'll call your parents later to apologize. And so will Mr. Williams." She glares at him.

"I'm sorry," he mutters.

Then she turns back to me and says, "You may go now. But please — do not hit anybody else."

I don't see Jimmy and his friends for the rest of the afternoon, but they're on the bus when I board it at the end of the day. I sit in the front, far away from their seats, my blood pumping. I'm on high alert, waiting for a revenge attack. But this time, no one else gets off at my stop.

I tell Mom what happened, and later, when the principal and Mr. Williams call, we listen together and I translate their apology for her. She shakes her head, then slams down the phone, hanging up in the middle, having none of it. "We fled monsters in our country," she says. "I didn't expect to be persecuted here in the land of the free."

I'm relieved to have parents who believe me.

The next day at recess I sit on the pavement by myself, away from the other kids. Andre is captain for touch football. He picks Jimmy and Juan José for his team. Then he spots me watching and yells, "Hey, Kenan, you throw as good as you punch?"

Is this a trick so they can all gang up on me one more time? I look away.

"You gonna play or not?" Juan José calls.

"C'mon, Kenan, we need eleven," pleads Andre.

Maybe it's not a trick, and they just respect me more since I stood up for myself. If they see I'm a good athlete, maybe they'll like me. "In my country, vee don't play this," I say as I stand up and walk over. "But I vatch on TV and tried at Vestport." I join in, excited but nervous. It's the first time I've played football on a team. I worry that if I drop the ball or get tackled, they'll never ask me to play again.

The other team kicks the ball toward us. It goes over Jimmy's head, but I catch it and run quickly toward the end zone, which is marked with two sweatshirts, not entirely sure what I'm doing. But somehow I score a touchdown. My teammates cheer, then tell me it's my turn to kick off. I punt, the way Miguel taught me, and the ball spirals into the sky.

"Man, check out those missile legs," Demetrius shouts, whistling.

When the game is over, Santiago comes over to me, saying, "That was the bomb!"

"Yeah, sorry we hit you, Bomber Boy," Andre adds. "But why'd you snitch?"

"In my country, bullies vith guns and tanks murder my people and try to kill me. No more!"

"Oh, snap. This kid saw some mad shit," Andre says. The guys seemed impressed by what I went through. Even Jimmy looks up and nods.

That night at dinner, I tell Mom, "I want to get a fade."

"What's that?" Dad asks.

"It's a haircut the American basketball players have," Eldin explains. "Shaved on the sides and in the back."

"No." Mom nixes the idea. "We don't need you looking like a soldier."

The next day at recess, Jimmy's spinning the football, looking right at me. His expression is unreadable. Is he going to jump me? Or ask me to play? Then Andre calls out, "Hey, Bomber, you with us?"

When I join their team, Andre gives me a high-five. Jimmy holds out his hand, but pulls it back before I can slap it and makes a move like he's combing his hair instead. Then he smacks my palm really hard and says, "Bomber Boy's in."

I run onto the field, grinning. My hand still stings, but I'm so psyched that Bomber Boy is taking the place of Bugs.

TWENTY-EIGHT

MAY 1994

"We can't live on what we're making," Mom says at dinner one night. "The first check I take home will be only one hundred dollars." She sighs. She has a new job at the Nivea factory, inspecting each makeup jar to ensure that the lids are properly sealed, but it's only twenty-five hours a week.

We're eating spaghetti with her homemade tomato and garlic sauce, which is cheaper than the canned supermarket version. "We barely have enough for rent, phone, electric, food," she goes on. "We can't afford a car. I'm trying to send twenty dollars a month to the International Organization for Migration to pay back the three thousand for our airfare."

"But Dad and Eldin both work forty hours a week. How can we still be broke?" I ask.

"After taxes, each of their paychecks is only three hundred every other week," she explains. "That barely covers our rent and bills. I might have to look for babysitting jobs on the side."

It upsets me that my parents and brother are working so

hard and we're still so poor here. I wish I could get a job too. After dinner, I put on the Rollerblades Miguel's mom gave me and skate in circles in the parking lot until it gets dark. When I come back in, I pick up our newly connected phone and call Miguel's number. I get the answering machine, but I don't leave a message. I don't want to sound needy or pathetic.

That Saturday, Dad and I ride our bikes to a nice new Shop-Rite store we've discovered, to buy groceries. At the checkout, he approaches a guy in a white shirt and tie wearing a name tag that says MANAGER.

"Are you hiring part-time?" Dad asks. "I'm a war refugee, new here. I work at the Polystar factory until three. I could get here by four during the week, earlier on weekends. Slice meats, stock shelves."

"I wish I could hire you," the manager says, "but the only opening we have is for a bagger. Minimum wage." He looks much younger than my father, closer to Eldin's age.

"I'll take it," Dad says, and I stare down at my sneakers, unable to watch him pleading with this guy for a position that's so far beneath him. He agrees to bag groceries from four to nine p.m. during the week and from one thirty to six thirty on weekends. I don't know how he's going to juggle two jobs without a car.

Late Monday night, after finishing both jobs, he comes home with a bag of stuff balanced on his handlebars. "Workers get a discount on food," he tells us, unpacking half-priced, two-day-old bread and cheese. It isn't as good as the Boston Chicken, but I break off a chunk of crust and eat it with a slice of cheddar, thanking him.

The next morning, he leaves at six a.m. and doesn't return until ten at night. He's so tired, he falls asleep at the kitchen table, not even finishing the leftover spaghetti Mom kept warm for him.

I miss having Dad home for dinner. In Bosnia, he'd get home from work at five thirty, full of funny stories about what happened at the gym, like the time a volleyball player's teammates hid all his clothes while he showered. Or the tall, skinny guy who downed thirteen rice puddings to win the team's contest to see who could eat the most. Now the only thing he says about his job is "a machine got jammed." He never mentions bagging groceries. He just does what he needs to do to feed us.

While Dad's at work, Mom lets me stay up late to watch the news with her and Eldin. She needs us for translation. One rainy night, Dad's late getting home. "I don't like him riding his bicycle in the dark," Mom frets. "That busy street is poorly lit and dangerous." When he still hasn't come home by eleven, we're really worried. It's pouring outside. I look out the window for the hundredth time and see my father getting out of a pickup truck, holding a wet, ripped bag. I run down to help him carry in the bruised tomatoes and soggy, smashed eggplants.

"What happened, Keka?" Mom asks, helping Dad out of his soaking wet jacket. He's drenched.

"I had grocery bags on the handlebars," he says, plopping down on the chair. "It started raining. My wheels skidded, and the bags fell. The groceries were all over the street. But this nice construction worker pulled over to help. He loaded my bags and bike in the back of his truck and drove me home."

I picture my father, helpless in the rainstorm, frantically picking up food that spilled on the road. In Bosnia, he was always in control, offering advice and assistance to everyone less fortunate. Now he's the one who's less fortunate. We all are.

"I'll work too," I offer, feeling guilty and useless. "Nights and weekends."

"No! Your job is to do well in school," Mom snaps. "I don't like that B you got on your last biology test. If you don't study hard and get As, you'll wind up on the assembly line at a factory, like us."

Jimmy and his pals aren't bullying me anymore, but they don't invite me to hang out with them outside of school either, so weekends are boring and lonely. I want to call Miguel again, but I'm not sure if I should.

"Want to go visit Dad at ShopRite?" I ask my brother early one Saturday afternoon.

"No. He's working. He won't be able to talk," Eldin says. "Besides, I have to study for my SAT test."

He's always busy now, working at the factory or meeting with Leah, the nice woman from Don's church who tutors him in English for free.

"Mom, can I ride my bike to ShopRite and see Dad?" I ask.

"Don't bother him," she says.

"I'll just go to the bookstore next door." I know she'll like that. "And I'll be back before dark."

She nods. "Okay, go read at Barnes and Noble. But be careful."

I've never biked three whole miles alone in America. I navigate the back streets to avoid traffic, remembering the route Dad and I took. It's hilly, and my legs get sore. At last I turn onto the main road, Connecticut Avenue. There are no bike paths or sidewalks like in Bosnia, just two lanes with cars zooming by at forty-five miles an hour. I'm afraid a truck will hit me, and I veer into a strip mall parking lot. I'm the only bicyclist in sight. It's scary but thrilling, weaving in and out of traffic, dodging potential dangers on all sides, like I'm starring in my own video game.

At ShopRite, I stare into the window and catch sight of Dad in his navy blue uniform. He smiles at the customers as he puts their things into a shopping cart. I look around for anyone I know—if the kids at school learn that my dad is bagging groceries, I bet they'll start making fun of me again. Then I lock up my bike in front and go inside.

"Hey, Kenji." Dad looks surprised to see me. "What are you doing here?"

"Just riding my bike around. What's up?" I ask him in our language.

"I can't really talk now," he says, turning to put a lady's eggs into a brown bag.

"When are you coming home?"

"I'm in a hurry," the lady sniffs, glancing at me. She has on a fur coat and a sparkly necklace.

"You know I get off at six thirty," Dad tells me. I look at the clock. It's only four.

"Be careful. They're organic," the lady says to him. "Last time, two were broken."

"Okay, I'll wait—" I tell Dad as the manager starts walking toward us, looking annoyed.

"You just had your break," he interrupts.

I stare at the rack of gum and LifeSavers. It hurts to watch Dad take orders from a young boss and snooty customers. How can a lifetime of respect vanish so quickly? I can't wait to move back to our country and reclaim our real lives.

"I'll read at Barnes and Noble next door," I tell him. "Will you pick me up when you're done so we can ride home together?"

He nods, then tilts his head toward the door to shoo me away as more people line up behind the egg lady.

At the bookstore, I browse the shelves and choose a hard-cover coffee table book on nature and a soccer magazine from the rack. I love sitting in their café, reading, looking at photos of forests, oceans, and mountains, saying the captions aloud to practice my English. I like the smell of the new pages and the hum of activity around me. With one eye on the clock, I wait for Dad. At ten to seven he comes in with a box of Entenmann's chocolate éclairs.

"They're old, half price," he says, opening the cover.

I take one and down it quickly. It's a little hard but still delicious. "You want one?" I ask.

He shakes his head. "Have mine," he offers. I eat a second. "But don't tell Mom."

Then we bike back to the apartment together, Dad leading the way, signaling with his right arm when he's going to turn, keeping an eye on traffic to protect me. It reminds me of when I rode bikes with him as a little kid back home.

The next afternoon, I get up the courage to call Miguel again. This time he picks up. "Hey, it's Kenan. Vee got phone."

"That's great. So how's your new school?"

"Rough time at Norvalk," I tell him. "Got jumped by five kids the first veek. But I punch one back."

"Jeez, sorry, man. Everybody here's been asking about you."

"Really? You still vant me to come play hockey and video games?" I ask.

"Of course! But my mom told me to give you some time to settle in first," Miguel says.

So that's why he wanted to wait a few weeks to call! What a relief. "How about this veekend?" I blurt.

"Let me check with Mom. Hold on." Moments later he comes back and says, "Okay, Emily will pick you up on Friday afternoon. You can stay the weekend."

That Friday, I'm so pumped, I quickly pack clothes in my backpack as soon as I get home from school and then wait by the window for two hours. When their green Jeep finally pulls up at five thirty, I dash outside. Miguel spots me, rolls down the car window, and calls. "Hey, man!"

Emily waves to me from the driver's seat. "Hi, love. Sorry I'm late. There was traffic," she says in her high, chirpy accent as I jump into the back seat with my pal. We high-five.

"Vhat should vee do over the veekend?" I ask.

"Basketball, video games, catch, maybe work out some new soccer plays. And watch a movie," Miguel suggests. "So, dude, you really punched someone out?" He looks impressed.

I nod. "I miss Bedford," I tell him. But I don't admit how much I've missed him.

—

"We're getting a car!" Mom announces when Nancie drops me off on Sunday morning. "Remember Laszlo, the Hungarian immigrant we met at Don's church? He's driving it over now."

A short while later, Laszlo pulls into our driveway in a slightly rusty blue four-door Pontiac.

"It's ten years old, with a hundred and sixty thousand miles on it," Laszlo says. "But you should be able to get another year out of it." He hands the registration and insurance papers to my father, saying, "I filled up the tank."

Mom insists on feeding Laszlo goulash, a Hungarian dish, to thank him. Then I go with Dad to drive him back to Westport.

I remember cruising the Bosnian roads, Uncle Ahmet speeding like a race car driver, one hand holding a cigarette out the window, the other waving at friends and beeping. Now both of Dad's hands grip the wheel. The car smells like mildew. He drives slower than the speed limit, leaning his head too close to the front window like an old grandma.

When we get back, Dad decides to drive us to the Trumbull Mall for a family outing. Mom hangs a lavender air freshener from the rearview mirror, and we pile in. Dad's worried about driving on the busy expressway, so he sticks to back streets, which takes an hour, but it's worth it when we get to the biggest mall I've ever seen, with more than fifty stores full of clothes, shoes, furniture, toys, and music.

It's crowded, with tons of teenagers. At the food court, we each have a slice of salty pizza with mushrooms and a fizzy ginger ale. Then we look through the sale racks at Sports Emporium, and Mom finds us hoodies on sale for $8.99. I eye the price on the team jerseys all the guys at school have: $89. I really want a Chicago Bulls nylon mesh tank top with Michael Jordan's number. If I save the dollars Mom gives me to buy milk at lunch and drink water instead, I can get a jersey like that in eighty-nine school days.

"Let's go soon," Mom says as Dad pays for the hoodies. "I don't want your father driving back in the dark."

We head out to the parking lot, pleased to be able to drive ourselves where we need to go at last. But when Dad turns the key in the ignition, the car shakes. Then it starts to slowly roll backwards.

"What are you doing?" Mom yelps. "You're going to hit someone behind you!"

Dad shifts the gears frantically, but it won't stop rolling the wrong way. "It's in drive. It's supposed to be going forward," he says.

"Great. How are we going to get home?" asks Eldin, sitting next to me in the back seat.

"It's okay," Dad says with a shaky voice. "I'll just ... try this way." He backs out of the parking lot slowly and onto a side street, then accelerates. I turn around to look out the rear window. It's as if I'm sitting in the passenger seat, but with no driver.

"You'll get in an accident!" Mom screams. "Stop the damn car."

"Then how are we going to get home?" Dad shouts, and he keeps going backwards down the street.

"You're going to hit something. You shouldn't do this," I plead.

"Everybody, calm down," Eldin says, sounding not so chill himself.

I picture the car veering into the wrong lane and somebody smashing into us. What if we get into an accident that winds up in the newspaper? I don't know which scares me more: that we could crash or that everyone at school might see an article about my immigrant dad going the wrong way on a two-lane street.

After about a mile of this, a police siren blares. Dad pulls the Pontiac over and puts it in park, then rolls down his window. Eldin, Mom, and I sit in horrified silence.

"What the hell are you doing?" the policeman yells as he approaches our car. He's a young, muscular guy with a crewcut. I'm afraid he'll throw Dad to the ground, handcuff and arrest him. I flash back to all the times we were stopped at checkpoints during the war.

Dad looks up at the policeman. "I'm sorry, Officer. The car won't go forward."

"Let me see your license and registration," the cop says sternly.

Dad reaches over and pulls papers from the glove compartment.

"I think the transmission's blown," Eldin says to the policeman. "We're war refugees, new in Norwalk. A member of Don Hodges' Westport church donated this old car to us. We didn't know how else to get home."

"It's illegal and unsafe," the cop tells Dad in a softer voice. "But I won't give you a ticket. I'll call the nearest auto shop."

"How are we going to get there?" my father asks him.

"We'll get the car towed, and I'll take you there," he offers. I'm grateful this kind policeman seems to understand how hard things are for us.

All four of us pile into the cop car. I feel cool riding with him, like we're in a *Law & Order* episode, rushing to a crime. "Can we get him to turn on the siren?" I ask in Bosnian.

"No! Don't ask for or say anything," Mom instructs, her teeth clenched.

At Jon's Auto Shop, the policeman speaks with the owner, a skinny guy who says, "Looks like I'll have to replace the carburetor. It'll take three days. Five hundred bucks."

"That's too much. We can't afford it," Mom says, shaking her head. But we have no choice. We need a car that works.

The policeman's radio goes off, and he rushes back to his patrol car. "Good luck," he says as he gets in. I can tell he feels sorry for us. I do too. It's a twenty-minute walk to get back to our place.

The next day, Jon calls to say that the engine won't start at all, and he'll have to charge Dad an additional three hundred bucks to get it running. Then, on Wednesday, Dad pays Jon a hundred more to fix an oil leak, emptying our bank account.

"He's ripping you off," Mom says.

"No, Jon is a good guy," Dad tells her. "I trust him."

I'm on Mom's side here: Dad's too trusting, giving everyone the benefit of the doubt. We almost didn't escape the war because he couldn't believe our old neighbors would betray and steal from us. He never called out Barbara for stealing from us. And now he's defending another thief.

When we get the car back from Jon's and it still barely runs, Dad gives in and calls Don to ask for advice.

"Take the car to my place, Westport Getty. I'll introduce you to my mechanic, Jay."

I ride there with Dad that weekend. It's a half hour away, an automobile repair shop connected to a gas station. Don's standing at the entrance, waiting for us. I hug him, and he shakes hands with Dad.

"Sorry about this lemon." He seems annoyed that his church member gave us such a clunker.

"I'll fix it on the house, since you're a friend of Don's," says Jay. "And you come here from now on. Next time you have a problem, I'll charge you for parts, no labor."

When we leave the auto shop a few hours later, the car drives smoothly. Jay's kindness makes up for Jon's price gouging, the way Don's generosity balanced out Barbara's stealing.

I used to think all Americans were good guys. But now I'm learning it's a crapshoot, just like in Bosnia: you never know who can't be trusted and who will surprise you.

TWENTY-NINE

Mom rushes into the apartment one evening after work, holding up a letter. "From my mother!" Eldin and I leap up from the couch and sit with her at the kitchen table. Dad's not home yet.

"Thank God she's okay," Eldin says as Mom carefully opens the light blue envelope. It's postmarked from Austria. Hands trembling, she pulls out a wrinkled page.

"How did it get here?" I ask, thrilled to see Majka Emina's loopy handwriting, proof she's alive. Two years have passed since we've heard anything from her directly.

"Someone fleeing to Vienna must have handed it to Ahmet, who sent it to us," Mom guesses. She reads Majka's words aloud through tears, her voice shaking. "'My dear daughter Adisa, I was so happy to get your letter, I cried.'" So she did get the letter Mom gave to a bus driver in Vienna ten months ago! I huddle closer, scanning the page, hoping she's not writing to say someone we know is wounded or dead. My eyes skip ahead, eager to find out when we can return home.

"'I'm fine, living in a house in safe Bosnian territory with six other refugees. I'd rather be in my own home with no roof than here, where I have to ask to go to the bathroom, but I have no choice.'" Mom wipes her eyes.

I'm crying from relief, too. Eldin leans in to take over reading aloud. "'After the area was bombed, your sister Bisera came here on foot to bring me bread. She got shot at by Serb soldiers, but luckily they missed her. It gives me solace that you and your family and Ahmet and his family left. I was overjoyed you made it out safely. Ahmet is not coming back. Neither should you. Our economy is destroyed, schools are closed indefinitely. Nobody's working, and we're all hungry. Stay where you are. Even if we win, there's nothing here for you to come back to. I wish I could join you. Love you always, Majka.'"

"How much would plane fare cost to bring her here?" my mother asks.

"We'd have to get her a visa and passport first," Eldin says, standing up, pacing around the kitchen. "Maybe Dad should call Don to ask how to apply."

Mom nods, holding the letter against her chest.

"I could call the Bosnian embassy here too." He goes to get paper to write a list of what we need to do to bring Majka across the world. "We'll save up and find a way," he promises.

"Wait. Do we have to stay in Norwalk?" I ask, piecing it together. I know Majka's not exaggerating about the war, but the thought devastates me. "We can't be stuck here forever."

"What do you want to do, go back there to die?" Mom asks. "We came to America for you boys!"

Are they crazy? Of course we'll return home. "Things can change there any day," I argue.

"We don't have a home there anymore, bro," Eldin says. "Our future is here, in the USA."

"But the fighting isn't over yet. You can't give up," I plead.

"We're not going back. You saw what Majka wrote," Mom says. "We have to bring her here."

I shake my head in disbelief. I have no words. I take the red, white, and blue soccer ball Don gave me outside and kick it as hard as I can against the wall of the apartment building. Then I boot it at the garbage cans lined up at the curb, knocking the lid off one. I argue with my family in my head: *You'll wind up working in factories here forever. We're far away from our relatives and friends. Nobody understands us in America!*

What do we have here in the States? Nothing. Staring at the deserted parking lot, I feel a jolt, thinking, *This is all there is.* It hasn't occurred to me before now that we might *never* regain our old lives.

I can't believe Uncle Ahmet and my cousins are staying in Vienna and never going home, that we have no home to go back to. I've always felt sure the Serbs would lose and we'd return triumphantly while the enemy soldiers were locked up in jail.

But now I imagine Vik, Ivan, and Marko breaking into my old apartment and stealing my G.I. Joes, my miniature cars, and my lucky soccer ball. How can their bad behavior be rewarded while good people like us are exiled forever? It goes against everything my parents taught us about fairness and why you have to be honest and kind.

I keep dribbling up and down the parking lot, as if I'm a professional soccer player getting blocked by a row of defense. The sun is setting, but the air is still warm. This perfect May weather reminds me of going boat racing on the river in Brčko with Dad and his buddies. Shutting my eyes, I feel like I'm still sitting at the outdoor café in town with him afterward, drinking tangy fresh peach juice through a straw as everyone we know comes by to say hello. On the walk home, shop owners would give me candy bars and wink, then nod respectfully to Dad. At night, with the allowance he gave me, I'd treat all the guys to ice cream and arcade games.

How can those days be gone forever? I'm afraid that summer was the last time I'll ever see my relatives and friends. That I'll never celebrate another birthday with my cousins, aunts, uncle, and grandparents. I think about Lena. Has she been hurt, killed, or dumped into a mass grave? I pray that she's escaped. Will I ever talk to her again?

As the sky grows darker, I kick the ball harder and harder. I wish I could blast myself into the air too, flying away so far and fast that nobody will ever find me. Then I punt so high, it flies over the three-story building and lands in the neighbor's yard on the other side of the chain-link fence. When I climb over to get it, my pants catch and tear. Sweat soaks through my undershirt, and suddenly I'm so exhausted I can barely move. I feel like my team is losing the most important championship of my life and I'm benched, not even allowed to play.

The light in the parking lot is out, and soon I can't see my ball anymore. I'm not myself in this lonely land. I'm always worried, trapped between who we used to be and the pathetic present where we have to remake ourselves from nothing. I sit on the building's stairs and lean against the metal railing with my head in my lap, sobbing.

Someone's hand on my back startles me. "Kenji, we're safe now," my brother says, sitting down next to me. "We're better off here, I promise. Just give it time."

More time? We've already lost years. "I can't," I tell him. "What if Grandma or Auntie gets old or sick, and we never get to say goodbye?"

"We can't control the future, but right now, everyone in our family's alive. Remember what Uncle Ahmet said? We're the luckiest Muslims we know."

"I feel the opposite of lucky," I moan. "I just want to go home."

"I know, it sucks," Eldin says. "But it's time to eat. Mom made us bean soup and the coleslaw you love." He stands and reaches out his hand to help me up. "Come on, Kenji. Let's go inside to eat and see what news Wolf has for us today."

THIRTY

JUNE 1994

"Stop here! Go back where you belong," I yell, smashing my green airplane into the camouflage-colored metal army tank that Uncle Ahmet bought me. I imagine that the tank sputters and crashes into the living room wall. "That's what you get!"

"You're way too old for this," Mom says, standing over me. "Enough with your fighting games. Do something useful, like draw or read a book."

I'd rather play soccer outside with friends, but I don't have any in Norwalk. So I spend the whole morning sitting on the living room floor, playing army by myself. I know it's babyish, but pretending I'm a captain in charge of checkpoints back home, throwing out the Serb soldiers until our side triumphs, makes me feel better. I miss the plastic army men I had to leave behind in the treasure chest in my old bedroom, and I wonder if some other boy is setting up my little green soldiers on my old carpet right now. I'm about to order another air strike when

Mom comes back in and says, "Get dressed. Someone's coming over to meet you."

"Who?" I ask.

"A lady named Diane who has two boys your age."

I've never heard of her or her sons. "From my school?"

"No. They go to a different one in Norwalk. Don't you want to make new friends?"

"No." I only want to hang out with Miguel.

"They know Reverend Don from church," Mom continues. "They're going out of their way to meet you. Quit frowning and being grumpy for one hour, please, Mister One Syllable?"

"Whatever." I roll my eyes and go into my room to get dressed and stash my battle toys back in the shoebox under my bed.

A half hour later Mom buzzes the visitors up. A woman walks into the apartment wearing sweatpants, sneakers, and no makeup, her curly blond hair disheveled. She's way less done-up than the other Connecticut ladies I've seen. Two guys my age follow her. "Hi, I'm Diane. This is my son, Bobby," she says, motioning to the one standing closest to her.

"Hi, Kenan." He holds out his hand, and I shake it. He's shorter than I am, with freckles and reddish-brown hair. He reminds me a little of Ivan, except cleaner, with a softer voice.

"Hey, I'm Steve," says his brother, shaking my hand too. He has the same copper hair, but it's longer, past his ears, and parted dorkily in the center. It turns out Bobby is thirteen like me, and Steve is one year older. But Steve's a lot taller and more muscular, like Eldin, who joins us at the kitchen table.

I don't know these people, and I'm not in the mood to be social. I'm sure we have zero in common. They seem like polite aliens beamed down from outer space. I assume the church put them up to this — visiting the poor, pathetic Muslim refugees in town. But I'm sick of being like a zoo animal on display, always having to be polite and perfectly behaved, answering questions and acting like it's such a treat to meet nosy new strangers.

Mom pours us Tropicana orange juice and makes coffee for Diane. Steve and Bobby are annoyingly friendly, smiling and chatty.

"We heard you just moved here. How do you like your new school?" Steve asks.

"Hate it," I mumble.

Mom glares at me as she puts out a plate of Fig Newtons for us.

"He's angry 'cause he got beat up by a gang of kids his first week," my brother reveals.

Now I shoot Eldin a look. "I punch kid back with my fist," I add, not wanting anyone to think I'm a weakling who can't defend himself.

"That's horrible," Diane says. "I hope you'll get to know nice boys here, like Bobby and Steve."

I wonder if there's something wrong with her sons. I mean, why is she going to all this trouble just to find them a friend?"

"So we heard you're a really good athlete," Steve says. "Some kids at church told us."

"Really?" I'm surprised.

"We want you to join our soccer team," Bobby jumps in. "Our league takes players from all four middle schools in Norwalk. What do you think?"

"We could use your help," Steve adds.

Oh! So that's why they came. I'm being recruited! They didn't say try out, they said *join*. I feel a smile leak out from behind my scowl.

"Vhen you play?" I ask. I would love to be on a soccer team here! School will be out in three weeks. Besides getting depressed watching Wolf and Christiane report on how my country is falling apart, I have no summer plans.

"Practices are Tuesdays at five p.m., and games are every Saturday morning at nine," Steve says. "The first one's in two weeks. We play on West Hill's field, on the other side of town. It's a hundred dollars to sign up."

Uh-oh. The fee and the distance are deal breakers. "Vee don't have money, uniform, or a vay there," I say. "My parents both vork, and Dad's car's a lemon that keeps breaking down."

Mom shoots me daggers again.

"What? I'm telling them the truth," I mumble in Bosnian.

"Don't worry about that," Diane says. "Coach Ted will cover the fee and get you cleats and an orange team shirt. And I can always give you a ride."

"What do you think?" Bobby asks.

I'm thinking: *I can show these guys some fancy Bosnian fudbal moves.* I nod, grinning.

"What size shoe do you wear?" Steve wants to know.

"Size seven and a half," Mom chimes in. I can tell she's thinking this will get me out of the house.

"Great! I'll pick you up for practice on Tuesday at four," Diane tells me as they finish their drinks and get up to leave.

After school on Tuesday I change into sweats, sneakers, and a T-shirt for my first practice and go outside to wait. Diane pulls up in her green station wagon at four o'clock sharp. "Hey, Kenan," Steve says as I open the car door. He and Bobby are in the back seat, wearing matching orange shirts. "Glad you're in," he adds as I join them. There are dirty T-shirts, empty water bottles, socks, and sports caps strewn all over the floor.

"Nice shirts. Vhy you pick six and four?" I ask, trying to make up for being a jerk when we first met.

"Six is my favorite number," Bobby says.

Steve shrugs. "Four was all they had left in extra-large."

With his height and heft, he's probably good at defense.

"Sorry about the mess," Diane says, glancing back at me. "Didn't have time to straighten up. Just kick it to the side."

The ride is twenty-eight minutes (I time it on the dashboard clock). I feel bad Diane has to go so far out of her way. I still can't figure out if they're doing this as charity for Reverend Don or if they're really desperate for a good player, or both. Their team must totally suck if they're willing to chauffeur a stranger they've never even seen play.

At four thirty we pull into a parking lot filled with minivans and station wagons and climb out of the car. I examine the grounds, impressed. The space is probably about half a mile square, with white lines painted on the short grass and corner flags ready. This isn't a dinky parking lot or a school yard—it looks regulation. The goal has an eight-by-twenty-four-foot net, like professional soccer teams have. This is a chance to play for real, practically pro.

We join a bunch of other kids wearing the same orange NORWALK JUNIOR SOCCER LEAGUE T-shirts as Bobby and Steve. A huge guy with curly black hair approaches us. "You must be Kenan."

He has wide cheeks and brown eyes that are set far apart. He's wearing the same orange T-shirt as the kids, with black sweats and cleats.

"Yes," I say, a little intimidated.

"Welcome." He shakes my hand firmly. "I'm your coach, Teddy Papadopoulos." His funny last name is even longer than mine. I can't imagine how you spell it.

"Just call me Ted. My family came here from Greece," he adds.

I don't know if he's explaining his long name or letting me know I'm not the only foreigner here.

"What number do you prefer?" he asks, showing me a box full of more orange jerseys.

I recall the one I'd wanted back home before the war, the one that Marko snagged. "Is ten taken?"

"It's yours," he says. "And here are size seven and a half cleats."

Diane must have told him my shoe size. He hands me black and white cleats that I quickly lace up. They fit just right. I take off my donated green shirt with the deer logo and throw on the new shirt, sleek and cool. I love the feel of the brand-new shoes and the jersey that's never been worn, not hand-me-downs.

"I hear you want to be a striker," Coach Ted says.

"In past I vas playing right ving up front," I say, wondering if that's too pushy.

"You got it."

That's it? I'm psyched. I don't even have to try out for my favorite position.

Coach Ted seems to trust me. But I'm afraid to trust him. Most Greeks are Christian Orthodox, the same religion as the Serbs. I learned that from an article in the Bosnian newspaper that showed photos of a volunteer platoon of soldiers from Greece who joined them to murder my people. What if Coach Ted uses me to win games but secretly hates Muslims? In America, he can't shoot me like Mr. Miran tried to, but he can still bench me for no reason.

I check out the other players, all wearing the same jersey and cleats, with different color shorts and socks. They're mostly white — there's one Black kid and a boy who looks Latino — all average height, except for one tall, skinny guy named James who must be six feet tall and towers over everyone. I'm surprised to see a girl in uniform. She has blond hair and a ponytail.

Bobby notices me staring at her and whispers, "The league's coed now, but she's the only girl on our team."

Coach Ted has us circle up, and he calls out each player's name from a list on a clipboard. Mike Schwartz and Stephanie Levine sound Jewish. Dan Kowalski is Polish and I bet Catholic, like the Croats from home. Mike and Nick Alexopolous look like they're brothers and must be Greek, like the coach and his two boys, Chris and Teddy Jr.

I'm the only Muslim. In my country, being surrounded by five Orthodox Christians is dangerous. For a second I picture them outnumbering me in a fight.

Then Coach Ted says to the rest of the team, "And this is Kenan. He'll be playing right wing forward today." Wary, I stay quiet as they each come up to me. One guy says "Hey, good to have you" and shakes my hand. Others introduce themselves and say "Welcome, Kenan." A few high-five me, smiling, and another pats me on the shoulder and says, "We're so glad you're here, man." They're acting like I'm an international soccer star here to rescue their team!

We start off the practice doing drills. The coach watches how I dribble up and down the field and how I shoot when the other guys pass the ball over to me. I'm nervous, eager to play well, running as fast as I can, sweating and dribbling fiercely. I put all my focus into controlling the ball so they'll keep me. I can't afford to fail.

"Strong legs. Sharp shooting," Coach Ted shouts from the sidelines. "You got this, Kenan!"

His praise gives me confidence. I keep tearing up the field. I'm impressed with the team's seriousness. The games I played at recess in Bosnia were just for fun, nothing organized like this. Now I'm part of a legit league that travels around town and plays in official competitions, the way Miguel does in Westport.

Two hours later, Coach Ted declares, "We have a new playmaker here, guys," as the other kids gather around me. I just hope I can make my new American team proud.

The next Friday, I'm waiting by the kitchen window for Emily to pick me up and take me to Miguel's place. I can't wait to tell him I joined the Norwalk Junior Soccer League. When the Jeep

Cherokee pulls into the parking lot at last, I'm surprised to see Nancie and Miguel get out of her car. I open the window to say, "I'll be there in a second."

But Nancie calls out, "We're coming inside."

I run to tell Mom, who presses the buzzer to open the door.

"Hi, Adisa. How's it going?" Nancie says warmly.

"Thank you for coming get Kenan," Mom replies. Her English is improving, though she still leaves out words.

"Oh, we're always happy to have him," Nancie says, then adds, "I need to talk to you and Keka about something important."

"Keka vork veekends now," Mom explains. "Something vrong?"

I hope I'm not getting in trouble for anything. We sit down at the kitchen table, and Eldin joins us. Mom offers drinks. Nancie has coffee. Miguel sips orange juice, bouncing in his chair and giggling. What's up?

"I have an extra ticket for a big soccer tournament in Chicago," Nancie explains. "My daughter has a dance recital and can't go. Miguel wants Kenan to come. We'd like to take him."

"It's the World Cup!" Miguel jumps in. "You have to come with us!"

My mouth drops open. The World Cup! It's the biggest soccer tournament of them all, and it only happens once every four years. In 1990, 116 teams played in Italy, and I watched it on television. The Yugoslavian team lost early, and West Germany won, beating Argentina in the finals. This year, my country won't play at all, since all our teams are disbanded. But I am so going to this!

"Ve don't have money," Mom says quietly.

"He'll be our guest, of course," Nancie insists. "I have a business meeting in Chicago on Monday anyway, so the room and my travel is all paid for. We'll be staying at a hotel in the city, near the stadium."

"It's the first time the World Cup is in America!" Miguel yells. "We have tickets to see my Spanish team play against Germany."

I've never been to a professional sports game. I've dreamt of being in the stands, celebrating the joy of winning a goal with thousands of other fans. I leap up from my chair, desperately willing my mother to let me go. But she stays silent.

"The game's opening ceremony will be on TV," Miguel continues, jumping up next to me. "The whole world will be watching, and we'll be there."

"That's really exciting," Eldin says, clearly jealous he's not invited.

"Vhen is it?" I ask, wondering how we'll get there: bus, train, plane, or a long car ride?

"The dates are June seventeenth to the twenty-first," Nancie says. "I have to work Friday morning, so we'll leave after school and get back late Wednesday night."

"Opening ceremony's Friday," Miguel tells her.

"I have meetings," Nancie says. "But you'll get to see your team play Germany on Tuesday."

"Wait — you'll miss three days of school?" Mom asks me in Bosnian. "Plus practice and a game with your new soccer team?"

"Vat I tell teachers and coach?" I ask Miguel.

"I'm missing my first game too," he says. "This is a once-in-a-lifetime chance."

"He just join," Mom, always a stickler for rules, says to Nancie.

All of a sudden I'm conflicted. I don't care about missing class, but I don't want to let down my new team. Yet there's no way I can miss out on this World Cup soccer adventure with Miguel.

"The first game is the least important game of the season. The record is zero-zero. You won't lose your spot on the team because of one absence," Miguel argues, turning to my mom. "Can he go? Please?"

"What if your teachers don't let you take off three days?" Mom asks me, sounding worried.

"Von't teachers fail me?" I ask Miguel.

"No. It's the last week of classes," Nancie explains. "I'll call Kenan's principal to work it out."

"What do you think, Mom? Can I go? Nobody will miss me. Please? *Please?*" I beg in Bosnian.

My mother starts to cry. That means she's saying no. I'm on

the verge of waterworks myself. I figure she feels bad because she's going to say I can't miss school and soccer, it's too dangerous, and she doesn't want Nancie paying. Or maybe she's scared to let me go without her. She's probably remembering the game Eldin went to before the war that ended in a riot. But then Mom says, "Yes, he go, Nancie. Thank you. Makes me happy he has such good friend in America."

For the first time since we've been in this country, I cry tears of joy too.

Looks like it won't be such a horrible summer after all. I have my own soccer team, and I'm going to my first professional game ever, *the World Cup,* with my best friend!

THIRTY-ONE

The last time I was at JFK airport, the day we arrived in America, I was terrified. This time, on Friday evening with Miguel and Nancie, I'm not at all scared. I speak decent English and feel relaxed strolling through the busy terminal, like I belong. Nobody's looking at me funny. No security people herd me in like a cow. For a minute I picture taking an international flight home to Bosnia with my family in a few years, sure that after we win the war, my parents will change their minds. But this day, on my way to the tournament with Miguel, I feel like I've won the lottery.

At the airport store, we get gummy bears and lime Gatorade. I take out the twenty dollars spending money Mom gave me, but Nancie won't let me pay. I notice Miguel has on a Polo shirt and khakis and Nancie's in a stylish gray pantsuit. I'm wearing hand-me-down shorts with my green deer T-shirt. In comparison, I look tacky and mismatched, though they don't seem to care.

When we board with our snacks, I see that the plane is much smaller than the one I was on before. They let me have the window seat. Miguel's in the middle, and Nancie's on the aisle. The New York skyline tilts and glitters below us as we take off. I'm looking forward to the meal, which I now know is free. But then the stewardess on the loudspeaker says they'll only be serving drinks and snacks.

"Vhy no dinner?" I ask Miguel.

"It's a short flight, an hour and a half. They only feed you on longer trips. We'll eat when we get there." He's an expert traveler who's been flying between the U.S. and Spain to see his father's side of the family all his life.

O'Hare Airport is just as busy as JFK. We only have carry-on luggage, so we head straight outside, and Nancie hails a cab. The airport is far from downtown Chicago, more than a half-hour drive, and as we get closer, we see more and more cars, buses, and people walking. In an area of tall buildings, we pull up in front of a silver high-rise. I've never been inside a skyscraper or a hotel. Aside from a cabin at camp and Dad's friend's bungalow by the seaside, I've only stayed in people's homes.

Miguel and I look around the clean, sparkly lobby while Nancie goes up to a counter and checks us in. The elevator zooms up so fast, I get dizzy and my ears pop. We walk down a quiet hallway, and when we find our room, Nancie swipes a card to get in, no key needed. We step into a suite that's the size of my entire Norwalk apartment. She shows Miguel and me the bedroom we'll share.

"If we eat the food in the mini-fridge, they charge us extra for it," Miguel warns.

In the bathroom, there are wrapped up mini-soaps, tiny toothpaste tubes, and little shampoo bottles. I'm afraid Nancie will have to pay if I open those too, so I don't touch anything until after Miguel does. As we're unpacking, Nancie says, "Let's go get deep-dish pizza. Chicago's famous for it." My mouth waters. I'm starving, and I love regular pizza, so I'm sure I'll like the deep-dish kind too.

We take another taxi to a place called Gino's and sit at a booth. The walls are covered with graffiti, and the waitress gives us Flair pens to add to the art. Miguel finds a blank spot above the table and scrawls *Miguel was here*.

Underneath it, I write *Kenan was here too*.

A waiter brings us menus, and Nancie lets us each get our own mini-pie. Miguel has extra cheese with pepperoni, which I can't eat, because it has pork. I order one with extra cheese and mushrooms, and a large Coke. The thick pizza comes already cut up, in a metal dish. The bread is salty, and there's so much cheese I have to eat it with a knife and fork. It's the best pizza I've ever had, even better than Pizza Hut. I can only finish half of it before I have to stop, I'm so full. The waiter comes to take my dish away, and I blurt out, "No! I vant to eat it later."

"We'll get you a doggy bag," Miguel says.

"Not for a dog. I vant it for myself," I say.

Nancie and Miguel laugh. "It's just an English expression for how we take food with us to go," she explains, and we put the rest of Miguel's pizza in my dog bag too.

Back at our hotel, Miguel and Nancie point out the high ceilings and the wraparound windows that overlook an ocean and pier, and spiky rows of silver buildings. But they tell me the water is actually an enormous Great Lake called Michigan.

"Don't forget to call your mother to tell her we got here safely," Nancie reminds me.

I know it costs extra to use the hotel phone too, so I try to be fast. As I'm saying goodbye, I hear Dad say in the background, "We miss you."

"I'll catch the game on TV," Eldin calls out. "I'll look for you and Miguel in the stands!" It's mind-bending that this time my brother will be watching on TV while *I'll* be there in person.

"Make sure you don't chew with your mouth open," Mom says before we hang up. "Always say thank you. And don't leave your socks on the floor. Nancie isn't your maid."

Late that night, we finish our leftover pizza, which is delicious even when it's cold, and watch two old *Police Academy* movies on the large-screen TV in the suite's living room. They crack me up, even though I don't get some of the jokes Miguel chuckles at. The guy who makes all the sound effects is amazing.

"This is the only movie I've ever seen where the cops aren't serious," I tell Miguel.

"That's because you watch a lot of war movies," he says. Good point.

There are two queen beds in our room, so we each get our own. It's the comfiest mattress I've ever slept on, way nicer than my squeaky secondhand bed. There are four soft, fluffy pillows and a comforter that makes me feel like I'm sleeping on a cloud.

The next three days are a blur of sightseeing, buildings and museums, eating out, shopping, going to the zoo, and walking everywhere. On Monday, when Nancie's busy in meetings, she lets us watch movies in our room and order hamburgers, hotdogs, french fries, and milk shakes from room service.

Our game is at four on Tuesday. Miguel and I pack water bottles and hats in our backpacks. Nancie puts the tickets, hotel key card, and her money in her purse, and we go out to breakfast. Then we walk down Michigan Avenue to Chicago's Shedd Aquarium, the largest in the world.

Tons of people are out, brushing past one another on the sidewalks, car horns beeping. The noise and bustle reminds me of Brčko.

At the aquarium, we watch sharks in a giant glass tank. "Vhen I was nine, I once saw a dolphin in the sea at camp," I say. "But I never saw a shark in person." We take pictures of seals doing tricks with a trainer in a scuba diving suit. She orders them to jump up, and when they do, she claps and feeds them sardines from a bucket. But my favorite animals in the entire place are the dark-billed penguins, huddled against a window.

"How do they survive the heat in this building when they come from a place that's so cold?" I ask Miguel, worried.

"Good question," he says. "Don't know."

I feel sad for them, far away from the mountains and frozen lakes of their South Pole home, stuck inside these humid walls where they've been brought against their will.

Miguel and I check our watches every five minutes, anxious to make sure we're at the game by four. In the aquarium gift shop, I use six dollars of my own money to buy postcards for Mom and Eldin and a dolphin key chain for Dad.

On the way back to the hotel we stop at a store that sells soccer team jerseys. "I'm getting Spain!" Miguel says, finding one with his team's red and yellow stripes. "Which one do you want?"

I look around.

"Which is your team?" the salesman asks me.

"Vas Yugoslavia, but the team is no more," I say, my eyes cast down.

"Want a Spain jersey?" Miguel asks, finding another red and yellow one for me.

I shake my head, trying not to cry. I feel left out, like I belong nowhere. But then, as we're walking out amid rows of international flags by the door, I spot the new blue, gold, and white flag from Bosnia. It's the first time I've seen our independent flag up close. I can't believe they have it here in America! Wow. This shows that we're not just a republic anymore, in a country that's trying to kill us off. Though we're battling for our lives, we're our own separate country. It seems to send an important message: the world is recognizing that we're no longer under Yugoslavia's control.

"Wait, Miguel, look!" I touch the blue nylon, five feet wide, eight feet long, as big as a blanket, the only one there. I want to own it, to bring it home to show my family. "It's Bosnia's. They have mine!"

Miguel turns to Nancie. "Can we get him his flag, Mom?" I look at the price tag. It's twelve dollars, same as his T-shirt.

"Of course." Nancie pulls out some cash.

"It's my flag, so I pay vith rest of my money," I say.

"No, it's our present for you," she insists.

I'm ecstatic to have the symbol of my people. I take my Bosnian flag from the salesman, draping it over myself like a cape. I can't wait to wave it high over my head at the game. Even though my team can't play, I feel proud. I imagine I'll be the only one in the stadium holding up my nation's colors, showing the world that those Serbs can't kill us off. We've survived.

"We have two hours until the game. Let's take the bus back," Nancie says as we leave the store, pointing to a bus stop nearby.

We sit on a bench in the sun to wait. She takes off her sweater and puts it down next to her purse and the shopping bags from the soccer store and the aquarium. In a few minutes, a really long bus pulls up in front of us. It's like two buses connected with a black accordion in the middle. I've never seen one so big. We rush inside and grab seats in front. From the window, I watch people on the street. Whenever somebody looks at me, I hold up my flag.

We're heading to the elevator in the hotel lobby when Nancie shouts, "Oh my God, where's my purse?"

Miguel and I look at each other.

"Oh, no. I must have left it on the bench at the bus stop!" She rushes to the concierge for help. "I lost my wallet with all my money and credit cards," she tells him.

"Our World Cup tickets are in there!" Miguel flips out and runs off to notify the police officer we've seen stationed outside the hotel.

"Do you remember where you left it?" the cop asks when Miguel brings him back.

"I think so," Nancie says, flustered. "By the bus stop near the aquarium."

"Come on, get in my squad car," says the cop. "We'll go check."

Nancie motions for us to join her. I'm scared, picturing the bad cops in my country who Mom paid off to take us to our apartment. But then I recall the nice officer in Norwalk who drove us to the auto store. I cram in between Nancie and Miguel in the back seat, where the criminals usually sit.

"Can you turn on the siren?" Miguel asks the policeman, just like I wanted to in Norwalk.

"Great idea. That'll make it easier to beat the traffic and red lights," he says, winking at us.

We speed along the streets, his light blaring and the siren on. But at the bus stop, Nancie's purse isn't there. We sit in the back seat, demolished, as the cop drives us back to the hotel.

"How could I have been so stupid?" Nancie mumbles. "I'm so sorry, boys. I have to cancel my credit cards. We'll have to find a different way to watch the game."

"Can't we just explain we lost the tickets? I memorized our seat numbers," Miguel tries.

"Tens of thousands of fans will be at Soldier Field," she says. "Without tickets, we can't get in."

I picture telling Eldin I went all the way to Chicago just to watch the World Cup on TV, like he's doing in Connecticut.

What a nightmare. I blame myself. I should have paid attention at the bus stop. I glance over at Miguel. He looks even sadder than I feel. I realize his connection to soccer and Spain is his father, who he sees only a few times a year. "Sorry, dude. Vish I could fix," I say.

"Thank you for trying," Nancie tells the police officer, who also looks bummed as he walks us to the elevators. I feel lousy. As we wait for the doors to open, the young woman at the front desk rushes over to us.

"Somebody returned your pocketbook," she tells Nancie, handing her the purse. We all stare at her in disbelief. I bet the tickets will be gone. I close my eyes for luck.

"Oh, thank God! the tickets and all my money are still here." Nancie holds them up. Miguel and I jump up and down, bumping each other's chests, high-fiving. "Who found it? Did they leave a name? I want to give them a reward," Nancie says.

"They didn't leave a name or a card or anything. They just said they found it on the bench and to make sure we got it to the rightful owner."

"How did they know vhere to bring?" I ask.

"The hotel key card," the cop says.

"Vhy they didn't keep the money or tickets?"

"We have very fine people in this town," the cop says, shaking our hands. "Enjoy the game, folks."

Mom's right: there's bad and good people everywhere. Sometimes the same person can be both. If I'd found a purse full of cash and tickets to the World Cup, I would have returned the money, but I'm not so sure about the tickets. I would probably have gone to the game.

We check the clock: it's three. Miguel whoops. "We're still going to see Spain play!"

We take another taxi to Soldier Field, fighting traffic, following a herd of people walking toward the stadium. Holding up my flag, I feel grand, waving it when anyone shows theirs.

Our seats are only twenty rows behind the goal, to the left. "There's more than sixty-three thousand people here," Miguel says, reading from the program. I stare at the throngs of fans from all over the world, with all different shades of skin, everyone talking in different languages. I don't feel like an outsider anymore.

I look up at the gigantic scoreboard above the field. When a man in a tuxedo sings "The Star-Spangled Banner," we put our right hands over our hearts, the way American Olympians do. I don't know all the lyrics, but I try to sing along anyway, to pay respect to the place that has taken in my family, treating us nicer than our own country.

"I vonder how many people here are from the USA," I say to Miguel.

He scans the crowd. "Maybe ten thousand? Look at all the

Spanish fans in their red shirts and the Germans in white. I bet there's more of them here than Americans."

Before the kickoff, a marching band comes out, and hundreds of dancers in glittery costumes perform graceful moves on the field; they must have practiced for years. After the starting whistle, fans cheer in Spanish, German, and English. The adrenaline of the crowd is insane and catchy. Miguel points out his heroes. Spain's players are short, with dark hair. The Germans are taller and blonder.

"You know, number eleven, the midfielder I told you about, is a Muslim Turk," Miguel says. "Sometimes before the games, he prays. He looks into the sky and puts his arms out wide."

I'm amazed. "Vhy they let him play for Spain?"

"Madrid—he has citizenship," Miguel says. "It's like how you could play one day for the U.S."

Growing up, I dreamt of playing on a Yugoslavian team. Now, as I watch the players sprint toward the goal, I'm trying to remember their moves to try out later. I'm awed by how strategically they play, everything choreographed, from the tight passing in the defense to the sudden bursts forward. It's insane how far they can pass the ball.

A guy walks by selling something called Cracker Jacks, and Nancie gets us a box to share. The caramel corn and nuts are delicious. Miguel digs his hand in and pulls out a temporary tattoo of an elephant.

"Each box comes with a prize," he explains.

"You keep it," I say.

"No, you. I've had them lots of times before."

I lick the back and press the tattoo onto my hand, screaming "Go go go!" when Miguel's team gets the ball. In minute fourteen, they score. Miguel leaps up, pumping his fists. I get goose bumps. We double hand high-five and stay standing for the rest of the first half, shouting *"Vamos"* and *"Rapido."* It ends with the score of 1 to 0, Spain. I love how everyone waves their flags, like I do. I hope the cameras will zoom in on me holding mine.

During halftime Miguel and I look for the bathroom. When we find it, somebody's throwing up in the sink. Gross. Two rowdy drunk guys shout at each other in German by the urinals. I'm glad to see a security team escort them out. I stay on the lookout for more troublemakers. Luckily, Nancie's waiting for us right outside.

As we make our way back to our seats, Miguel spots a guy painting the Spanish colors on his girlfriend's cheeks. He asks Nancie if he can get stripes drawn on him too.

She gives the go-ahead, and the guy draws on Miguel. He looks hilarious, with half of his face red, the other half gold. Nancie takes his picture. Then we get Cokes and hotdogs. I inspect mine closely.

"Don't worry, it's beef, not pork," she says. "Hebrew National. I asked."

"Thank you," I say.

Miguel puts ketchup and horseradish on his, so I do too. I've had hotdogs with mustard in Bosnia, but never with this *horseradish*. Does it come from a horse? I take a bite, and it's not bad; it gives the hotdog a little kick.

We get back to our seats just as the second half begins. Right away, Germany gets the ball and scores. We boo. I secretly like some of the players on their team, but I don't tell Miguel —whatever side he's on is the side I'm on. Whenever he jumps up to cheer, I do too.

In the end, Spain and Germany tie. For a minute I worry Miguel will be furious, but he takes it in stride.

As we follow the crowds out of the stadium, I'm thrilled just to be here, representing my nation with my flag. I keep it draped around me, showing it to everyone we pass. A blond woman nods. Three cute German girls shake their yellow, black, and red striped flag back at me. An older man offers a thumbs-up.

When we get out to the street, two guys point at my flag through a car window and hold up their fingers in a V sign, for victory. I'm sure they're my countrymen. Like me, they've made it to America alive. But we'll never forget those who were left behind.

—

When we get back to Norwalk that Wednesday night, the flag is the first thing I show to my parents and Eldin. "Look what I found in Chicago!"

"Woo! We never had a chance to see one in person," Dad says, taking it in his hands.

"I saw a picture of it in the Vienna newspaper," Eldin pipes in. "Our soldiers were holding it."

"What pretty colors," Mom says, running her fingers over the silk.

"This flag and the American flag are the most beautiful," my brother adds.

They're all smiling, patting me on the back. It's as if I've brought home the best present imaginable: our Bosnian pride.

THIRTY-TWO

Thursday is the last day of the school year. "You weren't in class this week. Were you sick?" Mr. Bauer asks when I walk into American history that morning. "Everything all right?"

Oh, no. When Nancie told Principal Vatelli I'd be away, she must not have shared the details with my teachers. "I vent to the Vorld Cup in Chicago," I tell him. "A friend from Vestport take me."

"Oh, lucky you. I watched the opening game on television," he says. "I love soccer."

"You do?" How cool to have a Connecticut teacher who's a soccer fan! "We vatched Spain-Germany tie," I tell him.

"My daughter plays high school soccer in Westport," he adds. "She'll be jealous to hear you were at the World Cup."

"History vas my favorite class in seventh grade," I tell him.

"You've certainly seen enough history in the making," he says. "I hope your family's okay back there. So, you're sticking around for next year?"

"Yeah, I guess vee are," I say, still not believing it. "For now."

"Great work these last two months, Kenan," he says, shaking my hand. "See you in the fall."

I'm proud he's noticed that my English is improving, and that I even raised my hand to answer questions in class.

Saturday morning I wake up early and put on my Team Orange jersey and cleats. As I chew on my blueberry Pop-Tart, Eldin joins me at the kitchen table.

"Why don't you come watch me play today?" I say to him. "It's my first game."

"I wish I could. But I'm doing practice SAT tests in the library with my tutor all day."

"Can't you miss one?" I beg.

"I missed two years of school. I don't know if I'll ever get into an American college, let alone be able to pay for it. If not, I'll have to work at a factory or fast-food joints my whole life, Kenji," he says in Bosnian, then finishes his juice and gets up from the table.

I'm surprised by how rattled he sounds. He's more stressed-out than I am.

I wait outside my building for Diane, Bobby, and Steve to pick me up. We're playing against the Yellows. When their station wagon pulls into the parking lot, I get in the back seat with Bobby and Steve and we high-five.

"How vas last Saturday?" I ask. I hope they're not annoyed with me for missing the first game of the season.

"We won," Steve says.

"One to nothing," Bobby adds. "Slow game."

"We missed you," Diane says. "So are you ready to score some goals today, Kenan?"

"Hope so. Vill try hard," I tell her.

When we arrive at the field, Diane goes to sit in the stands with the other parents. I wish my family were there to root for me, but Dad's working at ShopRite, Mom's taken a babysitting job to make extra money, and Eldin's studying. Teams Red and Blue are still on the field, finishing their match. I spot Coach Ted setting up a water cooler on a bench next to a stack of paper cups. I walk over to him, feeling guilty I was out of town.

"I can't believe you went to the World Cup in Chicago. I'm jealous! How was it?" he asks.

"It vas fun," I say, eager to make up for last week.

"Did ya pick up any moves from the pros?"

"Yeah." I nod, relieved that he's not angry with me.

Coach Ted shows me formations he's drawn with a marker on his erasable clipboard. He puts me in my favorite right wing spot, and his son Chris in center forward. James, the tall kid, is left wing. As the previous teams walk off, the Yellow Team takes the field, the players eyeing us, smirking, giving us dirty looks.

"Vhat's their problem?" I ask.

"Ignore them," Steve tells me. "They're trying to intimidate us."

"It's vorking," I say.

"The Yellows were champs last season," Bobby says. "They're supposed to be even better this year."

"Last year is history," says Chris. His goal is to cream them.

"Just remember to keep the ball moving, guys," Coach Ted says. "If you lose it, get right back on defense. Look for James, Chris, and Kenan, the fastest sprinters we have. Chris will take close free kicks, Kenan gets corners. James steers the ball into the goal. Now let's stretch and warm up."

As we march onto the field, our opponents are already in position. Chris warns me that the Yellows are aggressive and have a strong defense. Their coach is from Poland and has an accent as strong as mine. His sons and two other Polish cousins play defense, and they have two Spanish-speaking kids from Colombia in midfield.

"Watch out, they're tough and scrappy. It's a team of immigrants," James says in admiration.

We immigrants aren't all the same. Yet I don't mind him thinking that people who migrate here are worthy opponents who'll be hard to beat.

I'm breathing heavy, wanting the game to start already. "Let's get it done, guys." I clap my hands the way Coach Ted did, walking over to each player, chest bumping and slapping strong high-fives before we line up in our formations. After talking to Chris, I'm most concerned about the Yellow Team coach's son, Lukas. He's the smallest kid on the field, thinner and shorter than I am, but quicker; a striker who can tear through the defense like a speeding bullet. He has the same haircut as Vik, though his hair is blond, not brown. Bobby told me Lukas came here from Poland at age eight, younger than me. But he hasn't been through a war like I have.

When the whistle blows, we take off. Within minutes Lukas tears apart our defense and scores a goal, as if it's nothing. He looks right at me and smirks. But then James gets the ball and passes it to me and I kick it to Chris and he makes the shot. *Yes!*

The next time I get the ball, I pass to James, and he also scores. I feel good about my assists, but I'm holding back a little, trying to be a team player and not a showoff, so they'll keep me. By halftime, we're tied, like the Spain-Germany World Cup game. I really want to win.

"Spot-on passes, right on point, Kenan," Coach Ted says in the team huddle, rubbing my head with his big palms. "Now go get yourself some goals."

I feel like he's a general giving a new soldier marching orders. "You can do it," he adds right before the referee blows the whistle for the players to return to the field for the second half. It's just what I need to hear.

"Let's go. Let's do this!" I shout to my teammates. I try to forget how much is at stake for me. Imitating the fast crisscross dribbling of a Spanish player in Chicago, I go for it. After a perfect assist from Chris, I fake out Lukas, dribble right into the penalty box, and score a goal.

Zing! The parents in the stands cheer and applaud.

Chris plays center forward the way Miguel does, the ball glued to his feet, making it impossible for anyone to steal it. When he's ready, Chris shoots the ball over to me, kicking from inside like lightning. We feed off each other. *Boom!* I clip it into the net over the goalkeeper's outstretched arms, scoring my second goal!

Lukas and one of the Colombian kids each score a goal, and we're tied up again. But then I steal the ball from one of the Yellow's defenders, dribbling around him and booting it into the lower left corner for my third goal. I'm sizzling like a pizza. Then I do a volley shot with my right foot under the crossbar, shaking the aluminum. It hits the crossbar, and I hear a ping when the ball zooms in off the post to nail my fourth goal. The whistle blows. Final score is 6 to 4, our victory!

I scream, dancing around, my teammates chasing me to celebrate. I run down the field with my arms spread wide. I'm soaring like an airplane, flying toward my teammates, who spin me around in a crazy orange swirl.

"Bravo, Bravo!" Coach says, clapping his hands, stomping his big feet. "What a turnaround. Excellent job, guys." He hugs his sons.

I wish my dad had seen me win. I can't wait to get home to tell him all the details.

"Terrific game," Bobby tells me. "Four goals is ridiculous."

"I didn't know you were *that* fast," Steve adds.

These guys are growing on me. "Vee a good team. Thanks for the strong defense," I tell them. "Couldn't have scored vithout your help."

"We'll practice more Tuesday," Coach says. "I bet we'll see the Yellow Team in finals this year."

"The Norwalk *Hour* newspaper prints our soccer league stats," Bobby tells me on the drive home.

"Yeah, they'll have your name in it tomorrow," Steve says.

"Really?" I think about what a big deal it was when I won the drawing contest in the international Bosnian paper. Being recognized for a sports achievement by an American paper feels way bigger.

As I get out of the car, Diane smiles and says, "Great playing today, Kenan. We're so glad to have you on the team."

I'm so glad they didn't waste their cleats on me.

As we're eating breakfast the next morning, Betsy knocks on the door and hands the Sunday edition of the Norwalk newspaper to Mom, who must have asked her to get us an extra copy. I quickly flip through, searching for the sports section. There, on the page with league standings and Saturday's game summaries, I see my name. Underneath, it lists my four goals and two assists, along with other team statistics.

"Super. Show 'em how it's done," Dad says, kissing my forehead.

"Nice," Eldin offers. I hope he's jealous.

I keep reading over the game summary and stats, admiring how my name looks in print. I hope my Norwalk classmates will see it and give me respect. The news might even travel to my pals in Westport.

When Mom cuts out the article to save it, I recognize our silver scissors from Bosnia, the ones she used to cut our hair. It's strange what made it here and what we had to leave behind. Objects like her scissors, the bottle opener shaped like a cannon, and Grandpa's Swiss watch have become more important, as if they're survivors too.

"I'm proud of you, Kenji," Dad says. "I'm sorry I couldn't be there to watch you. I asked my boss if I can switch my Saturday schedule at the end of the summer. Next season I'll come to all your games."

Hearing him say that is the best prize. As we sit around the table that sunny Sunday morning, I recount the play-by-play for Eldin and Dad. "Good job," my brother says when I finish, high-fiving me.

I realize how lucky we are to be safe in the United States. I'm still heartbroken about the war, but I don't dream I'm back in Bosnia as often. I can't wait to play soccer in the fall, with my father watching. I don't need Vik or Mr. Miran anymore. I have good friends, an awesome coach, and a team that respects me. Staying in Connecticut for a while doesn't feel so bad, after all. It feels warm and safe.

I ask Mom if I can have the page from the Norwalk *Hour* and the article from the Bosnian newspaper too. She looks at me oddly but hands over both. I carry the clippings to the bedroom Eldin and I share, testing how they'd look taped to the side of the bookshelf or on the wall near the dresser. I debate whether they should be displayed or kept hidden in a box of treasures under my bed, to be taken out only to lift me up when I'm feeling sad or discouraged. I picture inviting Miguel over to show him my two best achievements so far.

Finally I decide they should hang above the corner of my desk, by the lamp. That way, every morning when I wake up in America, I'll see my name in the paper twice, a reminder that despite all we've lost and will never get back, I can still be a winner. Though maybe just being here with my family means I win.

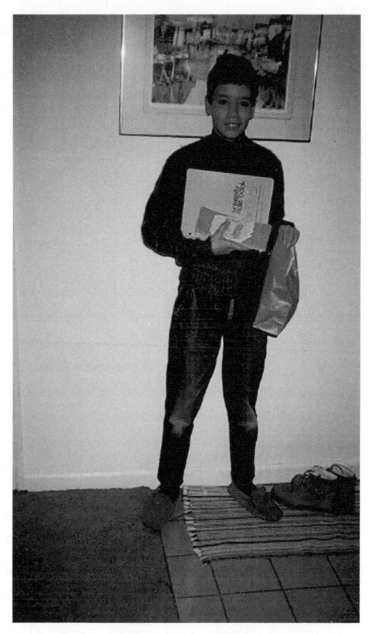

Kenan's first day of seventh grade in Connecticut,
November 3rd, 1993

AUTHOR'S NOTE

World in Between is an autobiographical novel where everything in the book really happened in my life, from age eleven to thirteen. All the historical events are true. Some names, dates, and details have been condensed or changed to protect privacy, and for literary reasons (like not wanting to confuse young readers with a thousand characters who have similar long hard-to-pronounce Bosnian names). To learn more about Yugoslavian history, my adult memoir *The Bosnia List* contains many pages explaining the complicated background of my region and relatives — along with charts, maps, and embarrassing old photographs.

I wrote that book with my coauthor and former teacher, Susan Shapiro, too. When she encouraged me to explore my Bosnian past in her first class assignment, to "write three pages about your most humiliating secret," I laughed. "You Americans! Why the hell would anybody reveal that?" I asked. She answered, "It can be healing." I wasn't fluent enough in English, my second language, I insisted. And I could barely recall much about the war that ruined my childhood.

The next day, I showed her forty-three pages. I suddenly couldn't stop remembering. I confessed how horrible it was to be exiled at twelve: I'd never driven a car or gone to a bar in my native land, or seen our capital, Sarajevo, or kissed a girl from home, and I was jealous my older brother, Eldin, had. I admitted holding a grudge against my old buddies who'd betrayed me, along with all the bad guys who hurt my people, Eldin, and my parents, Adisa and Senahid. I was afraid my grammar, spelling, and memory weren't good enough.

"This knocks my socks off," Susan said.

"No good?" I asked, bummed she didn't like it, unfamiliar with that Western expression.

After it turned into a memoir, I met Mirela, a beautiful Sarajevan woman who was moved by my story. The happiest day of my life was proposing to her in my homeland (she said yes!). So maybe putting my pain on paper *was* a little healing. Going back to my past led me to my future. As a duel citizen of the U.S. and Bosnia, I now feel lucky to live — and love — on both sides of the globe.

This book, *World in Between,* began with a *Newsday* essay, "My Own Coming to America" in 2017, when threats of a ban and detainment of refugees from Muslim countries were in the news. After having barely survived the ethnic-cleansing campaign in the Balkans that killed many of my countrymen, I feel blessed that so many kind people — of all backgrounds and religions — came to our aid. I'm especially grateful for our wonderful agent Samantha Wekstein, brilliant book editors Lynne Polvino and her HMH colleagues, and Wendy Wolfe (at Penguin Books), along with Eli Reyes, Honor Jones, Sheila Glaser, Mark Laswell, Will Dobson, Sarah Hepola, Leigh Newman, Erol Avdović, Barbara Hoffert, Ian Frazier, and others who first championed my work.

Since my coauthor, Susan, is Jewish, we see this as a Muslim-Jewish collaboration that celebrates the benevolent Christians my family met in Connecticut, like the Reverend Don Hodges and his wife, Katie Hodges, who proved my mother's belief in human goodness. I hope this book sheds light on how hard it is to leave your country behind, and offers ways to help other immigrants feel at home, while honoring the quiet heroes who treated me and my relatives with respect, generosity, and kindness that we'll never forget.

— Kenan Trebinčević